W9-BGD-909

And The Bride Wore Plaid

By Karen Hawkins

And the Bride Wore Plaid
How to Treat a Lady
Confessions of a Scoundrel
An Affair to Remember
The Seduction of Sara
A Belated Bride
The Abduction of Julia

KAREN HAWKINS

And The Bride Wore Plaid

AVON BOOKS
An Imprint of HarperCollins*Publishers*

AVON BOOKS
An Imprint of HarperCollins*Publishers*
10 East 53rd Street
New York, New York 10022-5299

ISBN: 0-7394-4291-0

Printed in the U.S.A.

Chapter 1

I pity people who think to fool their fellow man. Take poor Mary Gillenwather. She stuffed the front of her gown with paper in an effort to appear better endowed. We all knew she'd done it, but no one said a word; you simply cannot work that sort of thing into a genteel conversation. But it wasn't necessary after all. Last night, at the Pooles' dinner party, she sneezed and dropped an entire issue of the Morning Post *into her soup.*

Lady Mountjoy to her friend
Miss Clarissa Fullerton,
while sipping chocolate at Betty's Tea House

It was raining. Not a soft, whispering rain, the kind that mists the world into a greener, lusher place, but a harsh, heavy deluge that sopped the earth and saturated the very air with unending grayness. Water pooled, collected, swirled, swelled, and then burst into fields, raged through ditches, and rampaged across roads.

It was in this heavy, unending torrent that the

lumbering carriage finally reached its destination late at night. The driver and footmen were exhausted, the horses straining heavily as they pulled the mud-coated ornate wheels through the muck and mire that had once been a road.

Ten minutes later, around the curve of a hill, appeared a looming stone castle that stretched up into the blackness of night. The coachman didn't even bother to wipe the rain from his face as he halted the carriage at the door. Too wet to do more than tilt his hat brim to empty it of whatever water had collected, he squinted at the dark edifice that loomed in front of them. "Gor," he said softly, awe overwhelming the tiredness of his voice.

Beside him on the seat was Paul the footman, a relatively new arrival to Mr. Devon St. John's rather considerable staff. Paul was inclined to agree with John the coachman. "Dark, it is. It fair makes me shiver in me boots. Are ye sure we've come to the right place?"

"Mr. St. John said to go to Kilkairn Castle and to Kilkairn Castle we've come." The coachman shook his head disgustedly. "Though to tell ye the truth, I think Mr. St. John has bumped his noggin."

"Why do ye think that?"

"Just look at the facts. First he leaves his own brother's weddin' afore it even begins and then he orders us to bring him here, drivin' through godforsaken rain fer days on end. And when we do get to this lumbering pile of stone, there's nary a light on!" He sourly regarded the bleak building in front of them. "Looks deserted and hainted by ghosties, if I ain't mistaken."

Paul stood, stealing yet another glance at the dark edifice before them. While he wasn't a great believer in ghosties, the castle definitely left him with an uneasy, spine-tingling sensation that was as unnerving as the constant pour of rain.

Biting back a sigh, Paul made his way down from the seat, landing in a huge puddle of muck that sank his wet boots up to his ankles. "The drive's a rank mess."

"I only hopes they've a barn, though I daresay it is as leaky as a sieve, judging from the looks of things. Didn't they knowed we was comin'?"

"They was tol'. I posted the letter for Mr. St. John meself." Paul tugged his hat lower, though it was so wet it no longer protected him from anything the elements had to offer. He hoped the owner of the castle was not as ramshackle as his edifice and had a place prepared for them all.

Holding this warming thought in place, the footman trudged back to open the door for his master, stopping to collect a lantern from a side hook. It took a while to get the blasted lamp lit.

He carried the lantern to the door and hung it on a hook there, the golden pool of light greatly diminished by the weather. He tugged on the door handle, opened it, and then let down the steps.

Inside the plush carriage sprawled a long, elegant figure dressed in a well-fitted coat and breeches, sparkling top boots, and a perfectly starched and folded cravat, set with a blue sapphire. The jewel echoed the master's blue eyes in an uncanny manner. There was no mistaking a St. John—black hair and blue eyes, a square, determined chin, and a sharp wit marked them all.

At the moment, though, Paul couldn't make out his master's face in the shadows, which left him momentarily anxious. Though it was rare that Mr. St. John took an irritation, he could be cold and cutting when occasion called for it. Paul cleared his throat. "Mr. St. John, we have arrived at Kilkairn Castle."

The figure inside stirred, stretching lazily. "It's about time. I fear I had fallen into a stupor when—good God!" Mr. Devon St. John's blue eyes widened as he looked at Paul. "You're drowned!"

"Just a bit wet, sir."

"That is an understatement if I've ever heard one. Go ahead and say it— it's wretched, horrid, awful, godforsaken rain and you wonder why we're arriving so late at night."

Paul hesitated, then nodded. "Aye, sir. All that and more."

"Indeed," the master said. "The reason I pushed us so hard was because I mistakenly thought we'd be able to outrun the family curse."

"Curse, sir?"

"The St. John talisman ring. It's a curse if there ever was one. It seems that whoever holds the bloody thing is doomed to wed."

Paul had heard of the St. John talisman ring, and it

sounded horrid indeed. "Do ye hold the ring, sir?"

"Unknowingly, I've held it since before we left England. My brother Chase hid it in the blasted carriage. He must have known I'd flee before the wedding, the bastard. I didn't discover it until we were well on our way."

Paul shook his head. "Then ye're doomed."

St. John smiled, a peculiarly sweet smile, one that made Paul stand a little straighter despite his tiredness and the wetness that trickled down his back. "Like hell I'm doomed. I was not made for marriage. Not now, not ever. I'm afraid the fates will have to wait a few weeks to deliver their verdict."

"Weeks, sir?"

"Until I can get this blasted ring into my oldest brother's hands. Marcus is the last of us to remain unwed other than myself."

"God help him then, sir. Marriage is a horrible thing indeed." Paul shuddered, thinking of all the near misses he'd had. "I don't envy you, sir."

The master's blue gaze twinkled. "I don't envy myself, Paul. At least not on this occasion."

Not a single one of Paul's previous employers had bothered to remember his name, so he was impressed that Mr. St. John had bothered to do so. Not that his new master was overly familiar in any way; he wasn't. He might stand for an occasional exchange of quips, but he brooked no nonsense when it came to disrespect, thievery, or slovenly behavior.

It was that special combination of familiarity and

stern but fair grace that made Paul and all the other servants loyal unto death for Mr. Devon St. John. It was well known throughout the servant circles in London that there was no more plum spot to work. Had Mr. St. John's last footman not succumbed to an unfortunate stomach complaint that had turned fatal, Paul would not now be in such a wondrous position. Even with the rain, he could scarcely believe his luck.

Smiling, Paul opened the door wider. "The rain has let up, so ye shouldn't get too wet."

"Thank God." St. John placed his hat over his black hair, grimacing as he stepped into the thick mud. "Tipton will be appalled when he beholds my lovely new boots."

Tipton was Mr. St. John's valet, and a more starched, outraged person Paul had yet to meet. "Indeed, sir. Wouldn't surprise me a bit if the sight of yer boots don't put him to tears." Paul grabbed the lantern and held it aloft to light the way as they proceeded to the large wooden doors.

"I am sure Tipton will not hesitate to tell me what he thinks of the mud upon my boots. He has a tongue in his head that could scorch your soul if you were so silly as to bare it."

They reached the portico and stepped beneath the overhang, the rain dripping steadily behind them. St. John stood on the covered steps and frowned up at the stone castle. "Bloody hell, the place looks deserted. Is no one up?"

Paul set aside the lantern and went to the large knocker. "Per'aps they thought ye'd be delayed 'cause of the rain. I'll knock and see if we can't rouse someone." He grasped the knocker firmly and rapped. After several more raps, each progressively harder, a light finally appeared between the cracks of the large oak doors.

After what seemed an eternity, the door creaked open to reveal a rather scrawny-looking woman wearing a coat hastily donned over a night rail, large unlaced boots sticking out from beneath the hem. An assortment of keys hanging about her neck on a cord proclaimed her the housekeeper.

She stood in the opening, a brace of candles in one hand, her thick, gray braid flopped over one shoulder, squinting at the two men as if they were gargoyles come to life. "What do ye want?" she asked in a thick Scottish brogue.

"Is this Kilkairn Castle?" Paul asked in a haughty voice that made Devon smile.

"Indeed 'tis. And who might ye be?"

The footman drew himself up to his most impressive height and announced, "Mr. Devon St. John to see Viscount Strathmore."

The housekeeper's gaze traveled from Paul to Devon. After a grudging moment, she stepped out of the doorway and motioned for them to follow her. "I don't know any St. Johns, but ye're welcome to step inside a bit whilst we sort it out." She set about lighting the lamps in the hallway, muttering as she went. "Where is that blasted butler? Never where he should be, that's where."

James, one of the St. John underfootmen, came with the luggage. Devon watched as James stacked the valises beside the door, bowed, then left. Really, it had been a simple plan—all Devon had wished to do was leave England for a few weeks. A few simple weeks, and all would be well.

But fate was not cooperating. First the rain, then he'd found that blasted ring hidden among the carriage blankets on the seat, and now no one was awake to greet him at Kilkairn Castle. What was supposed to be a haven was rapidly becoming something quite different.

Devon met the minatory stare of the housekeeper and managed a smile. She sniffed and turned away. Devon had to hide a grimace of his own as he gave the castle a quick appraisal. They were not in a foyer, but a great hall of some sort. Heavy timbers hung overhead, while stone made up the outer wall. In contrast, the inner walls were heavily plastered and hung with battle antiquities, augmented by a scattering of standing sets of armor.

But what stood out the most was the fact that the whole room was thick with dust, a faint musty odor permeating the air. Two mismatched chairs stood by the fireplace, one sporting a broken arm. One of the tables by the entryway had a dirty glass left on it, the scent of soured wine evident even from where Devon stood. And the rugs were ashy in color as if it had been years since they'd been cleaned.

James brought the last of the baggage, bowed, and then left.

"Whot's this?" the housekeeper demanded, her affronted gaze on the pile of valises.

"I wrote to Viscount Strathmore," Devon said

coolly, deciding he was too tired to deal with impertinent servants. "He is expecting me. I assume you have a place for my servants and horses?"

The housekeeper's sullen expression did little to assure him. Devon stifled a sigh and turned to Paul. "Return to that inn we passed down the road. Have you money enough left for room and board for yourself and the others?"

"Yes, sir. Of course."

Devon nodded. He was not a man who was miserly with his blunt. When the time came to spend it, he spent it and regretted not a penny. "Thank you, Paul. Return in the morning, then."

"Yes, sir. At ten?"

Devon's brows rose. "I said in the morning. My morning will not begin until well after noon."

Paul managed a reluctant smile. "Yes, sir."

"And Paul . . ."

"Sir?"

"See to it that everyone gets a hot meal and all the ale they can hold. We made excellent time, and I am most grateful."

Paul brightened. "Yes, sir." He bowed, sent a sharp glance at the sulking housekeeper, and then left, the door closing behind him with an ominous thunk.

Devon shrugged out of his wet coat. Thank God he was only staying for three weeks before continuing on to see to some business for Marcus. "May I ask when Lord Strathmore is expected?"

"Expected? Why, he's here now."

Devon couldn't help glancing back at the shambling state of affairs in the main room. From what he remembered of Malcolm Macdonald from their school days, this disorganization was a bit of a surprise. What had caused Kilkairn Castle to be in such a state of disarray?

The housekeeper harrumphed, the keys about her neck jangling. "I wisht Davies was here."

"Davies?"

"The butler."

"Ah."

The housekeeper made a face. "The wretch is off a-sleepin' somewheres, if I know him."

Devon immediately had an image of an elderly individual reeking of gin.

"I suppose ye'll be wantin' a room to sleep in."

"Please," Devon said, removing his gloves and laying them, with his wet coat, on the table in the entryway, ignoring the thick layer of dust that was sure to cling to the fine wool. "And some food, if it is not too much trouble."

The housekeeper shook her head. "There's nary a crumb to be had till breakfast. Cook locks up the larder each night."

Wonderful. Devon began to think, with something akin to envy, of his servants holed up in that dry, snug inn. "Just a bed, then. My valet will be arriving shortly in another coach."

"Och dearie! Ye brought a valet? Whotever for? This isn't Edinburgh, ye know." The housekeeper scratched her chin. "Ye'll be needin' a room, won't ye? Blast Davies fer dodgin' his duties."

Devon swallowed a sigh. "I'm certain you know better than he which rooms are ready and which aren't."

That appeared to mollify her some, for she nodded. "'Tis unlikely the gold chamber is ready, though it might do in a pinch. Mayhap the green one isn't too bad off. I suppose we can put yer man—"

"I wrote Strathmore last week," Devon broke in, a little frustrated. "He should have received my letter stating the date of my arrival and—"

"Don't ye fash' 'bout His Lordship. I'm sure he forgot aboot it, whot with—" The housekeeper clamped her mouth closed, as if swallowing something unpleasant. Devon waited, but she just looked away. That was interesting. What was happening at Kilkairn Castle? Devon wondered if perhaps he'd made an error in coming to Scotland after all.

The woman sighed. "Come with me, if ye please. Let's find ye somewhere to sleep." She picked up one of the lamps and began walking up the stairs, not once glancing over her shoulder to see if Devon followed or not. "No one ever said whist to me aboot a visitor, and I've too much to do to go guessin' as whot needs to be done and whot doesn't. I suppose we'll make a go fer the green chamber first and see if 'tis clean enough. I'd put ye in the gold chamber, but the sheets haven't been turned in I don't know how long and . . ." She rambled on and on, only pausing for a quick breath now and again.

Devon followed her up the stairs, realizing with each step just how tired he was. His back ached from traveling so far, his shoulders were stiff, and his temper was wearing thinner by the second.

They reached the landing and walked down what seemed an interminable length of dark, dank hallway before the housekeeper stopped. She held the lamp high and opened a large oak door. Thick, dusty air crept around them. Devon looked about the large chamber and noted that not only was the fire unlit, but a swath of cobwebs stretched in every corner. Worse, there was a damp spot beside the window, the rug black where water had seeped.

The housekeeper caught the direction of his gaze and waved a dismissive hand. "Whist! Tis naught, that leak. Ye should see the one in the dining hall. It fair gushes when there's a good rain." The housekeeper moved forward to finger the linen on the bed. "Seems to me 'twas three months or so ago when last we changed this bed, so it can't be too bad."

Months? Devon raised his brow.

Before he could form a reply, she sighed. "It won't do, for ye might catch yer death of the ague. I daresay the linens could do with an airing."

To say the least. Devon struggled to control his impatience. "Are there no other bedchambers?"

"This is a large castle, make no mistake," she said proudly. "There are ten guest chambers on this floor alone."

"Good! Surely one of them is made up."

"Och, I wouldn't go so far as to say that. Indeed, 'tis a sad truth to admit, but as Her Ladyship prefers to stay in Edinburgh, we've no reason to upkeep every room."

Devon had to clamp his mouth over a curse. "It's late. I'm tired. There has to be one room, at least." He took the lamp from the housekeeper and began walking down the hallway, throwing open doors and peering inside. "I'm not picky, I just want something dry and—" He paused inside a doorway. Unlike the other rooms, it didn't smell musty.

Best of all, an especially large bed draped with thick blue velvet curtains and piled high with white lacy pillows filled the center of the room. While there was no fire, logs were already in place, ready to be lit. The air, too, was refreshingly clean and spicy, smelling of lavender and something else.

"Perfect," he said. And it was.

The housekeeper appeared at his side. She took the lamp, grasped his arm, and firmly led him out of the room. "Perfect or no, ye canno' stay here."

Devon planted his heels in the doorway. "What's wrong with this room?"

"Nothing but—"

"Are the linens clean?"

"I changed them meself just yesterday, but—"

"Any leaks in the floor, walls, or ceiling?"

"No, but—"

"I'll take this one." He reclaimed the lamp and held it over his head to better illuminate the room. "Yes, this will do nicely."

"Yes, but the room is—" She bit her lip, faltering at his stubborn expression. "I suppose one night won't hurt. I can always get another room ready on the morrow."

"Of course you can," he said, though he had no intention of giving up what he suspected was the only decent room in the entire castle.

She eyed him sullenly, then walked past him, pausing at the candelabra that decorated the nightstand. "If ye promise not to move anything, I'll let ye stay here." She lit the candles. "That door leads to the suite for the mistress of the house, though Lady Strathmore prefers the new part of the castle and has never slept there. This room was built to be the maid's room, which is why 'tis so small."

"I don't mind that it is small." Devon wondered why it was so clean while the others were not. "Small rooms are easier to heat."

The housekeeper nodded. "Ye're right aboot that. And it doesn't smoke, neither. Lord Strathmore had the fireplace rebricked to keep it from wheezing."

"Wonderful," Devon said. He smiled his most winning smile. "Thank you for your assistance. I am so dreadfully tired that I would have fallen flat on my face had I been forced to wait for that Davies fellow to appear."

Her expression softened as if she'd just conjured the room on her own. "Then off to bed wid ye, my good sir. As soon as yer man comes, I'll send him up. And in the mornin', when Lord Strathmore awakens, I'll tell him ye're here." She curtsied, and then left, closing the door behind her.

Devon was all too glad to finally be alone. He lit the fire and, to his immense satisfaction, the wood took instantly, blazing a toasty warmth.

Bone-weary, he kicked off his boots and pushed them under the bed. Then he shrugged out of his coat, untied his cravat, and tossed them into the far corner of the room. Tilton would collect them in the morning and see that they were washed. Yawning, Devon removed his waistcoat. Just as he pulled it from his arm, a faint plink sounded and something silver fell from his pocket and rolled across the floor.

Devon followed the small circlet, catching it just as it headed for a wide crack in the hearth that led to God knew where. "Oh no, you don't," he muttered, picking up the ring and tossing it into the candle dish on the night table. Heaven knew he didn't want the blasted thing, but the ancient ring was an heirloom of sorts, and if he lost it, his brothers would kill him. Worse, they'd do it one at a time just to make certain it hurt.

He glanced at the St. John talisman ring, a feeling of unease tightening about his throat. Blast his brother Chase for hiding the damned thing in his carriage. Devon had thought that if he was nowhere to be found, then Chase would be forced to trick their oldest brother, Marcus, into taking the ring.

Devon, of course, didn't believe in curses. It was all nonsense. Just a fairy tale his mother had woven to entertain her six busy children.

But still . . . Devon paused, glancing out of the corner of his eye at the ring, a pinch of disquiet nipping at him. So far, the legend had proven itself true. Three of Devon's brothers had fallen victim to the ring already; Chase, Anthony, and Brandon were all three married. "Good for them," Devon told the ring. "But not for me."

Some men were made for the wedded state. But not Devon. Sometimes, late at night, on the few occasions he happened to be alone, a horrid thought would creep in. One he never spoke aloud. He was almost thirty years old and so far, the grand passion had missed him. Completely. Oh he'd fallen in love numerous times, but he had never been in *love*, the kind of passion his parents had had, the kind that might last forever . . . or at least longer than two months, which seemed to be the maximum length of time he was able to stay interested in a woman no matter how beautiful, how witty, how acceptable she might be.

Every time Devon thought he'd found the perfect woman, the second he won her and held her in his arms, he found himself looking over her shoulder for another challenge. It disturbed him sometimes, far more than he cared to admit.

Which was why the ring rattled him. What if he succumbed to the ring and got married, only to wake up a month later to the heart-chilling realization that he'd made a horrid mistake.

Thus it was, on the trip to Kilkairn, Devon had formed a plan designed to protect himself; he would eschew the company of women—all women. At least until he could return to London and deliver the ring into Marcus's unsuspecting hands.

Devon removed the last of his clothing and tossed them along with his waistcoat into the farthest corner with the rest. Then, naked and warmed by the fire, he fell into the bed, pulling the covers up over him. The pillows were plump and lace-edged, the sheets soft and cool against his skin. He turned his head and took a deep breath of the feminine scent of lavender, thinking how nice it would be to twine his legs with the smooth, rounded legs of a wo—He caught himself. No, damn it. Not until he got rid of that blasted talisman ring.

Pushing the thoughts away, he snuggled deeper and closed his eyes.

But sleep eluded him. Tired as he was, the thought of being without a woman, any woman at all, for several weeks, depressed him. He loved women. He loved their smiles, their fascination with ribbons and bows and jewels, the way they'd get irked over something trivial, yet had large enough hearts that they could forgive the grossest indiscretion with just a few well-chosen words. He loved the scents they used, the sound of their laughter. He loved the feel of their soft skin, the taste of their rosebud mouths. He loved the giggles and the sighs and the ease with which they showed their feelings. He loved them all.

Only . . . it wasn't real love. It couldn't be. But it was the only kind of love Devon was able to feel—exciting, thrilling, and lamentably brief.

He thought of the way his younger brother, Chase, had looked at his soon-to-be wife, Harriet, at their wedding. There had been something intense and almost magical about it. Devon had asked Chase how he'd known Harriet was the one, and he'd answered, "Because life without her would be worse than death."

"Drama," Devon said disgustedly, even as a flicker of jealousy touched him. Drama or no, it seemed as if Harriet and Chase had indeed found something special, something lasting. Something forever.

But that was not for Devon. The backs of his knees

itched with a sudden yearning to burst into a full out-and-out run, away from the thought of being leg-shackled to a woman who would eventually come to bore him. Once the magic of discovery was over, there simply wasn't enough feeling left to sustain a relationship of any kind. Perhaps that was an ugly truth Chase had yet to discover.

Tiredness pricked at Devon's lids, and he pulled the curtains more tightly closed about the bed, hoping the pitch blackness would lure him to sleep.

Perhaps he didn't need to give up *all* women. Perhaps he could avoid only the ones who might be a threat to his heart.

Hm. Now that was a far more worthy plan. All he would have to do was define exactly what qualities were common among the women he tended to develop feelings for, brief as they might be, and avoid prolonged contact with those types of women. In his mind, he made a list of his past conquests and began comparing traits.

Half an hour later, Devon had to admit that he had a certain inclination toward petite, very feminine types of women. Women of birth who knew the benefits of guile.

Devon decided he wouldn't have too much difficulty staying away from vixens of that particular cut. He would instead amuse himself with only ineligible, hoydenish women.

There. That should take care of that blasted talisman ring. Life was not too difficult after all. His eyes slowly slid closed and he fell weightless into a deep, deep sleep.

Chapter 2

Devon St. John is no better than any other man. It's true, I suppose, that he is quite handsome. And everyone knows his family is both wealthy and well connected. I suppose it is also accurate that there is something charming about a man who knows his own value and is so very willing to appreciate yours. And God knows I'm not immune to that smile of his; it quite melts me where I stand. But other than that . . . oh blast it! I suppose he is better than other men.

Miss Clarissa Fullerton to her sister-in-law,
Viscountess Mooreland,
while watching the waltz at Almack's

Morning dawned, and with it a fresh, stiff breeze that rippled the grassy moors and chased the rain clouds to distant regions far beyond Kilkairn. Sunlight shone through the narrow windows of Devon's room. Full of golden mischief, a beam slipped through the single crack in the curtain to tickle his nose.

Devon rubbed his face with both hands. He yawned, then blinked into the sliver of light, slowly becoming aware of where he was. The standing ruins of Kilkairn Castle. He was suddenly glad for the shroud of bed curtains that kept out most of the sunlight. It would have been dismal indeed to have to face the wrack and ruin of his surroundings before breakfast. The door banged open, and footsteps sounded as someone entered his room.

Ah, Tipton! Thank goodness. The valet had a knack for making things pleasant. By now he would have everything hung and ready for the new day.

Devon lifted on one elbow and raised the edge of the curtain. But it wasn't Tipton at all. A woman stood with her back to him, a housemaid from the look of her rather nondescript clothing.

She threw open the wardrobe, the door banging against the wall. Just as he began to ask her what she needed, she sighed aloud and ran a hand through her hair, moving ever so slightly into the sunlight. Her hair gleamed brightly, red and gold threads vying for the light.

Devon was caught by the sight, the color almost mesmerizing. He wondered if her hair was as soft as it appeared, so thick and curling, as if it had a life of its own. She bent over to drag a bandbox out of the bottom of the wardrobe. She yanked off the top and then began digging through a tangled waggle of ribbon, muttering as she did so.

Devon raised his brows. From his vantage point on the bed, he was now at eye level with her rump. That was enough for the moment, for this particular rump was outlined very prettily by the thin, homespun material of the maid's gown. It was almost as if she were tempting him.

The red-gold hair . . . that lush rump. Was this what the arse of pure temptation looked like? It was certainly well rounded, he decided, cupping his hands at the approximate size of her cheeks. Lush. Sensual. Generous. Fleshy enough to make even his sleepy body stir to life. His manhood tightened in anticipation.

His curious gaze dropped lower. Her rump, in addition to being full and curved, was attached to a very long pair of legs. An instant image began to form in his mind—of the maid's firm, well-fleshed body against his own, of holding that rump while those long legs clutched at his waist. Beneath the covers, his manhood hardened even more.

A warm smile crossed Devon's face. This was something indeed! He'd gone to bed with the desire to pursue only the most ineligible women available, and then had awakened to find the perfect candidate within arm's length—a simple housemaid with hair the color of fire and a rounded, curvaceous body. She was so unlike the sophisticated, petite women he'd pursued in the past that she could well be his salvation. He'd be so busy entertaining her in his bed that he'd have no thoughts of love or anything else, for that matter.

He eyed her with new appreciation, suddenly anxious to get through the awkward first moments. She was deliciously different from his usual flirts. Not only was she a good head taller, but she was also wider of shoulders and hips. Quite a magnificent specimen, if he said so himself. Better yet, he'd never bedded a woman with quite that shade of red-gold hair. All told, it would be a daring, exciting new experience.

"St. George's dragon," the woman muttered, her voice rich and husky, like the smoky roil of fog across a morning moor. She kicked the bandbox as if utterly disgusted before turning toward the door, her profile presented against the deep cherry wardrobe.

Devon was given a glimpse of a straight nose, full, sexy lips; and long lashes shadowing eyes of an indeterminate color. Well! This was looking better all the time.

Grinning, he pushed back the curtains. "Good morning, love."

At the first rustle of the velvet, the woman whirled to face him. "Who are you?" Her brows snapped lower as she seemed to regain her breath. "And who let you in here?"

She didn't have the rich brogue he'd expected. Indeed, her tone would not be amiss in London. But what really caught his attention was her eyes—a deep and verdant green, they sparkled angrily.

Devon took the time to collect himself. "I am a friend of Strathmore's."

She returned his look with a flat one of her own, completely unimpressed. "Does he know you are here?"

Devon shrugged. "I sent him a letter, though it seems he kept the information to himself. No one seemed to know I was to arrive."

"And who are you?"

"Devon St. John." He waited to see if there was some flicker of acknowledgment in her gaze, but none came. Good. Curse or no curse, he'd be damned if he'd trade on the family name in an effort to win a chit to his bed. He'd never had to do so before, and he wasn't about to start now.

He gathered the pillows and piled them behind him so that he could lean back and still see the woman's expression.

She eyed him cautiously, but made no move to dash for the door. "Who let you in?" she repeated.

"The housekeeper, I believe. Short woman, rather thin." He held out his hand. "About this tall, with big feet and a thick, gray braid."

"That would be her," the maid said grimly. "I wonder why the devil she didn't show you into one of the guest chambers."

"None were ready."

"That is not surprising. Still, she had no right to give you this chamber." She met his gaze and said stiffly, "It is mine."

The housekeeper had said that it was the room of a lady's maid, which would explain the green-eyed woman's rather polished tones. "So this bed is yours, is it?" He smiled his most winsome smile. "I love the scent of lavender." And would have loved it even more if he had been inhaling the sweet scent from her bare skin and not just her pillows and sheets.

"How pleasant," she said in a tone that implied the information was anything but. "I'm certain someone has by now prepared a room for you. It is time you left."

The maid was as hospitable in manner as the housekeeper from the previous night. The help at Kilkairn Castle were poorly trained. They were, in fact, the worst Devon had ever experienced, with the exception of his brother Brandon's coachman, a not-quite-reformed thief.

Still, it behooved Devon to jolly the maid along, especially if he wished to visit her bed with her in it. He let his gaze travel across her, touching on the fullness of her breasts, the round curve of her hips. Rich like an oversoft mattress, her body beckoned him to while away a few pleasant hours. He imagined what she'd be like between the sheets and had to shift to get comfortable again. He didn't know if it was the faint air of challenge that clung to her very generous curves or the curves themselves, but he was quite ready to sample her bounty.

He stretched a bit, letting the sheet slip a touch lower. As soon as her eyes traveled over his chest, to his lap, he said, "This is a wonderful bed. The mattress is firm, the sheets sweet-smelling. Perhaps I should just stay here."

Her gaze jerked back to his face, and she plopped her hands on her hips. "Nay, you will not."

There it was, the faintest hint of a Scottish brogue. Apparently when my lady's maid was irked, her accent began to show. Devon hid a smile and shrugged. "We'll see."

"We won't see anything. You will leave now."

He looked down at his lap, barely hidden from sight by the thin sheet. "Now?"

Her gaze followed his to where his obvious reaction was visible against the folds. Her cheeks heated, a lush pink color beneath the creamy white. "Nay," she said hastily, "not now. But as soon as I've left. Then you can put on your clothes and be on your way."

He was not going to leave without at least a kiss—or something more—to give him the strength to fight off whatever enticements the blasted talisman ring had in store. He glanced down at the bandbox she'd been peering into. "What are you looking for?"

"A ch—" She snapped her lips closed, glaring at him as if he'd committed a sin of some sort. "None of your business." She bent down and plunked the lid back on the bandbox. Then she picked it up and returned it to the stuffed wardrobe, slamming the doors closed. "I'll leave you to dress and then I'll return and finish what I was doing."

"Don't leave yet." He patted the bed beside him, watching her from beneath his lashes. "Stay and talk a bit."

One brow raised in skeptical disbelief. "Talk?" Her gaze dropped pointedly to his lap. "That's not what you appear to be wanting."

He choked on an unexpected laugh. She was a brazen one with a wit to match. It was a pity he had so little time, for it would have been wonderful to luxuriate in that deliciously decadent body of hers. As it was, he was forced to immediate action.

Devon met her gaze directly. "I wish I had more time to spend here at Kilkairn."

"You aren't staying long?"

He ignored the satisfaction that threaded her voice. "I've business to attend to for my brother, so I must leave in three weeks. Which is a great, sad pity." He peered at her from beneath his lashes and waited.

She shifted from one foot to the other, curiosity rampant in her gaze. After a moment, she asked in a rush, as if the words were forced from her, "Why is it a pity?"

"Because if it were not for that wretched fact, I would stay here and spend days, weeks, slowly seducing you, teasing and tormenting away your frowns until you had nothing left but ecstatic gasps and contented sighs."

If she'd colored before, it was nothing compared to the blaze of pink that heated her cheeks now.

Devon leaned forward. "More than anything in the world, I want to kiss you. Right now. May I?"

She blinked, and he realized that her lashes were so long that they tangled at the corners. "A kiss?"

It wasn't an invitation exactly. But it would do. In one smooth movement, he slid to the edge of the bed, swung his feet to the floor, grasped the woman's arm, and pulled her into his almost-bare lap. It was unfortunate that the sheet had tangled about his hips or there would have been naught but her skirts separating them.

Without giving her time to react beyond a simple gasp, he lowered his mouth to hers and kissed her.

He kissed her deeply, thoroughly, his mouth opening over hers, his tongue pressing between her lips. He tasted, teased, poured every ounce of his longing and desire into that one touch.

She stiffened, but didn't move, neither welcoming nor fighting off his embrace, though he could feel her heat thundering beneath his hands as he held her close. Could taste the wanton desire that answered his own.

A soft moan sounded in her throat, and Devon deepened the embrace. But even as he did so, she went limp in his arms, her face turning away from his as she gasped for breath.

It was an unbelievably sensual moment, the feel of her in his arms, her taste on his lips, her heart beating so fiercely that his own raged in response.

Devon held her tight and didn't move. After a long moment of fighting off the heavy wave of desire that made his loins ache and his throat tighten with need, he caught his breath enough to lift his head and look down into her face.

He expected shocked surprise. Or perhaps a pretense of outraged virtue, all of which he was prepared to kiss away.

But instead, despite her flushed cheeks, she met his gaze directly enough and said in a rather breathless voice, "Bloody hell, not again." To his further astonishment, she seemed to school her expression into one of supreme disinterest.

Of all the hundreds—nay, thousands—of kisses he'd delivered, none had met with a reaction anywhere close to this—disinterest tinged with boredom. Nor was he used to seeing a tedious expression on the faces of the women he gifted with his expertise. Bemusement, yes. Wonderment, yes. Even awed excitement. But boredom?

He pulled back a little more so that he could see fully into the maid's face. "I beg your pardon, but did you say 'Bloody hell, not again'?"

"Aye," she said, her gaze even with his. Her cheeks were flushed, her lips swollen slightly, her chest still moving rapidly up and down—those few things assured him that she was a pretender.

But still, it was intriguing that she could manage such a disinterested look and tone. "What do you mean 'again'?" he demanded.

She struggled to sit upright, but when he refused to loosen his hold, she merely sighed, her breath sweet, brushed with cinnamon. "Every time Strathmore has a guest, I get mauled. I am damned tired of it."

Devon's lips twitched. The maid's breath might be sweet, but her language was not. "If you don't wish to be mauled, then perhaps you should try to be a little less tempting."

"Tempting? Me?" Kat Macdonald blinked into the blue, blue eyes of her captor, fighting a losing battle to appear unaffected. Her mind whirled around the fact that the handsomest man she'd ever beheld had swept her into his lap and bestowed an expert, passionate kiss on her astounded lips. Then she'd had to fight the fact that her body had immediately softened, her heartbeat had tripled, her chest had tightened with an unfamiliar emotion.

It had been all she could do to appear bored,

though she'd managed. It was the best way to depress unwanted attentions, something Kat excelled at. Something she was far too familiar with, as it was. But in a way, that was her own fault. She'd sold her reputation for something that had seemed far more important, only to discover that she'd been wrong, dead wrong. Now she was forced to deal with the repercussions of that decision, one made so hastily eight years ago.

He lifted a finger and traced the curve of her cheek, the touch bemusingly gentle. "You are a lush, tempting woman, my dear. And well you know it."

Kat's defenses trembled just the slightest bit. Bloody hell, how was she to fight her own treacherous body while the bounder—Devon something or another—tossed compliments at her with just enough sincerity to leave her breathless to hear more?

Of course, it was all practiced nonsense, she told herself firmly. She was anything but tempting. She looked well enough when she put some effort into it, but she was large and ungainly, and it was way too early in the morning for her to look anything other than pale. Her eyes were still heavy with sleep, and she'd washed her hair last night and it had dried in a most unruly, puffy way that she absolutely detested. One side was definitely fuller than the other, and it disturbed her no end. Even worse, she was wearing one of her work gowns of plain gray wool, one that was far too tight about the shoulders and too loose about the waist. Thus, she was able to meet his gaze and say firmly, "I am not tempting."

"I'd call you tempting and more," Devon said with refreshing promptness. "Your eyes shimmer rich and green. Your hair is the color of the morning sky just as the sun touches it, red and gold at the same time. And the rest of you—" His gaze traveled over her until her cheeks burned. "The rest of you is—"

"That's enough of that," she said hastily. "You're full of moonlight and shadows, you are."

"I don't know anything about moonlight and shadows. I only know you are a gorgeous, lush armful."

"In this?" She looked down at her faded gown with incredulity. "You'd call this gorgeous or lush?"

His gaze touched on her gown, lingering on her breasts. "Oh yes. If you want to go unnoticed, you'll have to bind those breasts of yours."

She choked.

He grinned. "And add some padding of some sort in some other areas."

"I don't know what you're talking about, but please let me up—"

"I was talking about padding. Perhaps if you bundled yourself about the hips until you looked plumper, then you wouldn't have to deal with louts such as myself attempting to kiss you at every turn."

She caught the humor sparkling in his eyes, and it disarmed her a bit more.

"Furthermore," he continued as if he'd never paused, "you will need to hide those eyes of yours and perhaps wear a turban, if you want men like me to stop noticing you."

"Hmph. I'll remember that the next time I run into

you or any other of Strathmore's lecherous cronies. Now, if you'll let me go, I have things to do."

His eyes twinkled. "And if I refuse?"

"Then I will have to deal with you myself."

"Oh ho! A woman of spirit. I like that."

"Oh ho," she returned sharply, "a man who does not value his appendages."

That comment was meant to wither him on the vine. Instead he chuckled, the sound rich and deep. "Sweet, I value my appendage, although it should be *your* job to admire it."

"I have no wish for such a job, thank you very much."

"Oh, but if you did, it would then be my job to wield that appendage in such a way as to rouse that admiration to a vocal level." Devon leaned forward and murmured in her ear, "You have a delicious moan, my sweet. I heard it when we kissed."

Her cheeks burned. "The only vocal rousing you're going to get from me is a scream for help."

A bit of the humor left his gaze, and he said with apparent seriousness, "I would give my life trying to earn that moan yet again. Would you deny me that?"

In all her years of avoiding the clutching hands of her half brother's friends, never had any attempted to woo her with words. Not a single one. The tactic surprised her, and very few things did. "Please let me go. It is very improper of me to sit in your lap." Improper, but comfortable for all that.

He pursed his lips. "I'm not sure I can. Not without a toll."

"A toll? To gain release from my own bed?"

His eyes glinted suddenly, a smile on his sensual mouth that left her heart trembling in her throat. His hands, so warm before, now seemed even warmer, almost hot through the material of her gown. "My sweet," he said, "you aren't in bed, but in my lap. Were you in bed, I'd demand much more than a kiss for your freedom."

She frowned. "That is not fair." And it wasn't, not in any way.

"Life is rarely fair," he retorted.

Kat couldn't very well argue with him there. Life had already proven that. Blast it, it wasn't fair if he was going to use logic. "I already gave you one kiss," she pointed out reasonably.

"You didn't kiss me—I kissed you."

"That's all you'll get from me."

"Really?" His lids lowered, and he regarded her with a sleepy, sexy look that quite stole her thoughts. "What a pity, for I enjoyed that kiss. More than I should have. Without a doubt, it was the most intriguing, most delicious kiss I've ever received."

Despite Kat's determination to appear unmoved, a tiny flicker of pride tickled through her. From the stranger's manner and appearance, she was certain he was quite used to being kissed . . . in fact, there had been something of a master kisser in his manner and ability. And yet *he'd* been impressed with *her* efforts. She hadn't even tried to impress him, either. She wondered what he'd think if she *did* try. He would be completely astounded and—

Kat blinked. St. George's Dragon, but if she continued on this line of thought, she'd talk herself into kissing him again. And all without him saying another word!

Her gaze narrowed on the stranger and she noted that he was watching her expressions intently, a pleased smile on his lips as if he knew exactly where her thoughts were taking her. *I'm playing right into his hands, blast it!*

"Enough of this. I will give you until the count of three to free me."

Amusement laced his blue eyes. "Or?"

"Or I will be forced to hurt you."

He chuckled, the sound rumbling in his chest. "Really? And how will you—"

"One."

"Oh come now. All I want is a kiss. You've already given me one, what can be the harm in—"

"Two."

He shook his head. "I vow, but you are a stubborn thing. Far more stubborn even than my sis—"

"Three." She lifted her foot and swung it back, hard. There was a solid thunk as the heel of her boot hit his bare shin. His arms loosened instantly. Kat was on her feet and across the floor before her captor finished a rather colorful string of invectives.

Once she reached the door, she wasted no time hurrying out and slamming it behind her. Then she continued on her way down the steps, through the great hall, and out the door, where she hurried on to the stables.

She didn't think Mr. Devon St. John would follow—he'd have to stop long enough to find some clothes.

But still, her heart was pounding as if he were hard on her heels. And perhaps, in a way, he was.

Kat found the stables thankfully quiet. She hurried by the nearly empty stalls, the scent of hay and oats mingling in the cool air. She went straight to the tack room, where she locked the door and then stood with her back against it, fighting for breath and the return of her usual calm thinking.

In all the times she'd fended off the groping hands of Kilkairn guests, never had Kat allowed anyone to touch her, much less hold her in his arms and kiss her. This man had merely caught her by surprise with his soft words and smiling eyes. But now she'd be cautious around him; very cautious indeed.

Certainly Kat had never *enjoyed* the attentions of any of Malcolm's other miscreant friends, yet this time she had to admit that she'd felt a definite trill of excitement. In fact, she'd felt many things while in Devon St. John's arms, and none of them was safe.

That thought firmly in mind, she waited only until her breath returned to normal before leaving the tack room and finding her horse. Then she mounted and left, riding through the forest and hills as if the hounds of hell were indeed following her.

Chapter 3

I am not here to argue, sir. I am here to inform you of my wishes and to see to it that you consent in all matters forthwith.

Viscountess Mooreland to her mirror,
practicing for an upcoming "conversation"
with His Lordship regarding
his wasteful gambling habits

The chit had kicked him. Hard. Devon's temper went from amused interest to astonished outrage in the space of a few seconds, his irritation complete when she swept from the room in seemingly righteous indignation, slamming the door behind her.

All told, it was a new, and unpleasant, experience. Women rarely refused his requests for a dalliance and never bothered to kick him before leaving the room.

Damn it, what was wrong with the woman? A simple "No, thank you" would have sufficed. Although . . . He rubbed his shin and winced. Perhaps he'd been too determined to keep the damned effect of that blasted talisman ring at bay by holding the chit in his lap. Truly, he had meant no harm. It was just the realization that she was so absolutely perfect for his plans—and right there, at arm's length—that had made him reluctant to heed her request for release.

Of course, most women he knew wouldn't have complained had he kept them in his lap for much longer than a few miserly minutes. Had he offered, many would have stayed and even suggested additional amusements to accompany such a luxuriously naughty position. But apparently London misses were something less particular than Scottish misses. Perhaps some small part of that was due to his position in London society . . .

An insidious idea crept into his mind and latched about his thoughts. What if all the women who had bedded him had done so merely because they had known who he was, that he was a St. John?

He glanced down at his ready "appendage," as the chit had called it, and relief swept through him. His name might have been the reason some women had tumbled into his bed, but it wasn't the reason so many of them clamored, cajoled, and begged to return.

Feeling a bit more himself, Devon rose and began to dress. He didn't have Tilton's way of decreasing wrinkles, but Devon managed quite well. His cravat was sadly crushed, of course, but here in the wilderness, who would know? He tied it as best he could and then pinned it in place with a sapphire pin. He'd just bent over to fish his boots from under the bed when he caught sight of the St. John talisman ring where it still rested in the candle dish on the night table. His gaze narrowed, and he reached out and touched the slender metal band.

The ring was warm beneath his fingertips, and surprisingly smooth despite the runes carved on the side. For some reason, the feel of the silky metal reminded him of the maid. She was every bit as prickly on the inside, and then just as surprisingly soft to the touch.

He traced the curve of the band, his mind lingering on the memory. Suddenly he caught himself, stepping hastily back from the table and ramming his hands into his pockets. Bloody hell, if he wasn't careful, he'd be bedded and wedded before the day was out.

Not to the saucy maid, of course—not only was she completely unsuitable, but she had also apparently developed an unreasonable dislike for his presence, as indicated by the bruise on his shin. He realized that she'd bruised far more than his shin; his pride was injured as well.

He shrugged into his waistcoat. Devon knew there had to be other unsuitable women to dally with, though he doubted any of the others possessed the creamy skin, red-gold hair, or pure audacity of the one he'd let escape.

Damn. He turned his back on the ring and pulled his boots from beneath the bed, grimacing at the mud on the once shiny leather. Sighing, he crossed to a window and opened it, pausing as he leaned out to dust his boots onto the gardens below. The scent of the flowers and herbs rose to meet him. For all the mismanagement inside Kilkairn Castle, the gardens were glorious. The green of the grass reminded him of the eyes of the wench who'd kicked him.

Damn. I'm doing it again. Apparently he had a weakness for women with green eyes and pointed shoes. He closed the window, then held up his boots to the light. They were now mudless, but covered in some sort of gray grime. Tipton would not be pleased.

Devon swiped them with the hand towel on the night table, stomped his feet into the boots, and shrugged into his coat. The sooner he lured the serving maid into his bed, the sooner he could relax and stop worrying he might meet a paragon of feminine virtues—the exact type of woman one might feel compelled to marry.

A woman he might not be able to refuse.

Fate might be conspiring against him, but she had not beaten him yet. Devon whistled softly to himself as he stepped out of the cozy confines of the room into the hallway, pausing a moment to get his bearings.

If he had thought Kilkairn Castle disreputable during his brief view of it the night before, it was even more forlorn in the bright sunlight. At first glance, the wide stone-lined hallway benefited from a brace of large, high-set windows, the tall ceiling arching gracefully over a set of elaborate iron chandeliers. But closer inspection revealed the layering of dust that piled in the corners of the hall, and the thick bracket of cobwebs that stretched from cornice to chandelier bracket. He followed a particularly long cobweb where it stretched down to the corner of the rug that ran the center of the hallway. In all probability, the runner had once been a rich red, though now it was an indiscriminate brown.

All told, it was a strange state of affairs considering that while at Eton, Malcolm had been so fastidious about his possessions that he'd taken a ribbing from his classmates on more than one occasion. It had taken the force of Malcolm's hot fists and ready temper to silence most of the naysayers.

Since then, of course, Malcolm had married, a supposedly "blessed state" that seemed to have the effect of immediately turning a sane, logical man into a quivering, starry-eyed impostor. Devon had seen just such a transformation occur in no fewer than three of his own brothers.

Thank God he was prepared to fight off the talisman ring's curse. He was a man who favored a more lively way of life. His needs were simple—enjoyment of life, an occasional flagon of brandy, and the warm company of a large number of the fair sex.

His stomach rumbled and he sighed, then made his way down the stairs. He wondered if there was to be breakfast or if he would have to procure his own. Considering the state of the castle, he would not be surprised to discover that there was ham for breakfast, but first he'd have to catch the pig, strangle it with his bare hands, and dress it himself.

The unmistakable clank of a serving dish sounded at the very bottom of the great stairs and alleviated his fears. Devon followed the sound, his stomach growling louder as the wafting scent of bacon reached his nostrils.

He didn't even pause on reaching the room, but entered forthwith. Only two occupants were inside. One was a bent-over, hunkered old man dressed in a footman's livery who stood beside a sideboard filled with steaming platters. He didn't even look around when Devon entered, but continued to move a water pitcher slowly toward an empty water glass.

Across the room sat the other occupant, a slender, well-dressed man with an expressive face and deep auburn hair. A rather small, solitary figure at the huge gleaming table, he occupied an ornate chair, a plate before him.

The man was just lifting a bite of egg to his mouth when his gaze fell on Devon. The man's eyes widened, and he dropped his fork. "Damn me, but I'll be drawn and quartered!"

"So you shall, Strathmore," Devon said. "An event I've predicted on more than one occasion."

Malcolm grinned from ear to ear as he jumped up from the table. "Devon St. John! How are you, you pox-ridden, swiving, crimped-ear dog!"

Devon took the hand Malcolm thrust toward him. "God save us all, but it is Malcolm Macdonald, scourge of Scotland and bane of Britain. Hide your money and your women!"

Malcolm laughed. "Och, laddie! You haven't changed a bit! When did you arrive? I didn't expect to see you till after this rain quit us."

"Last night, rather late. Didn't anyone inform you?"

"No one has informed me of a bloody thing! Who was up to greet you?"

"The housekeeper. Your butler was apparently unavailable."

"Davies," Malcolm said with a disgusted snort. "He's never where he should be. Still, I'm surprised one of the footmen didn't mention it." Malcolm looked at the humped-back old man who stood by the buffet and said loudly, "Damn it, Ketron! Why didn't you tell me St. John had arrived?"

The old man didn't look up but continued with his task, his blue-veined hands trembling as he lifted the pitcher to pour water into the glass. Large droplets splattered everywhere, sizzling on the ham plate.

"By St. Brennan's boat, I am surrounded by imbeciles and deaf mutes!" Malcolm sighed, then shrugged as if to move past his irritation, a pained smile touching his mouth. "There's naught for it now. Accept my apologies, St. John. I shall have to force you to drink a bottle or two of my best port as a way to offer solace for my shortcomings as a host."

"I accept," Devon said without hesitation.

"Thank you. You always were a generous man." Malcolm glared at the elderly retainer. "As I'm sure you've noticed, things are in a wee bit of disarray."

That was an understatement. Devon cleared his throat and said politely, "I'm sure it's not as bad as all that."

"Yes, it is. These servants are horrid. They were m'father's, most of them. The only ones who would stay. Except that one." Malcolm nodded toward the ancient footman who was now slowly wiping up the spilled water using the corner of his coat. "That one was a wedding gift from Fiona's mother. The harridan swore she was doing us a great service and claimed that he was indispensable to her household. At the time I thought she was being too generous, but now I am not so certain."

"A parson's gift, hm?"

"Aye. I think the real reason she sent him here was to cause us the greatest inconvenience she could. Devon, honestly, the man cannot hear a word."

Devon chuckled. "How inconsiderate."

"Aye. But enough of my misfortunes." Malcolm gestured to the table. "Come and eat!" He waited for Devon to sit before he took a chair. Then he said in a very loud voice, "Ketron, bring another plate!"

The old man didn't so much as blink, but continued, ever so slowly, to wipe yet another bead of water off the sideboard.

Malcolm closed his eyes, a deep crease appearing on his forehead. After a moment, he opened his eyes. "Perhaps I should just get it for you."

"Oh no—"

"Nonsense," Malcolm said, standing up with the air of a man who has suffered long and sees no end in sight. He made his way to the buffet, where he startled the butler by reaching past him to get a plate and then piled it high with a spoonful of every dish available.

Devon blinked at the amount of food that was eventually set before him. "I am overwhelmed." He supposed he could get used to the drafty halls, damp beds, and cobweb-strewn corners if his sojourn at

Kilkairn Castle promised food like this. "I don't believe I've seen a more lovely sight."

Malcolm resumed his seat and beamed affably. "Breakfast is my favorite meal of the day. Fiona has the ordering of dinner, so I have to—" He broke off at Devon's expression. "Never mind that. Just eat and enjoy." He glanced over at the elderly footman and then said in a loud voice that was a hair from a yell, "Ketron, could you inform Lady Strathmore we have a guest?"

The footman turned from the sideboard and put his hand to his ear. "Eh?"

Malcolm muttered under his breath and then repeated his request, even more loudly.

"Aye, my lord," the old man said. He straightened his shoulders, then lifted his foot. He shuffled more than walked, and it took him forever just to reach the door.

The second he passed through, Malcolm pulled his plate closer and reclaimed his fork. "So, how are those brothers of yours?"

"Chase just wed. Brandon returned just a few months ago from his honeymoon, and Anthony and Anna are talking about having even more children."

"Chase just wed? And Brandon as well? Saints, but it sounds as if the whole lot of you have gone daft." Malcolm eyed Devon up and down. "You don't have that bloody ring, do you?"

Devon nodded once.

"Blast! I knew it."

"Why does it matter?"

Malcolm drew back a little, his eyes wide. "Because it means that your goose is cooked, my friend."

"It means no such thing," Devon said much more firmly than he meant to.

A crack of laughter met this. "How do you plan on escaping?"

"By staying busy." Devon shifted in his chair, his shin hitting the leg of the table right where his morning visitor had kicked him. He winced.

Malcolm's brows lowered with concern. "The table has odd-placed legs."

"It isn't that. I merely struck a previous injury. A bruise caused by a rather spirited mare."

"A mare?"

"Yes. One with very intriguing green eyes." It was somewhat odd, but every time Devon thought about the sassy maid, he smiled.

Malcolm grinned in return. "Oh ho! An armful, was she?"

"And then some." Devon rubbed his shin once more. "She wears pointed boots, too. Apparently she took something I said in an unfavorable light and delivered a kick worthy of my new gelding."

"What did you say to cause such a reaction?"

"Nothing that I can think of. I merely told her she had to pay a toll to leave my room. A kiss. Inexplicably, she took offense."

"Och, you found a spirited one!" Malcolm spread some marmalade on a piece of toasted bread. "Where did you meet this maid? At a tavern along the way?"

"No. It was here. In the blue room."

Malcolm's laughter froze on his lips, something flickering in his gaze. He looked down at his toast, a strange expression on his face. "Did you . . . did you say the blue room?"

"Yes," Devon said cautiously. "Why?"

Malcolm shook himself, as if waking from a deep sleep. "Och, nothing. A thought, 'tis all. How did you come to be in the blue room?"

Reassured, Devon reached for the salt. "It was the only one clean enough to inhabit. When I awoke this morning, the maid was there and claimed the room to be hers. So, in return for vacating the premises, I asked for a kiss."

Malcolm started to take a bite of his toast, but then apparently thought better of it and returned it to the side of his plate. "What did this, ah, lass say to your price of a kiss?"

Devon grinned. "She didn't say anything while I was kissing her."

A faint flush crept up Malcolm's neck. "She *let* you kiss her?"

"Yes. Then I decided I wanted another kiss, and that was what caused our little disagreement."

"But she let you kiss her once," Malcolm repeated as if unable to believe his ears.

Devon frowned at his host, a sense of unease prickling along the back of his neck. "Why? Is she maid to your wife?"

"Maid to—oh no!" Malcolm apparently found that comment amusing for he snorted a laugh, then said, "She's no one's maid, is Kat. Tell me more about this encounter."

So the chit's name was Kat. Most likely a short version of Katherine. Devon shrugged at Malcolm's interested gaze. "There's not much more to tell."

"What do you think of this lass? Do you think she is pretty?"

"Pretty" wasn't quite the word for it. In comparison to the woman's true attributes, "pretty" was a pallid, winter shadow. " 'Lush' is a better word. She was well rounded with red gold hair and green eyes and—" He broke off, uncertain how much to reveal. "She was quite a noticeable woman." Which was understating the truth by a wide mark. Still, it never behooved one to bare all of one's secrets. For all Devon knew, Malcolm might have an interest in the maid himself. Devon regarded his friend for a long moment. "Why do you ask?"

Malcolm waved an expansive hand. "No particular reason. Did the two of you speak for long?"

"For several minutes. She was quite sharp-witted." And had a body that had begged for further exploration. "I take it you know this woman."

Malcolm's lips twitched. "Oh yes. I know her. That's why I'm surprised that all she did was kick your shins. It's amazing she didn't blacken your lights, too."

"She's a feisty one, I'll admit that. At one point she threatened to, ah, remove a certain 'appendage.' One I'm very fond of and have no wish to go without."

Malcolm burst into laughter. "She didn't!"

"Yes, she did. I tried to talk her into admiring my appendage at a closer distance rather than threatening to remove it, but she refused—" Devon frowned. "Good God, what is wrong?"

Gulping great gusts of air, Malcolm rocked back in his chair, his face red as he struggled to contain his laughter. "D—don't tell me any more, please! Let me—have to—catch my breath!"

It was too much. Malcolm had always been a laughing soul; it was one of the things Devon liked best about him. But for some reason, this time Devon had the feeling that Malcolm was actually laughing *at* him and not *with* him.

So it was that he said in a rather frosty voice, "I beg your pardon, but while it was certainly an amusing moment, it wasn't that funny."

Malcolm wiped his eyes, chuckling. "Ah, laddie! If only you knew!"

Devon threw his napkin on the table. "Knew what?"

"Th-that—by the saints, I c-can't talk." Malcolm fell into yet another paroxysm of laughter.

Devon was forced to wait while his host composed himself. It took several moments and three or four gulps of tepid ale before Malcolm finally gasped a calmer breath.

The Scotsman wiped his eyes and said, "Here's the whist of it: the woman you were kissing in your chambers this morning was none other than Miss Katherine Anne Macdonald."

Devon stilled. Surely Malcolm didn't mean . . . "Katherine Anne *Macdonald*?"

"Aye. My half sister."

"That tall Amazon is your sister?" Devon repeated, too bemused to do more. Bloody hell. And Devon had thought she was "safe."

Malcolm read his look of chagrin as something altogether different. "Aye, 'tis a sad thing my father had such a short one for his male child and then sprung a giantess for his daughter, but so 'tis, her mother being a wee bit on the English side."

"That explains her lack of accent."

"Lack? You mean it explains why she has one to begin with."

Devon smiled. "That, too."

"She's a wild one, is Kat. My parents' marriage was not pleasant. After one particular fight, my father stormed out and didn't come back for three months. Seems he found a seamstress in a nearby town, an impecunious English woman who made her way doing fancy stitch. She was tall with green eyes and red gold hair and was rumored to be a lady of some birth, though that was never substantiated. Kat is the spitting image of her."

Devon's spirits began to climb once again. So Kat Macdonald was the result of an illicit affair. Perhaps she was yet a good candidate for a dalliance after all. As long, of course, as Malcolm didn't mind. Devon didn't know what Malcolm's feelings about his half sister were, but judging from the mirth he'd thus far displayed . . . well, things weren't as grim as Devon had thought. "Tell me about this half sister of yours . . . Katherine."

"You'll call her Kat lest you are fond of bruised

shins. She dislikes the name Katherine and has never used it."

Kat it was, then. "Did you grow up with her?"

"In the same house? Lord no. My mother couldn't stand the sight of her. My father asked and asked to have her live here, but my mother was not a forgiving sort of woman. Eventually he quit asking and instead had a snug little cottage built in the woods near here for Kat and her mum. Kat lives there now."

Devon lifted his brow. "But she has a room here, in the castle."

"Indeed she does. She oft comes for dinner and stays the night. I had the room made up for her after I came into the title. My mother had a fit, but I thought it was only right."

"Your mother sounds like quite an opinionated woman."

Malcolm made a face. "You don't know the half of it. At first she flatly refused to have anything to do with Kat, even though it was painfully obvious that the girl needed some guidance. Eventually, I was able to talk sense into my mother."

"After your father died, I'm sure some of her hard feelings must have dissolved."

"In a strange way, it only made it worse. I think Mother blamed Kat's mum for the problems in the marriage even though they were in existence long before she came along."

"How awkward."

"For me, it was difficult." Malcolm's expression sobered. "For Kat, it was painful. But I brought my mother round eventually. I told her that if she wished to continue living in the Strathmore Dower House in Edinburgh, she'd make Kat welcome and present her to society."

"So Kat is a society miss."

Something flickered across Malcolm's face, but was quickly suppressed. "Hardly. Kat didn't . . ." The Scotsman hesitated, then shrugged. "She didn't take."

There was something more to that story, Devon was sure of it. Still, it seemed equally obvious that Malcolm did not want to tell him.

Of course, it was entirely possible that Kat had not been accepted based on the circumstances of her birth. That and she was far too bold, too bright to be welcomed into the tepidness offered by society. Small, prim-mouthed beauties were lauded by the *ton*, not tall, strong women who possessed enough red gold loveliness to make even a soggy morning appear fresh and intriguing.

Devon found himself nodding. "I imagine she didn't take at all."

Malcolm opened his mouth as if to say something, but then his gaze locked with Devon's. After a charged moment, the Scotsman apparently changed his mind, for all he said was, "Aye. I'm just surprised she was so lighthearted with you this morning."

"Lighthearted? I would hardly call her that."

"She let you kiss her and didn't remove your appendage. That is lighthearted where Kat Macdonald is concerned."

The words intrigued Devon all the more. It had

been a bitter pill to discover that his perfect flirt was the half sister of his host. But the fact that she was illegitimate, had apparently been shunned by society, and now lived tucked away in a cottage in the woods not far from the castle, seemed to make her the perfect object for a flirtation once again.

All Devon knew was that he needed a diversion to protect him until he removed to Edinburgh. Someone passionate enough, and challenging enough, that he would not be tempted to fall victim to an eligible woman, one with strong familial connections and a name in society . . . *If* there were any other eligible women about. So far, the castle seemed unusually free of feminine charms.

Hm. Devon wondered if he was to be blessed with peace, after all. "Malcolm, I hope I did not come at a poor time. I'd hate to bother you when you've other guests about."

Malcolm looked up from his plate with apparent surprise. "Other guests?" He glanced about them, Devon's gaze following. While the dining room didn't suffer from the obvious neglect that tainted the rest of the castle, it was still far from perfectly tended. The rugs could do with a beating and two dusty cobwebs hung in opposite corners.

"We used to entertain weekly," Malcolm said. "But not as often now that—" He gestured towards the cobwebs. "Now only a few of Fiona's closer friends come to visit, though rarely overnight. I only wish Fiona's sister, Murien, wouldn't come so often. She's a—"

The door opened and the aged footman returned,

face flushed as he huffed and puffed. The footman come to a wheezing halt beside Malcolm and cleared his throat. As this rather noisy and elaborate process seemed to steal all the man's available air, he didn't speak for quite some time.

Malcolm gave an explosive sigh. "For the love of St. Brennan! Just tell us what Her Ladyship said!"

The footman looked disapprovingly at Malcolm and wheezed out a rather breathless "Yes, my lord. Her Ladyship says she will not be joining you for breakfast."

Malcolm frowned. "That's it?"

The aged footman's color faded to a more pasty tone, his breathing easing somewhat. "I believe so, my lord."

"You *believe*? In other words, you don't *remember?*"

The old man's wrinkled lips pursed thoughtfully. "I think . . . I'm fairly certain Her Ladyship didn't say anything else."

Malcolm threw his napkin on the table, disgust in his voice. "You are *fairly* certain? You *believe* she didn't have anything more to say?"

The footman nodded, seeming rather pleased with himself. "I usually forget something if I'm told more than one thing, but this time, I remembered it all." His smile faded. "I think."

"Thank you, Ketron," Malcolm said tiredly. "I'll see Lady Strathmore myself as soon as I'm through here."

"Yes, my lord." Still looking pleased, the elderly man turned slowly, then shuffled out of the room.

The second the door closed, Malcolm flashed a look at Devon. "Do you see what I'm saddled with? Do you see?"

Devon chuckled. "You need new servants."

"I had new servants. Well-trained servants. Excellent servants. But they all left because Fiona—" He broke off, his face red. "I suppose there is no hiding that things are not as they should be. We were doing well, Fiona and I. But then, six months ago, we had an argument about Kat, of all things."

"Kat?" Devon raised his brows.

"I dislike Fiona's sister, Murien, and I made a disparaging comment. I didn't mean it, though if you ever meet Murien, you'll know why I said what I did. She's a beautiful woman on the outside, but she has ambition beyond what is acceptable."

Devon would take care that he didn't meet Murien. She sounded exactly like the sort of woman he wanted to avoid.

Malcolm shook his head. "So Fiona took offense and said that at least her sister hadn't ruined herself like Kat had by running off with a—" He stopped and his face pinkened. "Never mind. You don't need to hear our family problems."

Ah ha! Devon was intrigued and wished to hear more, though all he said was, "All families have problems." And they did. For example, his family had a horrid curse of a ring to contend with. Which was why, in a way, it was fortuitous to confirm his suspicions that lovely, impulsive, passionate Kat Macdonald was a ruined woman. Ruined women could not demand marriage if a dalliance became something more. Of course, Devon had no intention of going anywhere he wasn't invited; he wasn't a man to take anything that wasn't freely offered. But the passion behind Kat's kiss made him believe that there was the potential for that something more.

He stole a glance at Malcolm. His friend's usually joyful expression was somber now. He sat silently staring at his half-finished plate, his shoulders slumped. He caught Devon's gaze and managed a painful smile. "I apologize for my wife's absence."

That, Devon decided, *is why I will never marry*. It suddenly seemed silly to be uneasy about the talisman ring. Magic it might be, but Devon had his own protection against such tomfoolery. Just seeing the expression on Malcolm's face as he contemplated his troubled marriage added yet another line of impenetrable bricks to an already thick wall around Devon's reluctant heart.

"Blasted female," Malcolm said with a sigh. He raked a hand through his hair, a quiver of emotion flashing over his mobile face.

Devon thought of all the times from years past that he and Malcolm had laughed at those men who seemed in the clutches of the deadly disease of matrimony. Now it seemed that Malcolm had himself become a victim. It was a damned shame.

Malcolm's smile stretched awkwardly over his cheeks. "I know what you're thinking and—"

"You have no idea what I'm thinking. None at all." Devon pulled his plate of now-cold food forward. The food might be cold, but Devon's thoughts were just heating up. "Let us eat and talk of more cheerful things."

But in the back of his mind, a plan was forming. A plan that had to do with the reclusive, ruined-to-society Kat Macdonald. A plan that would guarantee that whatever muslin-dressed pitfalls fate might throw in front of him, Devon would be ready to meet them all.

He smiled at his friend. "Tell me about your stables. I brought that gelding with me, the one I wrote to you about."

"Did you? I cannot wait to see it. Kat's mad about horses, too. She has almost two dozen of them, eating their heads off in her stables."

Devon filed that bit of information away and made another comment about horses. Soon the conversation turned toward matters of sport and the hunt and didn't falter once. But even while discussing the seeming dearth of fox this season, Devon was planning how he would find the location of a certain cottage nestled deep in the woods beside Kilkairn Castle.

Chapter 4

I-I have something to say to you, sir, a-and I hope that you will . . . what I mean is that, I-I am not here to argue with you precisely—nor at all because arguing is not what I had in mind but—I mean, I want to discuss something—but—oh blast it all! Never mind! Just pass the stupid mint sauce and let's talk some more about the weather.

Viscountess Mooreland to Viscount Mooreland,
while having a rare, private moment at dinner
before attending the theater

To one side of Kilkairn lay a winding river, a slash of silver ribbon across the deep jewel-green fields that surrounded the castle. The river provided a source of fresh, sparkling water as well as negated the need to fence the entire north side of the property.

To the other side of the castle lay a deep, dark woods filled with huge craggy oaks and thick green moss that carpeted large awkward boulders and the rich black loam of the forest floor.

Some of the villagers said Kilkairn Wood was enchanted, a rumor given credence when Kat Macdonald moved into the abandoned cottage. Long ago it had housed her mother, a woman said to have bewitched the last lord of the castle.

To the villagers, the wood was reported to be enchanted and enchanted it remained.

"Blasted, ill-mannered, arrogant Englishman!" Kat told her horse, her tones ringing over the clopping of Merriweather's hooves on the packed earthen pathway. "I vow, but I am done with Malcolm and his houseguests."

She'd have to eschew all visits. At least this last visitor hadn't been as bad as Fitzhugh who tried to squeeze her knee beneath the breakfast table even after she'd darkened his lights once already. "Men. Always taking more than you want to give them."

Merriweather tossed her mane as if to agree that such behavior was beyond the acceptable.

Kat patted the mare's neck. "That's exactly what I think, too." She relaxed a little in the saddle, her nerves still a-jangle from this morning's contretemps with the handsome stranger. She wouldn't think about it any more. It was too fine a morning to let go to waste.

The lazy sun flickered through the leaves overhead as they meandered ever deeper into the forest, dappling the mare's reddish sides with touches of amber and streaks of gold. Kat lifted her face up to where towering trees laced branches over the path, wide boughs of green leaves soon encompassing them completely.

The air was even cooler here, in the deep woods. Kat loved being among the trees and away from the hard words and groping hands of Kilkairn. Calmness began to sift into her soul, though one part of her mind continued to dwell on this morning's confrontation.

Normally, though she resented such treatment, she didn't let such things bother her. But this time things had been different. For one, she'd actually allowed the stranger to kiss her, and for two, the truth be told, she didn't think she'd ever seen a handsomer man. Well, perhaps once. But that one time should have taught her to beware such men.

She thought wistfully of the prettily turned compliments that St. John had spoken, all with a disturbing glint of sincerity in his gaze.

It had been that glint that had given her pause. Most of Malcolm's guests knew her past history and came with the intention of luring her farther down the path of lost virtue. They used empty, quickly blurted suggestions and grasping hands, neither of which had any effect on her except to raise her ire.

St. John, in contrast, had seemed to genuinely admire her.

She glanced down at herself now. Not only was she taller than most women, but she had an abundance of flesh that she greatly disliked. When she'd first been introduced to Edinburgh society, she'd quickly learned that the women who garnered all the attention were smallish, slender, and delicately made.

"I felt like an ungainly, ill-dressed bull in a china shop," she told Merriweather. Her brother, Malcolm, had done what he could. He had not stinted on her clothing or anything else. He'd purchased the best the modistes had to offer. The problem was that fashion itself pandered to the slender and delicate and left healthy, normal women like Kat looking and feeling uncomfortable and less than attractive.

She smoothed a hand over her gown. Of plain worsted, it was not at all fashionable. Instead, she'd had it cut to fit her form, with a waistline at her waist and not tied directly beneath her breasts, a style that made her chest and hips appear twice their normal size. Really, did the fashion mongers think that all women were like Fiona, as tiny and delicate as a doll?

Kat snorted. "They need to look around. Most women are like me, a little too wide here and a little too wide there to be able to wear such nonsense."

Merriweather pranced a bit.

Kat chuckled. "My thoughts exactly." She was fortunate that she'd left society's frivolous expectations behind and now had complete freedom to be and wear what she wanted. She took a deep breath, the cool, fresh air sending a grin all the way to her feet.

They rounded a sharp turn in the pathway and came out into a clearing. The trees and foliage had been cut back, then kept at bay with a meticulous hand so that the sun shone freely here, bright and warm, bathing all in a golden light.

The cottage, if one could call a twelve room structure thusly, sat in the heart of the forest. It was a tall, two-story house with a steep roof and large, square windows. The building was of hand-thrown brick, covered with mud wattle, the walls a foot thick to protect the inhabitants from the extreme weather that graced this portion of the country.

But despite a severity of design, the house was ringed with welcome. The thickly thatched roof was braided into an intricate, cheery design. Every window sported a window box filled with lavender and St. John's wort, while a bright red door beckoned one to enter. Most days, the shutters were thrown wide and singing could be heard, often a set of deep baritones, though more likely than not, Kat's own fine feminine alto.

Kat loved the place with a fierce passion. Not because of its beauty, though that was part of it. But because it was hers. Every last blooming inch. A fact she made known to any who dared say nay about her or her chosen way of life. For some reason, for as long as she could remember, there had always been people telling her what to do, how to look, which way to act, and who to be. But not here. Here she was just Kat.

She smiled in satisfaction. "It's a lovely place, isn't it, Merriweather?"

The horse jangled her bridle bells in agreement.

It was a sad truth of life that those who were born on the wrong side of the sheets spent the rest of their lives in a state of "almost." Almost an accepted part of the community. Almost a member of a real family. Almost, but never quite anything.

So it had been for Kat until she discovered her "gift," as Malcolm called it. Then things had changed forever.

She'd found her gift by chance. She'd been searching for something useful to do with her time. One day, while sitting in church and admiring the beautiful colors that filled the windows, she began to wonder if perhaps . . . just perhaps, she could find a pastime more significant than embroidery or watercolors, neither of which was bold enough to hold Kat's interest. What she needed was a pastime that would produce something glorious and beautiful. Something like the stained glass windows that cast such gorgeous shadows of red and blue and gold across the floor of the church.

The thought took hold and grew. She began to make inquiries, and to her delight, she found that one of the groomsmen in Malcolm's stable—a large, ruddy giant of a man by the name of Simon—had once apprenticed doing glasswork. Soon Kat was visiting that very glass shop and learning the craft herself. Though it took time, Kat had a natural instinct for color and design, and she found that she loved every painstaking minute.

The glasswork quickly became more than a pastime. It became a goal. With it, she would carve her own niche in the world.

The cottage had been a natural choice. Kat had grown up there, and though it needed some work after sitting empty after her mother's death, it was basically sturdy. Though Malcolm had protested loud and long, Kat had moved into the cottage a scant month later, taking Simon with her. His sister, Annie, came along soon after that.

Kat guided Merriweather across the clearing to

the barn. Sensing a carrot was waiting, the mare kicked up her feet and attempted to trot.

Kat laughed. "Easy now! You'll get your carrot in good time."

A large, red-haired man came out of the barn door, a plank of wood resting easily on his shoulder. He paused when he saw Kat, his craggy face softening slightly. "There ye be! Annie has been lookin' all over fer ye."

Kat grinned at Simon as she kicked her foot out of the stirrup and stepped down. "What does she want?"

Simon lowered his brow. "I don't know, but she has some of her bosom friends with her. Last I heard, they were talkin' aboot the new guest at the castle."

Kat undid Merriweather's saddle, hefting it off the mare's back and onto the fence rail. "I met him this morning."

"Did ye now? What do ye have to say aboot him?"

Kat had an instant image of mischievous blue eyes fringed in thick black lashes, her body tingling at the memory of strong hands moving sinuously over her body. She forced a casual shrug. "I don't have much to say at all." Not to Simon, anyway.

Why *had* she been so slow to react when the stranger had kissed her? None of Malcolm's other houseguests had managed to weasel a kiss out of her. But this guest . . . Kat had to smile a little. Whatever the reason, she wasn't really sorry it had happened. It was a lovely, warm memory, and as long as it went no further, there was no harm. No harm at all.

Besides, the man had been damned good at what he was about. The thought made her grin even more.

Simon's gaze narrowed. He set the wood against the fence. "Out with it, lass. What has ye smilin' so big?"

Kat's cheeks heated. "Nothing. I was just thinking about—" Good Lord what did she say now? "Things," she finished weakly. Things like strong, well-defined hands that could cup one ever so intimately and make one's stomach tighten with need. Things like a pair of firm, warm lips that knew all too well how to send one's thoughts to places they were better not going.

"Hmph," Simon said, eyeing her up and down as she rubbed down Merriweather and then led the mare into the coolness of the barn. Simon followed along, his gaze never leaving her. "Whatever ye're thinkin' aboot, 'tis makin' yer cheeks turn red."

Kat wisely ignored him. Though he was a scant two years older than she, she thought of Simon as a father. Certainly he'd been more involved in her life than her own father had been.

"I'm fine, Simon. Just a bit heated from the ride back." Kat closed the stall door on Merriweather, and then left the barn. "Where is Annie?"

Simon followed her outside. "She's in the kitchen with Fat Mary."

Kat curled her nose.

Simon nodded morosely. "That's what I thought, too. Fat Mary does nothin' but spread rumors, night 'n' day. I don't know why Annie puts up wid it."

Kat could have told Simon that his sister was addicted to gossip. While Annie rarely passed on any information she gathered in her meticulous cullings, she enjoyed knowing more than anyone else.

Simon crossed his arms and leaned back on his heels. "I've got the lads down in the workshop, finishing off the last window for the Earl of Argyll. I tol' the lads they'd best make it something to behold. If we do a good job, there'll be more where that comes from."

Kat nodded. "The earl has a new wife. She'll be wanting to put her own mark on his household. She told me she wants to commission a window for every child they have."

"Women," Simon said, shaking his head. "They can think of more ways to spend blunt."

Kat lifted her brows. "I'm a woman."

"Aye, but ye ain't all trussed up in the need to tell everyone what to do." Simon glanced at the house for a moment, before adding in an undertone, "Take Annie. M'sister has a bad habit of bossin' a man aboot until he's ready to bundle his clothes and run for the hills."

"Just see to it that *you* don't run," Kat said, leaning over to give him a quick hug. "Or if you do, at least promise to come back after you've enjoyed a pint or ten of freedom. I can't do without you more than one day. Perhaps two, if things are slow."

Simon's smile blossomed. "I have to come back, lassie. Who else'll make the windows bearing the coat of arms fer those fancy earls and dukes?"

"Who indeed?" She kissed his cheek and turned to the house. "Tell the lads I'll be with them directly.

I just want to see what Annie bought in the village today."

"I'll tell them," Simon promised. He retrieved his plank and hoisted it over his shoulder, then winked. "I'll tell them ye're in a rare mood, too. That should get them to hoppin'."

"I don't want them hopping, just working. We've more orders to fill than there are hours in the day."

"Don't ye fash, Miss Kat. We'll come aboot. See if we don't." He gave her a reassuring nod, then left, walking toward the workshop, a long, low building set on the other side of the cottage, back against the line of trees.

She watched him go, a fond smile touching her mouth. Simon possessed a heavy sense of responsibility and a natural tendency to step in and do what most needed doing. These were just two of the many things she loved about him.

Kat turned and crossed to the back door of the cottage. If there was any chance that mud or dirt was clinging to her boots, she always entered through the kitchen. As she stopped outside the open door to scrape her feet, Kat heard voices from inside.

"I seed him meself, I did!" said a woman in a breathless voice. Kat recognized Fat Mary, a kitchen maid from Kilkairn. As round as a barrel, there was no mistaking her rough voice. "He's as beautiful as Lucifer, all black hair and blue eyes."

"Is he tall?" asked another woman. That sounded like Lucy, who came from the village to help Annie with the cooking.

"Tall he is," Fat Mary agreed with so much enthusiasm that Kat found a scowl upon her face. "He has a fine arse, too."

Arse? How on earth could Mary know that? Kat leaned closer to the open door and tried to peek around the corner.

"Och now, how do ye know aboot the man's arse?" Annie asked, her voice sharp.

God bless Annie, Kat decided with rising satisfaction. The housekeeper never stood for any nonsense.

"Why, I walked into his room to stoke the fire and there he was, lying on the counterpane, sound asleep and as bare-arsed as the day he was borned."

Kat took a hasty step forward, then caught herself. St. John had arrived in the middle of the night, and Kat herself had been there when he'd awakened, so it was highly unlikely Mary knew anything more than the man's fully clothed appearance. Mary was lying; she had to be. But Kat knew that bursting into the room, ringing with indignation, would only draw undue attention to herself.

In the time Kat had known her, Fat Mary had launched and sailed several hot air balloons' worth of gossip. None of them landing anywhere near the truth. But if Fat Mary started such a rumor about Malcolm's new guest, every single maid in the countryside soon would be making excuses to visit Kilkairn in an effort to glimpse the handsome stranger. For some reason, Kat found that very annoying.

Lifting her chin, she walked into the kitchen and looked directly at Fat Mary. "I was at the castle this very morning, and you did not light the fires in any of the bedchambers."

Fat Mary flushed. She was a large, fleshy woman with pale, stringy hair and watery gray eyes. "I did the guest chamber!"

"Oh?"

"Yes. That's when I seed him, whilst I was lighting the fire."

Kat lifted her brows. "Which chamber did you say St. John was sleeping in?"

"Which—" Mary shifted uneasily. "I don't remember, exactly—perhaps 'twas the green one."

Lucy frowned. "But ye tol' me on the way here that he was in the gold room and—"

"Ha!" Annie plopped her fists on her narrow hips as she glared at Mary. "Ye were fashin' us, weren't ye? Tellin' us fibs aboot one o' Lord Strathmore's guests. Ye ought to be ashamed o' yerself."

"I'm not tellin' fibs," Fat Mary said, though her gaze shot to the door and back as if she were considering running for her life. "I seed him, I did. And his arse, too!"

"I don't know who you 'seed' or whose arse, but it wasn't St. John's," Kat said. "He was in the blue room because none of the others were ready."

"There!" Annie eyed Mary with disgust. "Isn't it time ye returned to Kilkairn? I daresay they've more dirty pots fer ye to scrub."

Mary stiffened, her plump shoulders rising almost to her ears. "I was just tellin' ye what I seed, was all."

"What you *wished* you'd seed," Annie amended. Though a good head shorter than any other woman in the room, she managed to maintain control of every conversation, simply through sheer force of her character. Even now, her hair tucked beneath a cap, her whip-cord thin body covered with a gray gown, and solid, plain shoes on her feet, she was plainly in command. "Off with ye. Mary, ye know where ye're wanted . . . and where ye're not. I'll have yer cart brought around. Lucy, thank ye fer the jelly. Tell yer mum we're grateful."

Kat watched while Annie bustled her guests out to their cart and waved them on their way. Then, wiping her hands on her apron, Annie returned and pulled out a wooden bowl and a sack of potatoes and began peeling them.

Kat found another knife and joined in. "I'm sorry your visit turned out so unpleasantly."

"Och, don't think on it. Fat Mary is as Fat Mary is. By this time tomorrow, neither of us will remember who was mad aboot what." Annie finished off a peeling with an expert twist of her wrist.

"She's a braggart, all right," Kat agreed.

"Indeed. Actin' as if she was the only one who saw him in the castle." Annie turned to Kat and eyed her up and down. "Well?"

"Well what?" Kat asked uneasily. She kept her gaze on the potato she was peeling so she wouldn't have to meet Annie's gaze.

"What do *you* have to say aboot the stranger at the castle?"

"I know his name is St. John." And that he had a mouth made for kissing. Kat cut the potato with more force than was necessary, the knife thunking soundly on the cutting board.

Annie eyed the flashing knife with some misgiving. "Indeed?"

"Aye. If I remember what Malcolm told me a while ago, I believe they met whilst the two were down at Eton." Or so she thought.

"Indeed?" Annie said. "Is that all ye know?"

"Aye," Kat said.

"Hm. I suppose I'll have to wait until my cousin Jane gets a look at him. She's ever had an eye for a handsome man."

Kat didn't like that at all. Jane was the upstairs maid at Kilkairn, and a more lascivious woman was difficult to find.

In fact, Kat was quite certain that Jane had bedded most, if not all, of Malcolm's guests. "I daresay St. John isn't the sort of man Jane would like to dally with."

Annie looked astounded. "He was breathin', wasn't he?"

"Aye, but—"

"Then Jane would enjoy dallyin' with him. She's not particular, is our Jane."

Kat cut another potato in two, this time slicing it so thoroughly that she buried the tip of the knife in the table top. "Oh! I'm sorry."

Annie's hand closed over Kat's. "Just leave the knife there. I'll take care of the rest of these."

"Are you certain? I can at least—"

"I'm certain. Besides, aren't the lads waitin' on ye?"

They would be, of course. Since housework had never held any appeal, Kat readily washed her hands in a bucket and dried them on a towel Annie kept nearby. "You're right. We have to finish the windows by the end of this week or we'll be good and behind."

"There is no 'good and behind.' There's only 'behind.' Get to work, Miss Kat." Annie flashed a smile, her angular, usually morose face lighting. "I'd never let the lads alone for a minute. You canno' tell what they'll be into."

Kat agreed, smiling in return. The men they'd gathered as glassworkers were a singular lot, all of them strong on personality. Simon had collected most of them, scrutinizing them carefully. Kat paid more than a fair wage, and she rewarded quality work, which meant the best of the best were drawn to her cottage.

Waving good-bye to Annie, Kat left. She lifted her face to the sun as she walked across the clearing to the workshop where the pleasant sound of hammering and male voices made her smile. All in all, it was a good thing she wouldn't be going to Kilkairn Castle any more this week. She'd spent far too much time mulling over the handsome Englishman as it was, and all for no more than a little kiss. Heaven only knew what state she'd be in if he'd done more. So to preserve her own peace, she'd stay away from Kilkairn. At least until St. John was on his bonny way.

The carriage swept into the drive and pulled up in front of Kilkairn Castle much as it had done the night before. Paul leaned forward and caught a glimpse of a solitary figure standing on the front portico.

"Mr. St. John's biting at the bit, ain't he?" John the coachman said.

"So it appears." Paul jumped down the second the coach came to a halt. He hadn't been entirely certain he'd find the master up and about. It was only eleven, after all. But there he was, pacing the front portico, hat in hand, dressed for riding.

As soon as Paul approached, St. John smiled. "There you are! How was the inn?"

"Adequate, sir." Barely. But it was better than staying at the castle.

"Excellent. I find Kilkairn just as satisfying."

A smile hovered over St. John's mouth, and Paul found himself responding. "I'm surprised ye're up so early, sir."

"What? Me? Why, I love mornings!" Devon waved a hand. "Just smell the fresh air. Taste the crisp coolness of the dawn."

Paul didn't point out that dawn had been hours ago. "Indeed, sir. I hadn't noticed."

"You'd better wake up, Paul. Such glorious mornings do not come often." St. John's eyes twinkled. "Almost never, where I am concerned."

Paul grinned. "No, sir. Did you wish us to take you somewhere today?"

"Actually, yes. But I'm not sure where."

"Sir?"

"I want to find a house located in the woods. A smallish house, from what I understand."

"A small house? Ye want one to let?"

"No, no, no! This house belongs to someone, and I wish to pay a visit."

Things suddenly became clear to Paul. He was beginning to smell a petticoat. "Sir, who might this house belong to?"

"Miss Katherine Macdonald."

From the look on the master's face, this was obviously a promising errand of a romantic nature. "If Miss Macdonald lives hereabouts, I daresay someone in the stable will know how to get there."

"Excellent idea! Furthermore, I believe I should ride there myself. All I need are the directions."

"Of course, sir. Shall I have the gelding saddled?"

"Yes. I daresay Thunder could use a stretch." Devon had paid a small fortune for the horse, and had never regretted it. Especially today when he could ride up to Kat's cottage astride a horse worthy of carrying a knight.

Paul bowed, then went on his way. In a relatively short time, he returned with directions, leading Thunder to the steps. The animal was huge, all gleaming black muscle and streaming mane and tail. Devon pulled on his gloves. Miss Katherine's head was bound to be turned.

Moments later, Devon galloped across the green fields of Kilkairn toward the forest. He was spurred forward by the memory of Kat's lush body in his lap.

Devon considered briefly the information Malcolm had let fall. There was an unspoken code of gentlemen that averred that one did not attempt to seduce the sisters of one's best friends. Malcolm must have decided that any flirtation of Devon's was nothing more than that—a flirtation, begun and ended with a kiss. Of course, Malcolm also knew that Devon would never go beyond the line of the acceptable, not without the permission and encouragement of the lady in question. What stung was that for some reason, Malcolm seemed to think his sister was immune to Devon's particular charms—that Kat would want nothing more from Devon than a kiss.

But Devon was not so sure; Kat seemed to possess a very passionate nature. Whatever the truth, it would certainly take more than a kiss to ease his lustful thoughts of Kat Macdonald, and to satisfy the curiosity and heat he'd seen burning in her eyes.

But the real beauty of it all was that the more time Devon spent with Malcolm's ineligible sister, the less chance there was that Devon might fall victim to the talisman ring's magical powers.

With Kat and her ruined reputation, Devon was completely safe, no matter how far their flirtation went. More proof that he was smarter by far than any ring ever made. Smiling to himself, he urged Thunder farther into the woods, certain he was on his way to dislodge an evil fate.

Chapter 5

It's really quite easy. As soon as you see the fires of wrath in their eyes and know your time has come, you begin the seduction. A brush of your hand across theirs when they reach for the crème pot. A heated glance. A lingering appreciation for how they look . . . smell . . . taste. Just try it, sir. I've been married fourteen years, and not once has she managed to ring a peal over my head without stammering and blushing like a school girl.

Viscount Mooreland to his uncle,
the Earl of Stempleton,
whilst viewing the horses for sale at Tattersall's

Devon had always believed that one's greatest strength was also one's greatest weakness. Such was his case, anyway. From the time he'd been a child, he had never been known for his lack of persistence.

Once, when he had attained the ripe age of five, his parents had left for a brief visit to London. Devon had begged to go with them, but had been refused.

Looking back now, he could see that perhaps his parents had desired some time alone. Even though they employed a squadron of governesses and tutors, six children had to have been a drain on their marital reserves.

But at the time, all Devon had known was that he was being left behind. Thus he'd waited until the trunks for the upcoming journey were sitting in the front hall and he'd opened the largest one, removed one of his mother's voluminous gowns and stuffed it beneath the settee in the front sitting room, and then paid his brother Chase a shilling to close the trunk and lock him in.

Moments later an unsuspecting footman had carried the trunk to the waiting coach and strapped it on the back. Neither Devon nor Chase had thought of such mundane things as food or air. Within thirty minutes of rumbling out of the long drive, Devon had begun to realize the shortfalls of his plan.

He became increasingly hot, the air stifling and then thin, and all the while he was aware of a horrid need to relieve himself.

By the time the first hour had passed, he'd begun to panic and tried to gain the attention of the coachman, but the noise of the creaking, swaying coach and the clopping of the horses concealed the thumping of his small fists on the trunk lid. No one heard him.

It was a good thing the trip to London was a mere three hours, though by the time Devon was discovered, he was ill from the heat and the confinement. It took almost two days before he could get out of bed.

Of course, he'd been thankful for his convalescence as it prevented him from receiving the switching that should have been his. As his father would later say when the incident was brought up, "Devon's determination will be both the making and the breaking of him. God only knows which."

Now here he was, not in London, but in a clearing in the forest, looking at what had to be Kat Macdonald's cottage, and that same determination that had caused him to ride in a trunk all the way to London was urging him forward.

The sun shone on the house and lit the clearing until he almost expected the door to fly open and little men in matching tunics to come tumbling out, turning buttercups into gold, or making mushrooms into sweet cakes, or some such nonsense.

"Either that or seven beautiful maidens," Devon said to himself, trying to remember the fairy tales his mother had so delighted in telling. Something about seven pairs of shoes and dancing . . . He frowned. Whatever the tale, he'd forgotten most of it. Not that it mattered. It was all childhood nonsense anyway.

Devon urged Thunder across the clearing. The gelding frisked and frolicked, prancing as if afraid of the splotches of sun that trembled across the ground in unison with the breeze. They were only about halfway to the cottage when Devon realized they had an audience.

A group of men stood outside a long, low building. The group was small, but the men were not. They were all huge. "Giants," Devon muttered. "One. Two. Three—good God. Seven giants."

He pulled Thunder to a halt. He wasn't afraid of the giants. The tall ones always fell the hardest. Still, it wouldn't do to be rude.

He led Thunder up to them and dismounted. "Good day," he called. "I am looking for—"

Kat stood in the doorway behind the men, dressed in the same drab gown as before. It hung gloriously on her curves, molding itself to her slants and slopes. The sunlight dappled her hair gold, muting the red and making her shine like a new guinea. Standing with the men, she looked petite.

"What are you doing here?" she asked, one hand propped on her hip.

It was hardly the welcome he wished. "I came to ask you a question." He glanced at the men, offering a smile to offset their glares. "In private," he added.

They didn't move. Neither did Devon.

"I don't wish for a word in private with y—" Her gaze wandered past him to Thunder, her eyes widening. "What a lovely horse!"

Devon hid a smile. Malcolm had been right; Kat loved horses. "Thunder is a lovely animal. And he knows it, too."

One of the men—a red-haired, burly sort with disapproving eyes and a grim expression—said, "Miss Kat, we've work to do."

"Aye, Simon," she said, though she continued to walk toward Thunder. "How long have you had him?"

"I purchased him a year ago."

She reached them and placed a hand on Thunder's neck. The horse pretended to shy. She laughed and grabbed the bridle, holding him still while she patted his side. "He's a high-strung one, isn't he?"

"Miss Kat!" Another of the men chimed in, a large, brown-haired man with a beard and thick brows. "We've glass to do and time's a-wastin'." He glared at Devon the whole time he was speaking.

"Glass?" Devon said quietly so that only Kat could hear him.

She started to answer, then hesitated. "It doesn't matter. A business concern, no more." She turned to the brown-haired man. "I wish to speak to Mr. St. John. Go ahead and begin on the next brace of cuts."

The men eyed him sullenly, apparently blaming him for Kat's answer. Devon took the opportunity to eye them all back. It was a strange assortment. Some were brown-haired, some red; some had freckles, some didn't. Except for their size and the glares on their faces, they were as different as the day was long.

Devon wondered if they were going to allow Kat to stay and speak with him. Hm. How did one deal with seven giants? He didn't recall a single one of his mother's fairy tales that gave instructions. If only he had some magic beans. The thought made him grin, a fact that did not sit well with the giant conclave one bit.

"Miss Kat," snapped the redheaded one. It was quickly becoming apparent he was the leader. "I don't think ye should be standin' aboot, talkin' to a stranger."

"Simon, for the love of—what could happen? We're here, in the middle of the clearing. If the man is foolish enough to attempt to molest me, I'll black his eyes and send him on his way."

Devon had to bite back a smile for the calm way she spoke. He didn't know of another woman who would have made such a statement in such an unemotional manner.

"Simon," Kat said. "Take the lads back inside; I'll be in shortly."

"We've two more windows to make," he answered, though his gaze never left Devon.

"I realize that," she answered, a note of steel in her voice. "Which is why you all need to get back to work. I cannot do the cuts until you've got the glass ready."

Whatever that meant, it must have been true, for the men began to shift uneasily. Finally Simon flexed his shoulders and nodded once. "Very well. If ye need us, ye've but to call." He cast a last, cold glance at Devon and then turned to the others. "Back inside, lads. The sooner we get the glass ready, the sooner Miss Kat can get it cut."

As soon as they shuffled back into the building, Devon glanced down at Kat. "Your servants?"

"No. Apprentices. Except Simon." She gave Thunder one last pat, then stepped away, her gaze meeting his. "Why are you here, Sassenach?"

"Sassenach?"

"Englishman."

He wasn't sure he liked the way she said that. "You're English, too. At least half."

Her mouth tightened, her green eyes accusing. "You've been talking to Malcolm."

Devon nodded.

A faint line of color touched Kat's face, and she turned away, facing the building. "I suppose I shouldn't be surprised."

Devon eyed a large wood curl in Kat's red-gold hair. He reached out to untangle the sliver of wood, but Kat yanked away.

She eyed him suspiciously. "What are you doing?"

He smiled and reached again, only this time more slowly. She held still, though her body was so stiff he could almost feel the tension seeping from her.

Apparently, when she wasn't surprised, Kat Macdonald was a bit shy of touch. He wondered if that was a result of the incident that left her "ruined" in the eyes of society, or because of Malcolm's other guests continually groping her when they came to visit.

He plucked the wood curl from her hair, then showed it to her. "What *have* you been doing?"

She took the sliver of wood and tossed it to the ground. "Helping Hamish with the frames."

"Frames?"

"Malcolm didn't tell you everything, then. I am not a lady, St. John. I make my own way, I do." Her firm chin lifted and she said with simple pride, "We are glassmakers, the lads and I. The best there is."

"If you're a glassmaker, why is there a wood shaving in your hair?"

"Because glass must be fit in a frame. And the right frame is as important as finding the right colors for the picture."

"You and the 'lads' do this by yourselves?"

"Aye. And we've more work than we can fill."

His gaze roved over her, from the pride in her eyes, to the strength of her body, to the broad grace of her hands. She was a conundrum, this woman, a strange mixture of strength and . . . was it vulnerability? Or pride? Something sweet and delicate rested deep in her eyes, and he was determined to discover what it was.

Despite Devon's determination to merely establish a dalliance with Kat, he had to admit that he was somewhat fascinated. Not too much, of course. He was no wet-eared halfling to think interest was love. It wasn't, of course. But it did promise to make the flirtation something special, which was fine by Devon. It had been a long time since a woman—any woman—had truly intrigued him.

Devon reflected that of all the women he knew, with the exception of a housekeeper, laundress, or maid or two, none had had professions of their own. Truly, everything about Kat Macdonald was larger than life—her size, her blazing color, even the gentle rasp of her husky voice—all were *more* in some way. More than he expected, and far more than a proper lady should be.

The thought was rather exciting. "Do you know what I think?"

Though her expression didn't change, he felt her withdraw, as if in expectation of a blow. Devon placed a finger beneath her chin and tilted her face to his. "I think you're an exceptional, astounding woman, and I want to know more of you."

Kat discovered that it was possible to stop breathing

even while panting. And she was panting. There was a fey magic about the stranger, something that made her body quiver the second he was within range.

If she looked back in her memory, there was only one other time she'd been so affected by a man. The memory tightened about her throat and halted her voice.

"Furthermore," Devon St. John continued, his voice low and smooth, "I wonder why you are the way you are." His gaze wandered over her, from her head to her feet, a question in his blue gaze. "Who are you, Katherine Anne Macdonald?"

She stiffened. "I am who I am. And I would prefer it if you did not call me by that name."

"Katherine? Why not?" His eyes twinkled. "It's your real name, isn't it?"

"Yes. But my mother never used it unless she was angry, so I prefer Kat. Or for you, Miss Macdonald."

He laughed. "Miss Macdonald it is. But only if you'll call me Devon." His gaze darkened the slightest bit. "I want to hear my name on your lips."

Kat had to rub her arms to stop the goose bumps that traveled up her skin at the silken tone of his voice. It took all of her composure to answer in a steady voice. "I hope you aren't counting on such. I will never say your name."

He leaned forward, his eyes so rich a blue that she couldn't look away. "Is that a wager?"

"No, Mr. St. John. It is a fact."

The man smiled then, a faint curve to his well formed mouth that drew the gaze and sent heated thoughts through her mind. "Miss Macdonald, may

I say that I look forward to the challenge of our continued friendship."

Friendship . . . was that what this was? Kat was held by the thought. It had been a long time since she'd thought of having a friend—any friend, even a dangerous one like Devon St. John. And he was dangerous. She stole a glance at him from beneath her lashes.

Kat was used to seeing rather robust men appear pallid beside the likes of her lads, especially Alistair and Simon, who had to dip their heads to enter the lower barn door. But this man carried himself with such masculine ease that she caught herself looking at his legs, his hips, his hands . . . wondering what he would be like in bed. She already knew his kisses were hot and lethal, a fact that only made her wonder the more about the rest of him.

Kat's cheeks heated. Bless her, but she was worse than Annie's cousin, Jane.

Well, perhaps not *that* bad, but bad enough. "I am exactly what you see, St. John. Can you say the same?"

"I think so," he answered, nodding thoughtfully. "I have never been one to dissemble."

Before she could stop herself, she snorted in disbelief.

His brow jerked lower. "I am serious. I do not lie."

"Never?"

"Never."

"Have you ever told a woman she had beautiful eyes for no other reason than to tempt her into your arms?"

He opened his mouth. Then closed it. After a long moment, he puffed out a sigh. "Up until now, I hadn't thought of that as a lie."

"No? What would you call it?"

"A hard-won compliment."

Her own lips twitched, but she swallowed the smile before it could blossom. "That is the problem with men like you. You lie so much and so oft that you no longer know the truth. Now if you'll excuse me, St. John, I've work to do."

She turned to go, but his hand was about her wrist before she could take a step.

"I came for a reason, Miss Macdonald. I came to ask you if you'd do me the honor of taking a ride with me."

"A ride?" She tried to pretend that the feel of his strong hand about her wrist wasn't making her stomach heat in a most disturbing way.

"A ride," he repeated. He gave her a rueful, lopsided smile. "That's all. One simple ride. I'm here alone, you know. And I've no place to go for three weeks. Surely you can spare a few hours of your time for something as innocuous as a ride."

For one blessed mad moment, Kat thought of agreeing. She could almost see the two of them, riding across the fields, laughing and talking. But then reality returned and she remembered another time, another man, also pleading for nothing more than "a few hours." At the time, she'd wondered what harm could occur in a few hours. Now she knew.

She pulled her wrist free. "No thank you, Mr. St. John. You'll have to find someone else to pass the time with. I'm not available." With that, pride stiffening her weakened will, she turned on her heel and quickly made her way into the shop.

Malcolm climbed the stairs to his wife's bedchamber, his boots landing heavily on the grayish runner. He tried to ignore the small puffs of dust that swirled with each footfall and the dusty slickness of the railing beneath his hand, just as he tried to ignore the cobwebs that hung unattended from the branched chandeliers displayed overhead, and the faint musty odor that was slowly permeating his once orderly household.

Though he'd been unable to explain the entire situation to Devon, the truth was that Malcolm and his wife were not arguing. Oh no, it had progressed far beyond that. They were now at war. What had begun as a difference of opinion had escalated into something far worse.

It was a simple matter, really. He wanted children; his wife did not. Worse, he wanted to stay here, at Kilkairn, and enjoy life at the castle, while she was determined to drag him to Edinburgh.

Normally, Malcolm had nothing against Edinburgh. He rather enjoyed a taste of town life on occasion. But after Fiona had denied his request for a child and refused to stay at Kilkairn for more than two weeks at a stretch, he'd dug in his heels and refused to go anywhere. Better yet, he'd refused to allow her to travel, as well.

He'd thought to wear her down, make her agree to his wishes—once she had his son, she could travel all she wished, and with his blessing. It seemed a fair enough request, but she'd been far from agreeable. What was worse was that he'd underestimated one small facet of his lovely wife's character—her overgrown sense of pride. It was equal to his own, if not larger and far more entrenched.

In response to his ultimatums, she'd done what she could to make Kilkairn Castle the uncomfortable mess it was today, irritating the capable servants until they left and neglecting to oversee the ones that stayed. Malcolm had uneasy dreams of Fiona dancing through the castle, tossing dust in the air. Then, once she tired of that game, resting in his favorite chair by the fire to knit cobwebs of every shape, size, and color.

Malcolm paused outside a wide oak door and straightened his shoulders. "Do not give an inch," he muttered to himself. His father would have never put up with such nonsense, and neither would Malcolm. Still, it was difficult to maintain his pride because he loved Fiona . . . didn't he?

A cold grip of uncertainty held him in place. As always, it was the one question he couldn't answer. What if his love for his wife only lasted as long as his father's love had lasted for his mother? Malcolm remembered his mother's pain each time his father strayed.

It was a long moment before he lifted his hand and knocked on the door and then entered.

The room was decorated in delicate blue and white, Fiona's favorite colors. A large bed sat in the center of one wall, an ornate dressing table across the room, near the large fireplace.

His bride sat at the dressing table, a lace gown tossed over her shoulders, her hair streaming down her back as her maid brushed out the long curls.

Fiona's gaze met Malcolm's in the mirror and a stubborn flush rose in her cheeks as she looked away.

Malcolm flicked a glance toward the maid. "Marie, I wish to speak with Lady Strathmore privately."

Marie's gaunt face reddened and she gripped the back of Fiona's chair in a protective manner. "I was just brushing Her Ladyship's hair and—"

"That will be all, Marie," Malcolm said firmly.

The maid sniffed and then looked at Fiona. "Madam?"

Fiona sighed. "You may go, Marie."

"*Oui*, but—" Marie glanced at Malcolm as if to ascertain his trustworthiness.

That irked him. By the saints, he was the man of this house, and he wouldn't stand for such impertinence. He spun on his heel and went to the door and held it open.

Head high as if she were on her way to the guillotine, Marie slowly went to the door. The second she crossed the threshold, Malcolm kicked the door closed behind her.

Fiona jumped. "Malcolm!"

"Sorry. My foot slipped. I meant to plant it in her arse."

Fiona's cheeks pinkened. "There is no need to be crude."

"I disagree." He met her gaze in the reflection of the mirror. "I came to speak with you about this morning. You, madam, are out of hand."

Fiona adjusted the cut-crystal decanters on the dresser. "I am no such thing."

"I sent you a request to join me and a guest for breakfast. You refused to attend."

She picked up the brush and began brushing her hair. "I was not yet up."

"Then send word that you had to dress! I asked you to attend us and you should have."

Her chin lifted. "You know how I prize my mornings."

Mornings. The thought echoed in his mind. At one time, he'd loved mornings. Mornings when he'd come into this very room and climb into Fiona's bed to find her warm and soft, snuggled deep beneath the blankets. A pain tweaked his heart. "It has been some time since I was allowed to share mornings with you."

Her cheeks turned a deep pink, though her gaze met his steadily. "You know the cost of returning to my bed."

Malcolm paused. A part of him wished to end this ridiculous standoff. To return to the warmth of their previous relationship. But he could not bend. "And you know the cost of returning to Edinburgh. I will have a son, madam."

Fiona pulled the brush through a long strand of hair. It was thick and as brown as the forest floor, with threads of gold glimmering in the silken mass. "As before, we are at an impasse."

Malcolm rubbed his neck where an ache was beginning to form. "Look, Fiona, I didn't come here to argue. I came to ask that you be polite to St. John."

"Oh!" She tossed the brush to her dresser where it clattered to a stop among a mass of crystal bottles. "When have I ever been rude to any of your guests?"

"Never. It's just that I happen to think that perhaps St. John is interested in Kat."

"They all are, at first. But you know what will happen. St. John will take one look at Kat and she'll set her fist in his eye for his impertinence. And then he'll want nothing more to do with her. Her attraction never seems to last past the first meeting."

"This seems different."

Fiona's delicate brows rose. "Oh?"

"They met this morning, and if I'm not mistaken, Devon is quite interested."

"But Kat is—" Fiona bit off the rest of the sentence.

Malcolm's gaze narrowed. "She's what?"

Her cheeks glowed. "Nothing."

"My sister may be a tad unusual, but she is right as rain. Give a man a chance to get to know her, and he'll come up to snuff. See if he doesn't."

"I've nothing against your sister, you know that. It's just that a man like St. John would be more comfortable with someone like . . . oh, Murien."

"*Your* sister?" Malcolm almost stuttered.

Fiona flounced in her seat. "You have *never* liked Murien!"

"That's not true—"

"Oh, just admit it!"

He paused, fighting to control the tight ball of anger that burned in his stomach. "I've never been fond of Murien and well you know it, though that has nothing to do with us."

Fiona met his gaze a moment. "Except that it is yet another way in which we differ. I vow, but I am sick unto death of our squabbles. If only there was a way to—" She paused, a light coming into her eyes. "Malcolm."

"Aye?" he answered, a faint quiver of alarm dancing up his neck. "What is it?"

The look she turned on him was almost blinding in its luminance. "I know what we need to do to end this argument between us!"

"What?"

"You and I will make a wager. I shall invite Murien here and we shall see whose sister is more to Mr. St. John's liking."

Malcolm frowned. Murien here? Under his roof? "I don't think I could stand it."

"There is nothing wrong with her!"

He shrugged. "If you say so."

"At least *my* sister knows how to dress."

"You have me there. Kat has never been one to toss her good sense after fashion."

"No," Fiona snapped, "just her virtue."

Malcolm's jaw tightened until it ached. "My sister may have made some mistakes in her youth, but you have to admit that she lives circumspectly now."

"Circumspect? You call living with seven men in the middle of a forest—"

"They are her apprentices. I have explained that time and again."

"Of course," Fiona said tightly. "Do we have a wager then? My sister against yours."

Malcolm considered this. He was so dispirited by

their disagreements. Perhaps this would be a way to regain at least a little of his peace. "Done," Malcolm said. "And the wager?"

"If I win, you will cease pestering me to have a child and we will spend every season for the next five years in Edinburgh."

"The whole season?" he sputtered. "For *five* years?"

"All of it. And you will spare no expense."

"That's a steep wager."

"Afraid you'll lose?"

He ground his teeth. "No, I am not afraid to lose. I know Kat, and there are things about her that you wouldn't understand. Things that make me certain she'll win hands down over your whey-faced sister."

"Oh!" Fiona stood in a faint rustle of silk. "Don't you dare speak ill of my sister! At least Murien has manners. Kat goes about in clothes covered in wood curls and smelling of burned metal."

Malcolm jammed his hands into his pockets to keep from reaching for her. "*Enough*! My wager, madam wife, is to be allowed back in your bed until you bear the fruits of that endeavor. I shall have my son. One way or another."

Fiona's hand tightened about the back of her chair, tears threatening. "I know what happens to marriages once a child is born. My own father—"

"I am not your father. I would never leave you."

"He didn't leave, either. Not physically. Once he had his heir, he was just more interested in other things."

Malcolm raked a hand through his hair. "Fiona, I will not—"

She took a step forward, her gaze almost pleading. "Malcolm, can you promise me that your feelings for me won't change? Not even when we have a child?"

He opened his mouth to say the word, but then it happened. Could he care for a woman forever? She saw it in his eyes, a flicker of his uncertainty, dark and fearful. Fiona's heart sank and it took all her pride to keep her head upright. She'd been right to deny him. Right to worry that his feelings for her were not immune to change.

She steeled her heart once again. He was angry with her decision not to have children. But she could stand his anger better than his absence. One day she might agree to have a child, just not now. Not while she was still desperately in love with her own husband.

Malcolm shook his head. "Madam, I await your answer. Do you agree to our wager?"

She hoped her lips didn't tremble as she resumed her seat and reclaimed her brush. "Yes, I agree. And I hope with all my heart that I win."

His jaw hardened. "We are settled then. I won't burden you with my company any longer." He spun on his heel and left, slamming the door behind him.

Fiona scarcely waited for his footsteps to fade before she dropped the brush, jumped up and threw herself across her bed, where she cried until she could cry no more.

Chapter 6

A man will vow to his dying day that he hates being chased by a woman. But let him meet one who will not chase him, one who barely knows he is alive, one who acts not only disinterested, but disgusted as well, and he will do everything in his power to fix her interest.

Earl of Stempleton to his neighbor Mr. Poole,
while sharing a glass of port after dinner
at His Lordship's London house

After riding Thunder another two hours, over hill and through valley, Devon returned to Kilkairn. His disposition had not improved on the ride. That was twice now he'd been rebuffed by Kat Macdonald, and it was twice too many.

Not that he was giving up. Bloody hell no. If anyone deserved to be brought down a peg, it was that golden-haired waif who thought herself better than the world. Devon now had *two* reasons to visit the glen in the woods. One, to escape the threat of the ring, and two, to teach a certain high-handed miss a much needed lesson.

Devon strode into Kilkairn, his mind on the problem ahead. What could he do? If only—

"Devon!"

He paused to see Malcolm standing in the doorway to a room off the great hall, a brandy glass in his hand. "Malcolm! How was your day? I took a ride—"

"Come and have a drink with me," Malcolm said, lifting his glass and gesturing. "Finest batch of brandy I've ever had. And there's plenty where this came from."

A glass of brandy would be welcome, Devon decided. He followed Malcolm into the room, finding a snug library of sorts, lit by a large, warming fire. It bore only a few signs of the slovenly care that infested the rest of the castle.

Malcolm went to a sideboard and splashed a generous amount into a fresh glass, then touched up his own drink. "There you go."

Devon took the drink and then made his way to the brace of leather chairs that sat by the crackling flames.

Malcolm joined him, stretching his legs before him. He eyed Devon a moment, then said, "Where have you been today?"

Devon thought about prevaricating, but something about Malcolm's expression made him pause. "I went riding. And I found your sister's cottage in the woods."

Malcolm's eyes brightened. "Did you indeed?"

"Indeed." Devon shrugged. "She was very busy, and I didn't get to speak with her much." It would be different next time; Devon would see to that.

"Busy?"

"Yes," Devon said in what he hoped was a firm voice. He really didn't want to continue this topic of conversation. "I rode about the lands some. You have a magnificent property here."

"It's nice," Malcolm said absently. "While you were visiting the cottage, did you get a chance to see some of Kat's work?"

"The stained glass? No. I'm surprised you didn't mention it at breakfast this morning."

"I should have, but I was rather taken aback that she'd allowed you to kiss her."

"Had I known she was your sister—"

"Pssh. It wouldn't have made any difference."

Devon met Malcolm's gaze. After a moment, Devon grinned. "You are right, of course."

Malcolm chuckled. "I know I am right. Kat's a lovely woman but she's stubborn as they come. Frankly, there's no way in hell you or anyone else will ever get more than a startled kiss out of her."

Devon paused in taking a drink. "No?"

"No," Malcolm said firmly. "She's a strong- willed lass, is Kat. She'll have nothing to do with a man who doesn't appreciate her for what she's worth. And most men wouldn't prize her Independence. Most men would stupidly want a woman who was more like Fiona . . . or that sister of hers, Murien Spalding."

"I don't believe I've met Miss Spalding."

"Count your blessings," Malcolm said darkly. He glanced at the open door, then leaned closer to say in an undertone, "She's a bloody witch, make no doubt. Oh, she looks well enough. Like Fiona, she exudes helpless fluttery womanliness. But unlike Fiona, Murien's heart is made of marble, her soul so chilled, the devil fears to take her to join him lest she freeze the flames of hell."

Devon chuckled. "Bloody hell, she can't be as bad as all that."

"Wait and see. Her grandest wish is to marry and marry well." Malcolm eyed him for a moment. "You might be safe, for you've no title. But then there is that blasted St. John fortune . . ."

"That sounds dire indeed."

"Aye." Malcolm shook his head. "I wouldn't be surprised if Fiona invites her to come. Best you avoid her like the plague, that's my advice."

And good advice it seemed. The thought of the talisman ring still resting in the candle dish on his night table made Devon shift uneasily.

"Meanwhile," Malcolm continued as if unaware he'd just caused Devon concern, "you might be able to help me with a small problem I have myself."

"Oh?"

"Yes. 'Tis about Kat, too. And since you seem to know her—"

"Barely."

"Enough," Malcolm continued, undeterred. "I thought you might have some insight to the problem."

"Which is?"

"It's become clear to me that Kat will never marry. Or so she says."

Good for Kat, Devon thought, silently toasting her with his brandy.

"But I can't help but think I should bring her to the notice of some potential suitors, just to be certain she's not rushing into a life of being a stained glass master and nothing else."

"Is she happy?"

"Doing her stained glass? Lord, yes. Do you want to see some of her work?"

Devon nodded before he could catch himself. He couldn't help but wonder what sort of work Kat did as it might give him another connection to her.

Malcolm brightened and jumped up. "She's magical, she is. Just look." He set his glass on a small table, then went to the farthest window and pulled back the drapery. There at the top was a round window, hidden by the uppermost foot of curtain.

Devon rose and went to stand beside Malcolm. It was exquisite. Even with his lack of knowledge, he knew it was quality work.

The glass formed a picture of a large stag on a bluff, antlers pointed toward the sun as he stood proudly surveying the rolling grasses and forest below him. There was something about the combination of colors, the line of the bluff, and the stag's proud head that drew the eye and kept it. "It's beautiful."

"She's a master of the craft. There are twenty-six such windows at Kilkairn; old arrow awls used to fire on attackers in the early years of the castle."

"Ah, the charm of an older residence."

"Indeed. They used to have wood shutters over them and let in far too much cold before Kat began replacing them. I'll have to show them all to you one day." Malcolm dropped the curtain, and he and Devon returned to their chairs.

Devon absently took a drink of brandy. Kat Macdonald was a complex woman, and he was only beginning to realize how much. "Do you think your sister is happy living in the woods?"

"No one is happy alone."

"She's not alone."

Malcolm's face creased into a sudden smile. "Och, you met her merry lads."

"Merry? They looked as if they wished to kill me." The next time Devon went to the cottage, he'd arm himself with a cudgel, just in case.

"Well, they're merry when you're not about. I've seen them myself and they don't mind me in the least. 'Tis to strangers that they're so forbidding."

"I suppose they're better protection than a pack of wild dogs."

"Aye. That they are." Malcolm took a drink of his brandy. "You know, if I was to mount a campaign to win over Kat, the first thing I'd do is gain the approval of her lads. Though she rules them with a velvet glove, they are a strong-willed lot and make no bones about telling her what they think."

Devon looked into his own brandy, the light of the fire reflected in the amber depths. There was something in what Malcolm was saying. Not that Devon wished to "win" Kat over. That sounded far too much like wooing and not enough like seducing.

"And then," Malcolm continued, as if unaware that anyone else was in the room, "then I'd work on Annie."

"Annie?"

"Kat's housekeeper." Malcolm glanced about the library, a wistful look on his face. "I tried to steal her away, for she's a stern hand on the household and keeps it neat as a pin, but she's loyal unto death to Kat."

"You tried to steal your sister's housekeeper?"

"I was desperate. I still am." Malcolm gestured to their brandy glasses. "You see these? I had to wash them myself. There wasn't a servant to be found anywhere."

Devon grinned. "I daresay it was good for you."

"Perhaps, but I'll be damned if I'll see to my own laundry." Malcolm scowled into his drink. "Devon, never marry a dainty-looking woman, for they're anything but. They'll ruin your peace of mind, empty your house of its comforts, and then complain they've naught to do and wish to return to town."

"Fortunately for all concerned, I don't plan on getting married. Ever."

"We'll see what the talisman ring has to say about that."

"I don't care what it has to say. I'm not getting married and that's that."

"Hm. Well, speaking of rings, I don't think Kat is at all fond of jewelry. If I was to get her a gift, 'twould be something for her glasswork, or for her house."

Devon set down his drink. "Malcolm, if you're

thinking I'm about to engage a campaign to win your sister, you're wrong."

Malcolm's eyes widened a ridiculous amount. "By the saints, what gave you that idea?"

"You did. You and your 'if I wanted to win Kat over' ideas."

"Well, you're far and away from the truth, my laddie. Know why?"

"Why?"

"Because you haven't a chance in hell of garnering her interest. You, my lad, are the exact type of man she is least likely to take up with."

Devon didn't know whether he'd been insulted or not. "What does that mean?"

"Only that she's run up against libertines before and she—"

"I am not a libertine."

"Rakehell, then. Or do you prefer rogue?" Malcolm asked politely, laughter in his gaze.

Despite his irritation, Devon found himself smiling a little at this. As soon as he relaxed, he realized, reluctantly, that there might be something to what Malcolm said. Devon sighed. "She's had a bad experience, eh?"

All of the laughter left Malcolm's face. "The worst. I think it hurt her even more than she let anyone see. Which is why she's turned her back on all men. Especially those with a silver tongue like yourself." Malcolm sighed. "There's only one thing that will remedy that."

"What?" Devon asked before he could stop himself.

Malcolm's gaze darkened. "The truth. She needs

someone who will never lie to her, no matter the cost."

The quiet words sifted through the silence. Devon looked at the glass he held in his hand, the edges smooth against his fingers. "I hope she finds him."

Malcolm opened his mouth as if to reply, but then shut it. "So do I."

"I don't mean to pry, but it seems as if your sister is doomed to spinsterhood."

Malcolm sighed. "I know. I have worried that—" He bit his lips, his shoulders slumping. "It doesn't matter what I think. Or you, for that matter. Kat is even more stubborn than you, and there aren't many who can make that claim. A pity you are the type of man Kat avoids the most. Otherwise . . . but no, I don't think you have a chance. She won't like you at all."

Devon slowly lowered the glass from his lips where he'd been about to take a sip. From the time he'd been old enough to marry, he'd been used to people trying to fix his interest with their sisters, cousins, family friends. This was the first time someone had told him that his sister, or even half sister, would not like him. Whatever else he was, Devon was always likable.

He opened his mouth to say something more when Malcolm unexpectedly asked about Thunder, mentioning that he'd seen the horse from the window earlier in the day.

The conversation never returned to Kat and her self-imposed banishment to the cottage in the forest. But Devon's mind remained firmly fixed on the woman, even more so than before. No one told him he couldn't do something—even his own brothers knew better than that. And Malcolm's words, as offhand as they'd seemed, had set up Devon's back a bit. Could he win another kiss from Kat Macdonald, one earned without surprise? Without guile? The thought was intriguing.

Across from him, Malcolm hid a smile behind his glass. Devon's answers were becoming increasingly vague, a clear sign his mind was already dwelling on Kat. Which was good because Malcolm feared that once Devon saw Murien Spalding, he might forget about Kat. Lovely as Kat was, Murien was exquisite.

Which was why Malcolm was determined that Devon spend as much time in Kat's company as possible. Murien might be beautiful, but she was no match for either Kat's force of personality or her intelligence. The problem was that most men felt with their eyes first, and their brain last.

If his wager with Fiona worked, then Malcolm would have all he desired—his wife back at his side, a son, and Kat happily married. As for his feelings for Fiona. . . . Malcolm frowned. Surely he was not so fickle as his own father. The love Malcolm felt for Fiona was so vivid, so much a part of him, that if he lost it, he thought perhaps a part of him would go with it.

Was that what his father had felt, too? A heavy weight seemed to press on Malcolm's chest, and it was with difficulty that he turned his attention back to Devon. His friend would make a fine brother-in-law. A fine one, indeed.

Other men might hesitate to put their sisters into the notice of a man who bluntly stated that he had no intentions of marrying, but Malcolm had three things in his favor. First, he knew that for all of Devon's philandering ways, he was a man of integrity. All of the St. Johns were, whether they realized it or not.

Second, there was the talisman ring. Those who didn't know any better might scoff all they wanted, but Malcolm believed. And when all was said and done, so would Devon.

And last, if by some miracle Devon was successful in breaking through Kat's rock-steady defenses, her brother Malcolm would be there to make sure the right thing was done. Friend or no, if Devon compromised Kat Macdonald, he would marry her, whether or not she or he wished it.

All told, it was a good, solid plan, and only Fiona and her be-damned sister could ruin things. Keeping his thoughts to himself, Malcolm got up to pour more brandy in his and Devon's glasses. It wasn't time to celebrate. Not yet. But judging from the thoughtful look on Devon's face, things were getting off to a fine start.

The next day, as afternoon approached, a coach and six rumbled up to the front door. As usual, the door was not answered on the first knock. But eventually the housekeeper came and let in the sole occupant, then sent a note to my lady's room, informing her of her visitor.

Moments later, a flurry of footsteps sounded on the landing. "Murien!" Fiona flew down the steps to the main hall, her dressing gown floating around her, a froth of pink and lace. Her slippered feet barely touched the worn runner. "You came!" She threw her arms about her sister. "And so quickly! I am so glad to see you!"

Murien grimaced. "Fiona, my hair!" She disentangled herself and then glanced at the dusty mirror beside the front door. What she surely saw had to have pleased her, for there was not a more beautiful woman in all of Scotland. Delicate blond hair swept back in a mass of shiny curls from a face of such perfection that no portrait painter had ever managed to quite capture it. Her skin shimmered white even in the dull light that shone through the dust-ridden windows, her figure perfect in the white pelisse and blue gown with matching bonnet.

Fiona clasped her hands together. "I am sorry! I was just so excessively glad to see you that I didn't think. Your hair still looks lovely." And it did. Every blond curl was in place, a ribbon artfully tied about the whole.

Murien patted an especially fat curl that hung to one of her shoulders. "It turned out better than I'd hoped, though I'm not sure why I bothered. There is no one in the whole of Scotland worth such effort."

"Oh!" Fiona gave an excited hop. "That's exactly why I asked you to visit!"

"Yes, well, I can only stay one night. I am on my way to Duart to stay with the Macleans."

"Can't stay? But—" Fiona bit back a sigh. "I really wanted you to stay at least a week. I *need* you to stay at least a week."

"Don't look so dispirited! We still have a good portion of the day together." Murien stripped off her gloves and looked around for the butler, the expression in her green eyes hardening. All she found was an elderly footman who stood half asleep on his feet.

Murien walked up to him. "You, whatever your name, pray put these in a *clean* place. And I hope you've washed your hands sometime in the last few days. The last time I left my gloves here, they looked as if someone had stored them up the chimney."

The old man blinked a few times, as if confused by her instructions. But after a moment, he bowed and took the gloves with but one finger and thumb. "Yes, miss."

Fiona barely waited for him to turn away before she took Murien's hand in hers. "Perhaps once I explain things, you will change your mind and stay for a while."

"As much as I enjoy chatting with you, I simply cannot remain out here in the middle of nowhere without getting a headache. It's the quiet, I think. It won't let me sleep."

"Yes, but—" Fiona bit her lip. How was Murien to ensnare Devon St. John if she wouldn't stay at Kilkairn? That was if Murien could be persuaded to make the effort at all.

The truth was, though Fiona had been brazenly confident in front of Malcolm, she wasn't sure she could count on her sister's cooperation in this venture. Murien was notoriously sure of her own worth and had turned down every offer of marriage that had been made to her. From beneath her lashes, Fiona regarded her sister for a covert moment. There really wasn't a more beautiful woman in all of Scotland. And Murien knew it, too; her confidence radiated from her like a beacon.

Filled with pride, Fiona hugged her sister yet again. "Come up to my room. I'll have tea brought and I'll explain why I asked you to visit." Talking rapidly, Fiona led the way upstairs.

Moments later, they were seated before the fire in Fiona's chambers. She poured some tea for her sister and handed her the cup. "How you are, Murien? Are you well?"

Murien's brows rose. "Don't I look well?"

Fiona sensed a rebuke and she instantly flushed. "Of course you look well! You look lovely—radiant, in fact. You always do, you know. Even when we were children, you would—"

"Fiona." Murien frowned over the edge of her cup, then placed it back in the saucer. "What do you want? Your note said it was dire. Have you decided to leave Malcolm?"

Fiona blinked. Leave Malcolm? Where had Murien gotten such a crazed notion? Had Malcolm said something? Panic flooded her. "Of course I'm not going to leave Malcolm. Why would I do such a thing?"

"Come, Fiona. Don't pretend you haven't thought about it. The two of you haven't ever gotten along as you should. He treats you abominably."

This was distressing indeed. Malcolm had treated her poorly? Had he? Fiona looked down at her teacup. "I don't think you understand how Malcolm and I care for one another. We've just had some . . . disagreements. That's all."

Murien looked unimpressed. "He's a monster to try and keep you locked up here, at Kilkairn. It's a wonder he doesn't make us climb up your hair just to visit you. It's my opinion that your marriage is already over."

Fiona gave a watery giggle, tears clouding her eyes. Good God, did Murien see what she, Fiona, did not? Had she and Malcolm grown so apart that they were doomed? Her throat tightened. Worse yet, was that what Malcolm thought, as well?

The thought pained her, a splinter shoved into the tenderest morsel of her soul. All she had was hope . . . hope that somehow, someway, Malcolm's feelings for her would return to the fervid passion he'd once had. Back when they'd been courting. Perhaps if they returned to an atmosphere not unlike that when they'd first met—surrounded by gay, happy people; brilliant amusements; and the constant thrill of a filled social calendar. It was a thin hope, but all she had.

Murien gave a graceful shrug. "Don't look so crestfallen; I daresay everyone knows how it is."

"Do you mean to say that a lot of people are discussing this?"

"I suppose so. Not to me, of course. No one would dare. But I hardly think it a secret that you and Malcolm do not see eye to eye on anything. It is certainly the first thing I notice whenever I come to visit."

The words had a strange effect on Fiona's heart, hollowing it out and making it thud painfully against her ribs. She managed a belated laugh. "Murien, you are so silly! Malcolm and I are fine. I just wrote you because . . . Well, I have a favor to ask."

"Favor?" Murien's pretty mouth turned down. "Really, Fiona, I hope this is not about money. I only have what Father left in trust and it's hardly enough as it—"

"No, no!" Fiona said hastily. "It has nothing to do with money. Murien, did you find anyone to interest you in Edinburgh?"

"Hardly. Provincials, every one."

Thank heavens! Just to be certain, Fiona said artlessly, "What of Lord Davies? He has been to Paris, and I'm certain he's the most sophisticated gentleman I've ever seen."

Murien sent her a fulminating glance, a frown on her pouting lips. "That shows how little you go in public. Once you've been to London, as have I, you will know there is little in the way of eligible men to be found in Scotland."

"You prefer Englishmen?"

"I prefer well-titled, wealthy, handsome, sophisticated men," Murien said, dissatisfaction radiating from her. "There are none to be found in this backward country. If I had the funds to stay in London, I would take the place by storm. I just know I would."

This was good news indeed. Had it not been for that depressing thought that perhaps her marriage was in dire straits, Fiona would have been ecstatic. As it was, she barely managed a smile. "That is precisely why I invited you to visit. Malcolm has an old friend from Eton visiting him, and I thought the man would be just the thing for you."

"A friend of Malcolm's?" There was just the tiniest hint of a sneer to Murien's voice.

Fiona stiffened. "Malcolm has many intelligent, well-bred friends. Why, he is personal friends with the Earl of Argyll, and I know not how many times the Earl of Carlysle has invited us to visit his country estate outside of Sterling."

"Really, Fiona, there is no need to be so argumentative."

"Yes, well, I think Mr. St. John is excessively well bred and—" Something gripped her arm. Fiona looked down and realized that it was Murien's hand. "Ow!"

Murien didn't loosen her hold. "Did you say *St. John*?"

Fiona nodded, pulling on her arm.

"Black hair? Blue eyes?"

"I don't know, as I haven't yet seen him. Murien, my arm—"

Murien released her, eyes ablaze. "But which St. John? Marcus? Never say 'tis the marquis!"

"No, it's Devon St. John."

"Devon. That is almost as good! He has no title, but—" Murien leaned closer, oblivious to the fact that the lace of her sleeve was now trailing in her tea plate. "Fiona, do you *know* who the St. Johns are?"

"No. I mean, Malcolm hinted that they were important, but I've never really heard—"

"They are the wealthiest family in all of England—all the world, perhaps!" Murien stood and began to pace about the room, the lace of her blue gown trailing the carpet behind her. Her green eyes gleamed.

"And to think that Devon St. John is here, of all places. I cannot believe—" She whirled back to Fiona. "For how long? How long will he be here?"

"I don't know. He hasn't really said. I just thought that you might—"

"You don't know?"

"A week, I think. Perhaps two—"

"I need more time." Murien came to kneel by Fiona's side, gripping her arm once again. "You *must* make him stay."

"How?"

"Oh for the love of—must I think of everything? Plan something in his honor—a hunt or a ball—and he will be forced to stay until it is done."

"Without asking his permission? Wouldn't that be rude?"

Murien grimaced. "Don't you *wish* to see me wed to one of the wealthiest men in the country?"

"Of course, but—"

"Don't you *wish* to see me wed to one of the handsomest men in the country?"

"Yes, but—"

"Then you must do this for me." Murien stood, swiftly walking to the mantel to inspect herself in the mirror that hung there. She rubbed her cheeks to give them more color. "This is fate, Fiona. I know it. He will be here for weeks, with nothing else to do. I cannot fail under such circumstances."

With all her heart, Fiona hoped Murien would succeed. If Murien was right about Fiona's marriage already being over, she had to win the wager. She simply *had* to.

Murien clasped her hands together, her eyes narrowed in thought. "Devon St. John at my sister's house. And with no competition to contend with."

"Well, there is some competition. A little, anyway."

Murien whirled on her, her eyes blazing, her face contorted in sudden fury.

Fiona drew back, saying hastily, "It's only Kat."

"What? Malcolm's half sister?" Murien laughed. "Good God, I thought you were serious."

"Well, I am in a way. You see . . ." Fiona hung her head. "Murien, this is more important than you know."

"Why?"

"Because Malcolm and I made a wager."

"A wager? On me?"

"I hope you don't mind, but he was so smug, saying that Mr. St. John had shown a decided interest in Kat and positively *gloating* about it, so I . . . well, I made a wager that you were more St. John's type and that you could attract his interest much quicker than his sister."

Murien merely smiled. "I hope you wagered something of great import."

"I did," Fiona said. She wet her lips nervously. "Murien, if I lose, I fear my marriage will indeed be over." It hurt, just saying the words aloud.

Murien frowned. "You aren't going to cry, are you?"

Fiona blinked back the tears. "No! No, of course not."

"Good. I hate it when you cry. But you needn't worry. If I have anything to do with it, I will not only attract Mr. St. John's interest, but I will secure it." She held up her hand and looked at it as if admiring a ring. "By this time next month, Mr. Devon St. John will be mine."

Fiona gave a sigh of relief. Once she and Malcolm settled this one argument, their relationship could go back to the way it had been when they'd first gotten married. She knew that once she got to Edinburgh, she would be merry again, and then so would Malcolm. "Thank you, Murien! I knew I could count on you."

Murien smoothed her hands over the front of her dress, pressing her breasts up, her eyes gleaming softly. "Indeed you may, Fiona. You will win this wager. Devon St. John won't know what has befallen him."

Chapter 7

I love you. I really, really love you. Like the stars in the sky, like the water in the oceans. You, my dear, are everything to me and there will never be another.

Mr. Poole to Lady Lucinda Sutherlund,
while stealing a kiss beneath the stars
on the veranda at the Sutherlund rout

"Ye're sure ye're feeling well?"

Kat turned from where she'd been supervising the loading of the cart. They'd finished the earl's final window late last night and had spent the morning grinding off the uneven edges and cleaning the glass until it gleamed. Now all the windows were safely packed in frames and were ready for delivery. "I'm fine, Simon. I'm fine now. And I was fine five minutes ago when you asked me then."

He reddened. "Sorry aboot that, Miss Kat. I was just wonderin'—" He clamped his mouth closed. "Never mind."

She waved good-bye to Alistair and Donald, who dutifully waved back. Alistair was, as usual, grinning from ear to ear, while Donald, ever the soothsayer of doom, was muttering about the bad roads ahead and how his left knee told him they were in for a fierce storm.

Kat waited until they were well down the path before she turned to Simon. "I'm ready now. You may begin."

"Begin what?"

"Whatever it is that has been worrying you all day. Out with it before you explode."

"Nothing's worrying me, Miss Kat. I was jus' wonderin'—" He scratched his neck. " 'Tis not my place to say anything, but from what I've heard aboot the Sassenach, you'd best have a care."

"Have a care about what? I've only spoken to him once." That Simon knew about. Kat didn't see the need to inform him of the other time as it would just raise unnecessary questions. Questions she wasn't sure she could answer.

"I know, missus. But he seemed a wee bit determined to take you for a ride when he was here a few days ago. I'd thought he'd be back by now." Simon's eyes narrowed. "I don't trust him as far as I can throw him."

"Well, I said no, didn't I? So you have nothing to fear."

Simon looked at her.

"What?"

He raised his brows, his gaze fastening on her gown.

Kat flushed, her hand smoothing her skirt. "So I

wore a different gown today than I normally do. That doesn't mean anything."

"Ye've worn a nicer gown every day since he last visited. Are ye wishin' he would return?"

"No! Not at all."

Simon raised his brows again.

Kat's face heated even more. "By St. George's dragon, I'm not about to apologize for wearing something other than one of my old gray work gowns! Besides, it's not as if I came to work dressed for a ball or anything ridiculous."

Of course, it was a better quality of gown than the ones she usually wore. Of soft dove-gray cotton, it fell in fuller, more graceful folds. And the neckline, while not precisely fancy, did have a thin stitching of trim.

Kat self-consciously traced the stitching. "I wear this gown all the time."

"To church, mayhap. But not to work in. 'Tisn't practical as ye'll get soot on it and the sparks'll mark it."

There was something in what he said; Kat didn't own a work gown that didn't have at least one small hole burned in the skirts.

Simon crossed his arms over his barrel chest. "Know what I think?"

"No, but I'm sure you'll tell me."

"I think ye were hopin' the Sassenach would come a-callin'."

"I did no such thing," Kat replied hotly. Although, to be honest, there had been a moment yesterday when she thought she'd heard horse's hooves clopping on the path and her heart had pounded a bit harder than usual. She sighed to herself. Very well . . . perhaps she *had* hoped to see the Sassenach again. He'd been much in her thoughts. But she'd be damned before she admitted such a thing to Simon.

Of course, she was a little chagrined that St. John hadn't returned before now. Perhaps he wasn't as interested as he'd pretended. The thought pricked at her pride.

"Lass, ye're dreamin' if ye think this Sassenach will come a-callin'. Not that ye're not a lovely woman, fer ye are. But the Sassenach didn't look like the kind of man who'd take the time to act like a proper gent—" Simon's gaze moved past her, his brows lowering until they met over his nose. "Bloody hell!"

Kat turned, though she already knew what she'd see. And there he was—Devon St. John, riding across the clearing. He was hatless, the sun gleaming off his black hair, limning the bridge of his nose and touching the plane of each cheekbone. Dressed in a blue riding coat with buff breeches, he looked far too handsome to be in the woods.

There! She'd been right to wear one of her better gowns. She cleared her throat. "Simon?"

"Aye, lass?" It was a testament to how upset he was that Simon's voice was more of a rumble than actual words.

"Why don't you take the rest of the lads and begin cleaning the workshop. I'll be there in a trice."

Simon glowered. "I don't like leavin' ye with His Namby-Pamby Lordship. Ye need a chaperone."

"Out here? In the middle of the clearing? What's

he going to do? Throw me to the ground and have his way with me in front of all of you and the house staff?"

"I wouldna put it past him, the bounder."

"Simon, you've gone daft, you have. Now off with you. I'll be there to help shortly."

"But—"

"Please."

Simon sighed. "Very well," he mumbled. He slowly turned on his heel, glaring at Devon as he went.

Devon pulled Thunder to a halt as Simon walked by. It didn't take a man of unusual discernment to read the message on Simon's craggy face. Devon hoped that the fact that he returned the look without flinching sent a message back.

He reached Kat and dismounted. She looked especially lovely today, her hair a little tousled by the wind, her gown hugging those luxuriant curves.

It made all his efforts worthwhile. He thought he discerned the slightest bit of excitement in her green gaze, a hint of warm welcome that was quite different from the calm dismissal she'd last given him. Good. Though he'd wanted nothing more than to storm back to the clearing after their last meeting, he'd decided that Miss Kat needed some time to decide what she wanted. He'd hoped that being alone in the woods with her work—doing the same thing she always did, talking to the same people she always talked to—would make her yearn for something out of the ordinary. Something special. Like an Englishman with a ready smile.

He smiled down at her now, bowing a little. "Good morning." Last night he and Malcolm had whiled away the evening playing billiards and drinking brandy. As soon as night fell, Devon excused himself and went to his room, where he began to formulate a plan, all the while feeling the onerous presence of the talisman ring. With the information he'd garnered from Malcolm, added to his own innate knowledge of women, and the little he knew about Katherine Anne Macdonald, Devon was fairly sure that by the end of the week, if he was not in her bed, he'd be close to it. She was a hot piece, and all he had to do was break through some of the barriers she'd erected around her heart.

Not too many, of course, for he had no intention of becoming the focal point of that heart. All he wanted was the pleasure of her body, a brief taste of her spirit. Her heart she could save for whomever she came to love, as long as it wasn't Devon.

But first, before he did anything, he had to win her trust. After that, he would woo her with a thoroughness that would leave them both panting and pleased. Malcolm had said Kat needed the truth and Devon was ready.

He bowed, glancing up at her through his lashes.

Her cheeks flushed pink beneath the cream, though her gaze did not waver. "Perhaps we should skip the civilities and go right to the reason you are here."

Devon had to smile. "I came to ask you once again if you would come for a ride with me."

"No."

"Poor Thunder. He would have enjoyed having such a lovely rider."

Her mouth formed a no, but it never came out of her mouth. Instead her gaze went over his shoulder to where the horse was tied, the sun gleaming on the gelding's pure, strong lines.

After a long moment, she turned her gaze back to Devon. He was amused, as well as chagrined, to see that some of the admiration that had sparkled in her gaze when she'd looked at the horse had disappeared when she focused on him.

Devon had to bite back a sigh. Kat was so different from the women he usually met; like Malcolm's sister-in-law, for example. Murien Spalding was everything Malcolm had warned of—she was small and feminine and exuded a helpless charm—exactly the sort of woman Devon knew he should avoid, though it had been difficult. Murien seemed determined to waylay him every chance she got, which made Kat's reluctance all the more appealing.

Kat looked at him now. "If I ride *your* horse, what will *you* ride?"

He shrugged. "I daresay you have any number of animals in your stable that could hold me."

"None are as fine as Thunder."

"No, but I will be justly compensated by your lovely company." He knew he'd made a mistake the second the words were out of his mouth. Kat Macdonald didn't want flowery phrases and empty words. She wanted . . . He almost frowned. What *did* she want?

Her expression had shuttered, and he could see

that she was already pulling away. There was nothing for it but the truth. "Miss Macdonald—Kat, please. I am a stranger in Scotland. And while I am thankful for your brother's hospitality, it is rather tense in the castle."

Her expression softened just the tiniest bit. "Fiona and Malcolm are still at it?"

"Oh yes. So far I haven't had the opportunity to witness them do anything other than snip at each other, though I'm sure they were a charming couple when they first wed."

She tilted her head to one side, curiosity making her eyes appear lighter. "You don't sound as if you approve."

"Of what? Marriage?"

She nodded.

"I don't believe in it. At least not for me."

A faint smile touched her lips, the first one today. For some reason, Devon felt as if the sun shone a trifle brighter just because of that tiny upturn of her generous lips.

"So you aren't a marrying man." Her eyes were bright with amusement. "I'm surprised you admit that."

So was he, though it was the truth. Had he made such a statement to a society miss in London, one with a matrimonial gleam in her eye, he would have been labeled crass and unfeeling. But Kat merely nodded. "I don't think I believe in it, either. Not anymore."

A faint hint of sadness touched her smile. Devon knew she was remembering her past, and he was hard-pressed not to ask her about it. He certainly didn't know her well enough to ask such personal questions, but somehow he knew that if he did, she would answer. There was no pretense or artifice about Kat. There was . . . just Kat herself.

Thunder whickered in indignation at being made to stand, and he pawed the ground impatiently.

Kat chuckled. "You had better go. He doesn't look happy."

"He can stay where he is until I've had my answer. Will you ride with me?"

She turned her head to give Thunder a final, lingering glance. Devon knew the instant she made up her mind, for her shoulders straightened.

"Very well. I will ride with you. But it cannot be for long. I've work to do."

"I know that. We'll make it an hour, no more."

She raised her brows.

"Half an hour then. Later this afternoon?"

"No. Best make it tomorrow."

He'd hoped for today, but if he wanted to breach the walls Kat had built, he'd have to let her set their pace. So instead, he took her hand and turned it over in his. "Shall we say morning? At ten?"

"Fine."

He uncurled her fingers and pressed a kiss to her palm. Her skin was warm and firm beneath his, her fingers roughened. He ran his thumb over hers and smiled into her eyes. "You work far too hard."

She pulled her hand back, her face shuttering once again. "Work is good for the soul, Mr. St. John. Perhaps one day you'll try it and see."

"I may not have cut firewood for a living, but I've done my fair share of work."

"Indeed?"

"I'm solely responsible for various aspects of the St. John holdings. More than any of my brothers other than Marcus, I have safeguarded the family fortune and helped it grow."

"That's not work."

He thought of the countless meetings he'd sat through, some lasting days, of the hard-won negotiations, of the endless hours he'd spent traveling to their holdings. "Tell me, Miss Certainty, have you tried it?"

She pursed her lips. "No. I suppose I shouldn't speak, then."

"No," he agreed. "Any more than I should make assumptions about your glasswork." He hesitated a moment, then added, "Perhaps one day you can show me the glass shop. I wish to see how it all works."

She shot him an uncertain look. "No one has ever asked me that."

"Well, I'm curious. Especially after your brother showed me some of your efforts."

"I could spit on a glass and tell Malcolm it was a lantern shield and he'd think it was the best thing he'd ever seen."

Devon smiled. "That's what brothers are for."

She nodded, her lips curving into a returning smile. For a moment, a simple sort of harmony seemed to build between them. Perhaps it was the cool breeze that kept tugging her dress and fanning the fringes of her hair. Or perhaps it was gradual realization that they were not quite as different as they thought. Whatever it was, Devon found himself lingering, wanting to stay a little longer. And a little longer yet.

Kat scuffed her toe on the ground. "How many brothers do you have, St. John?"

"Four. And a sister."

Her eyes widened. "That many?"

"My father said we were his army, and indeed our house was often like an army camp."

She looked at him wistfully, but didn't say anything.

"You and Malcolm seem unusually close."

"He's been a good brother to me."

"And I'm sure you've been a good sister."

"I try," she said softly, "though he does so much—" She bit her lip.

"I daresay you do more than you realize."

A horse could be heard coming down the path. Devon recognized Malcolm the same instant Kat did.

"Blast it," Devon said with a sigh. "Your brother has an uncanny way of showing up when he's least wanted."

"It's a trait he's had his whole life," she replied in a grim voice.

Devon pulled Thunder closer. "I shall see you tomorrow then?"

"At ten," she agreed.

"Excellent." He took her hand and placed one last kiss on the back of it.

Kat had to fight a shiver as his lips brushed her

skin. Her entire body seemed to tighten whenever he was about, and when he touched her, she had to clench her teeth against a tremor that traced her spine.

"Till tomorrow, Miss Macdonald." With that, he left her and remounted Thunder.

Kat watched him go, a dashing figure on the black horse. A horse that tomorrow she would be riding. And oh, what a horse. She eyed it greedily, almost giving a little hop of excitement. Only the knowledge that Simon was most likely standing in the window, watching, made her hold it back. She wasn't really excited about seeing Devon St. John, she told herself; all she wanted to do was ride that beautiful horse.

Still, she could not deny that it would be pleasant to have someone with whom to while away a little time now that the earl's windows were done. There were more orders to fill; there always were. But none so urgent.

Malcolm had pulled up to speak to St. John, and she stood there a moment, watching them and feeling strangely bereft.

All she had for company were the lads and Annie and Malcolm, whenever Fiona could spare him from the castle. While they were all good people, Kat sometimes wished for more. Something was vaguely disquieting about the way things had settled in her daily existence. Kat thought that perhaps a conversation or two with Mr. Devon St. John might help her discover what that was.

Of course, she'd make good and certain those conversations were held in broad daylight. She'd also make certain St. John's hands stayed closer to his person than to hers. Not that she was worried; she had experience in such matters, and St. John already had one bruise to prove it.

Malcolm and St. John said their good-byes, and Malcolm turned his horse toward Kat. He hopped down from the large bay and gave her a broad smile.

"What's that all about?" she asked, instantly suspicious.

"What?" he said, blinking innocently, though his grin dimmed not one whit.

"That smile. I don't trust it. You never smile like that."

Malcolm did a little jig, pumping his arms in a ridiculous way. "There," he said, coming to a stop, panting hard, though the smile still lit his eyes. "I never dance, either, but I am today."

She had to laugh; she felt a little giddy herself. For a mad moment, she wondered if this was all from St. John's presence. But then she realized how silly that was. "So, Malcolm, what has you in such a good mood? Did you and Fiona solve your differences?" Kat immediately wished she hadn't mentioned Fiona, as some of the light left Malcolm's face.

"Not yet." A set look touched his mouth. "But hopefully soon."

"I hope so, too." And she did. She knew how much he cared for his wife. Though Fiona didn't seem capable of seeing it, it was painfully obvious to everyone else.

"Did you get the windows off to the earl?"

"Aye. You just missed them."

"Excellent." Malcolm rubbed his hands together. "I have a favor to ask you, Kat. A big one."

"What?"

"I need you to entertain St. John a wee bit—" He held up his hand when she opened her mouth to deny him. "Only during the days. No more."

"Why?"

"Because Murien arrived at the castle earlier this week."

Kat pressed her lips together. "Murien has her sights on St. John."

Malcolm nodded. "And you know what she is. She won't stop until she has him."

"Surely he can avoid her if he wishes—"

"He might, but then there is that blasted talisman ring." Malcolm shook his head solemnly.

Kat caught him looking at her from beneath his lashes. "What talisman ring?"

"Didn't he tell you?"

"No."

"Och now, why hasn't he done so? I suppose he's a mite embarrassed." Malcolm sighed heavily. "Poor Devon. His family is cursed with a ring that seems to cause marriage."

"Marriage?"

"That's what happened to three of his brothers. And they each had the ring in their possession when it happened, too. Devon fled London, hoping to escape the ring, but he found it in his carriage after he'd left, and so here he is, stuck with the blasted thing."

"Malcolm . . . surely you don't believe in this ring?"

He shrugged. "Perhaps."

"I don't."

He eyed her shrewdly. "Not at all?"

"Not even a little."

"Good!" He reached into his pocket and withdrew a small object. "Since you don't believe in it, you won't mind trying it on."

Kat blinked down at the small circle that lay in the palm of his hand. Silver with tiny runes etched in the surface, it appeared innocuous. "Does St. John know you have that?"

Malcolm looked slightly shame-faced. "Perhaps."

"Perhaps? Och, Malcolm! He's your guest."

"Whist, Kat! I am going to put it back. I was just curious." He held the circlet up to the light. "You must admit 'tis pretty."

It *was* pretty, glistening in the sun. As Kat looked at the ring, the urge to touch it began to simmer through her.

She shook her head. "I want nothing to do with it."

"Damn, Kat! Must you be so stubborn?"

"Yes," she answered implacably.

A sigh burst from his lips. "You are the most irritating woman I know, with the exception of Fiona."

"Thank you. I'll treasure those words."

"I only borrowed the ring; I did not steal it, so you can stop glaring at me."

"Why would you do such a thing?"

"Because I was curious to see it. Don't you fash, I'll have it returned to his room before he knows what's toward. Meanwhile, hold out your hand and let's see if the ring fits."

"Fits?" Her brow lowered. What was he doing? "Why would you want to see if it fits?"

"Because I'm curious, is why." Malcolm reached out and grabbed her hand. Before Kat could say another word, he'd slipped the ring over her finger.

For an instant, she felt nothing. Not even the tang of cold metal against her skin. "It's noth—" She caught her breath. A slow, almost insistent heat was beginning to radiate from her finger.

"What is it?" Malcolm asked, leaning forward, his gaze fastened on her face. "What do you feel?"

"I feel . . ." Bloody hell, what *did* she feel? Her entire hand was warm, her arm tingled, and now her breasts were beginning to shimmer with heat.

Malcolm blinked. "Kat, love. Are you well? Your face—" He gripped her arms. "Kat?"

She gasped. Heat arced from her breasts to her stomach and then lower. Somehow, she saw St. John. Saw his face above hers . . . felt his hands on her body . . . felt his hips against hers . . . She clenched her teeth against the onslaught of emotion and feeling. It was as if every thought she'd ever had, every feeling, was suddenly thrown into her heart at once. It was almost too much to bear.

Her entire body trembled and ached, and it took every ounce of her strength to grasp the ring and yank it from her finger. The second it broke free, she sagged, her breath wrung from her lips.

"My God, Kat!" Malcolm's arm was the only

thing that kept her from falling down. He took the ring from her lax fingers. "Are you well? What happened? Is it your heart? Good God, Kat, talk to me!"

"I—I'm fine," she said, her voice trembling. "I just didn't have any breakfast and I—" She couldn't finish the falsehood. She took a shuddering breath and pushed his arm free of her shoulders, moving back, away from him, away from the ring. "I'm fine now. Really I am."

His face was pale. "Are you certain? Perhaps you should go into the cottage and lie down a bit."

"No, no. I'm fine. I just got a wee bit dizzy was all." Her entire body ached, her heart still raced.

Malcolm looked at the ring a long moment, a queer expression on his face. Then he slid it into his pocket as carefully as if it had been made of crystal. "I will return it."

"Yes." She pressed her hand to her forehead, trying to still the turmoil in her mind. What had just happened? She'd never felt such a reaction, such heat, and certainly never from a mere ring. It almost felt as if . . . Her cheeks colored. No. Surely not.

Malcolm untied his mount from the railing and led it forward. "I'm sorry, Kat. If I'd realized . . ." He paused, a dawning look spreading across his face. "Kat! If the ring gave you such a strong reaction, then you must be—"

"The wrong woman for Mr. St. John," she said, far more steadily than she felt.

Malcolm shook his head. "No, no! If the ring—"

"Malcolm, think a moment. If the ring finds St.

John's future wife, then it would have to be someone other than me. I am not going to marry. I've told you that time and again."

"Yes, but—"

"No buts. I have no need for a husband. I like my freedom and my solitude. Besides, what man would let me have my lads and the glasswork? I can no more leave that behind than you can stop caring about Fiona."

He grimaced. "Don't—"

" 'Tis true and you know it."

Malcolm sighed. "I had hoped that you and St. John—"

"Well, we're not. Besides, he's no more a marrying man than I'm a wedding woman." She smiled at her thin joke.

Malcolm pulled the ring from his pocket and looked at it. "I suppose you are right. It didn't seem to have a *good* effect on you, anyway. Are . . . are you certain you're well?" Concern tightened his expression. "You looked as if you were in pain."

It hadn't been pain, but pleasure. Pure, unadulterated pleasure. Kat managed a smile she was far from feeling. "I'm fine."

He eyed her a moment more, then tucked the ring back into his waistcoat pocket. "I hate to ask this, because you're still a little pale . . ."

"What?"

"Remember to keep St. John about this week. For his sake, if not mine."

A feeling not unlike panic nipped at her. "St. John is not in need of a nursemaid."

"You don't know Murien well enough, then. She's unscrupulous, that one, and I don't trust her."

"St. John can take care of himself."

"How can you say that? He's used to the frail misses of London. Murien would devour him with her tea and crumpets, and he'd never know what had happened."

"You're exaggerating."

"Kat, I would not put it past Murien to try and trick St. John into her net. I think she'd even claim ruin, if she had to."

Kat paused. The rules regarding a woman's reputation were murky and gray at best, which made them all the easier to break. In truth, since St. John's family was so high and mighty, all Murien would have to do was trick Devon into being alone with her and arranging for someone to "discover" them. All told, in a castle the size of Kilkairn, it was an easy enough feat. Especially if Fiona was to assist Murien.

Kat sighed. "If she cried foul, even if he'd done nothing, it's possible he'd be forced to marry her."

Malcolm nodded. "And a bloody, sad shame it would be, too, for I cannot imagine two worse matched people in all of the earth."

Kat had to admit Malcolm had a point. Her gaze dropped to his waistcoat where the ring was now safely tucked away.

There was so much she didn't understand. Why had that ring affected her so? Why did her body warm every time St. John was about?

Kat had never considered herself a particularly

sensual woman. But somehow, every moment she spent with St. John seemed to prove her wrong.

She had to find out more, discover what the ring was and what it meant. And she needed to know who Devon St. John really was.

"Very well," she heard herself say. "He's coming to ride tomorrow. I will see if he'll stay for a wee bit of lunch, too."

Malcolm's face cleared. "Thank you, Kat! You won't be sorry."

Kat wasn't so sure. All she knew was that she'd never feared anything the way she feared the St. John talisman ring. Except, perhaps, Devon St. John himself.

Chapter 8

I love you. I really, really love you. Like the stars in the sky, like the water in the oceans. You, my dear, are everything to me and there will never be another.

Mr. Poole to Miss Elizabeth Standon,
while stealing a kiss behind the shrubbery
of Standon House in Mayfair

"There he is!" Fiona exclaimed.

Murien rushed to the window and almost pushed Fiona aside in her determination to garner a look. "It's about time! He's been gone an hour."

"Aye."

A flash of satisfaction crossed Murien's face as she watched Devon. "He's magnificent. We shall make quite a pair, he with his dark looks and me with my fair ones."

Fiona smiled. "He is most presentable."

"Presentable? He's more than presentable." Murien began smoothing her gown. "How do I look?"

Fiona admired Murien's choice of gowns. It was

cream over white, the heavy, cream-colored lace draped over a white silk undergown. Small pale blue and pink flowers were woven into the lace, their tiny, pale green leaves adding faint touches of color.

The overall effect was one of fairylike delicacy, something Murien's own pink and gold coloring supported. And indeed, if one didn't look too closely into her eyes, Murien looked fresh and innocent and achingly beautiful.

Murien patted her hair. She'd pinned it up in a simple knot that emphasized the graceful length of her neck and the delicate turn of her shoulders. Fiona didn't think Murien had ever looked so perfect.

They could only hope it was enough. For some reason, Devon St. John hadn't been as enthusiastic about Murien as they'd hoped. Oh, he was pleasant enough, complimenting Murien on her beauty and paying her every attention. But he made the same efforts for Fiona, often including her in conversations that Murien obviously wished her out of. It was all rather confusing. Did he like Murien? Or was he merely being polite?

The sound of footsteps echoed down the hall.

"Quickly!" Murien said, hurrying to sit by the fire. She picked up her discarded embroidery frame and adjusted her skirts. "He'll be here any moment!"

Fiona took her place across from Murien, and together they waited. The footsteps walked closer . . . louder and louder. They paused outside the door, and then began to fade away.

"Blast it," Murien whispered. "I thought that footman of yours was going to direct him in here!"

Fiona stood. "Just wait. I'll fetch him myself." She smoothed her own gown of pink muslin before crossing to the door and opening it.

It wasn't Devon who was walking away, but Malcolm. He turned on hearing the door open, pausing with one foot on the lowest step. He'd had a smile on his face, but when he saw her, it faded from sight.

Her heart ached. At one time, he'd lit up every time she walked into the room. She swallowed her disappointment and made a quick curtsy. "My lord."

He nodded, his handsome face grave. "Lady wife." His gaze flickered past her to the door. "How goes your campaign?"

"Better than yours, I dare say. Which you would know if you had breakfast at a decent hour. Neither you nor our guest was there."

A faint hint of smugness crossed his face. "St. John and I agreed to eat earlier than usual so that we might have a morning ride. Then he went to visit Kat."

"You should have told me about that," Fiona said, wincing a little at the petulancy she heard in her own voice.

Malcolm smiled, that bright flash of teeth and a crinkling of eyes that always made her want to smile back.

He was a handsome man. He wasn't tall, but then she liked that, for large people overwhelmed her. He was quicksilver and charm, a lethal combination where Fiona was concerned.

She realized she missed him, missed their morning breakfasts together, missed his visits to her room . . . Tears threatened to well.

To hide her distress, she said, "Murien and I were waiting on St. John. I just saw him in the courtyard."

"I fear you are going to lose this wager before you even begin it. He seems quite taken with Kat."

Fiona stiffened. "Indeed, I am not. In fact—"

Footsteps sounded once again, this time slower and more shuffling. The elderly footman led Devon up the stairs. He bowed on seeing Fiona. "I was told you were expecting me."

She smiled and placed her hand on his arm. "Indeed I was. Pray come in. Murien and I wanted to ask your opinion on something." With that, she drew St. John to the drawing room door.

From where he stood on the landing, Malcolm could see Murien standing by the fireplace, her expression one of artful innocence. Damn it, but she looked beautiful . . . beyond beautiful, even. He thought of Kat this morning, in her plain gown and slightly mussed hair, and he grimaced. He was going to have to do something about that. And soon.

Malcolm's heart sank when he caught sight of Devon's admiring expression as he faced Murien. Bloody hell, there was no justice in this world.

Just before Devon went through the door, he paused and sent Malcolm a quizzical glance. "Are you coming?"

"No, no! Perhaps we can meet in an hour for a game of billiards?"

"Of course. I hope you are prepared to lose again."

With a grin, Devon followed Fiona the rest of the way into the room.

As Fiona moved to shut the door, her gaze met Malcolm's. For an instant, a tense silence bound them. Malcolm had never wanted anything more than to throw caution and his pride to the winds and reclaim her for himself. What would she do if he marched up to her and threw her over his shoulder, then took her to their room and locked them both away for a week?

The urge was almost overwhelming. But first he'd have to make a promise he didn't know if he could keep. He let the words die on his tongue. Fiona's gaze faltered and dropped. Her shoulders slumped and she turned away and then pushed the heavy door closed.

Grumbling to himself, Malcolm turned and made his way up the stairs, hoping against hope that Devon was made of sterner stuff than most men.

The next morning, Devon flipped one end of his cravat over the other, then twisted them in an intricate knot. It took almost fifteen minutes, but when he finished, his cravat was tied in a fabulous creation known as "the mathematical."

His valet, Tilton, watched a respectful distance away, preserving the utmost silence. As Devon finished, he cast an amused glanced at the valet. "You can speak, you know. I don't need silence just to tie a cravat."

Tilton sniffed. "They say Beau Brummell required absolute silence and that the slightest noise would cause him to go into a fit."

"Brummell was a fool. A well-dressed fool, but a fool nonetheless." Devon made the final adjustment to his cravat. "There. How's that?"

"Superb, sir. Simply superb." Tilton regarded the cravat a moment more, and then, nodding faintly, he picked up the coat he'd just brushed. "A pity you got so dusty yesterday morning."

"I was riding. That happens to my riding coat when I use it."

"You've been riding before, but never have I seen so much dirt."

"That's because I rode in the woods and not in a genteel park with tended pathways."

Tilton curled his nose. "How shabby of Lord Strathmore not to have a park for your amusement."

"I shall tell him you think so."

"Pray do. Otherwise I shall be forced to share my opinion with the upper footman in the hopes that he might tell the second housemaid, who is, I have been informed, sleeping with His Lordship's valet. I would hate for Lord Strathmore to hear my opinion in such a hodgepodge manner."

"Consider it done," Devon said, waving a hand.

Tilton paused. "Would you indeed, sir?"

"Of course. One should never ask a servant to do what one is not willing to do oneself. I may want you to spread some gossip for me one day."

The valet sniffed, his thin nostrils flaring. "I suppose next you will be offering to iron your own waistcoats. What a delight for me."

Devon raised his brows. "I wouldn't take it that far."

"Then I'm to understand that in return for my extra services, you are only going to claim such duties as carrying gossip and, if pressed, an occasional note for a tryst, and not such duties as laundry, pressing the creases from your shirts, or polishing your boots?"

"I have to leave something for you to do. Otherwise I might realize I don't need you, and you could lose your position."

"Don't tempt me, my lord," Tilton said. "The Duke of Claridge has been asking for my services for years now."

"That old clod-digger? You'd be miserable. He doesn't dress, he merely rolls into his clothing. Besides, I have it on good authority that his funds are tied up on the 'change and he pays his servants in a very clutch-fisted manner."

"Then Viscount Addinton. He cuts a good figure."

"When he isn't drunk. If that's the turn you wish to take, I wish you well." Devon knew Tilton would never leave his service; the valet had far too high an opinion of himself to work for anyone with less style. Besides, Devon paid handsomely and Tilton had little to complain about.

Devon glanced about the room Tilton had just moved them into. The valet had arrived the day after Devon and had wrought a miracle in one of the less damp chambers. Gone was the dust, grime, and gloomy air. The sheets and coverlet were fresh and crisp and even the rug was a brighter color than the others in the castle.

Truly, Tilton was worth his weight in gold. Devon

picked up his gloves and tucked them into a pocket. "I'm off to ride with Miss Kat."

"Cat, sir?"

"Miss Katherine Macdonald. Kat."

"Ah. That would be His Lordship's half sister."

Devon cut him a glance. "You've heard about her?"

"Indeed, sir. I've heard all about Miss Macdonald *and* Miss Spalding."

Devon cast a glance at where the ring had been on the night table. He frowned. "Tilton, I thought I put the ring in the candle dish. Did you move it?"

Tilton's gaze followed his. The ring was no longer in the candle dish, but beside it. "No, sir. I did not move it."

Devon crossed to the table and picked up the ring. "Perhaps I just forgot. Take this and put it somewhere safer."

"Of course, sir." Tilton took the ring and placed it in a box with Devon's cravat pins. "There. It's fortunate you do not believe in the power of the ring, for I have it on the best authority that you have come to Kilkairn to meet your future bride."

"Just what have you heard?"

"Only that speculation is rife over who you will choose, Miss Macdonald or Miss Spalding. Wagering is heavily favoring Miss Spalding."

Devon frowned. "I favor neither. I've no wish to get married." Which was why he was on his way out of the castle now. It was a good thing he had Kat to while the day away with, for he could not be certain he'd escape Murien's spell otherwise.

"Sir, I am well aware of your feelings toward matrimony. And so I informed the other staff, but I fear I come into the servants' hall too late to have any influence."

For some reason, it irked him that the servants were speculating on his future. "Old gossips, the lot of them."

"They are quite antiquated, sir. I feel as if I've stepped into a world filled with gout and a disturbing fascination for flatulence." Tilton cast a glance about the green room. It was still a long way from meeting Tilton's standards. "I shall attempt to organize your room a bit more today, although I have little hopes of actually causing an improvement."

"You've already wrought miracles," Devon said. Though there really wasn't much to be done about the smoking chimney or the stained walls.

Devon glanced at his pocket watch, then started. He'd be late if he didn't leave soon. Now all he had to do was get out of the castle without being forced to pay homage yet again to Fiona's sister. "Don't expect me to return until after dark."

"What a long ride. I do hope your horse will be able to maintain such a pace."

"I hope *I* can maintain such a pace," Devon said. He grinned at the valet and then left the room, hat tucked beneath one arm.

He ran lightly down the stairs and had just reached the front entryway when a door opened off the great hall. Fiona stood in the opening. "There you are, Mr. St. John!" she said in a breathless tone.

Devon stifled a feeling of impatience. "Good morning, Lady Strathmore."

"I'm so glad I caught you. Murien and I were just sitting here talking about how pleasant it would be if you visited."

"I am on my way out, so I can only stay a few moments." And that was all. He followed her into the room, bowing to Murien when he entered.

Murien was standing beside the pianoforte, holding some sheet music, looking as beautiful and radiant as she had the day before. Devon knew what the music sheets portended; she wished to play for him as evidence of her correct upbringing. All women were raised the same, and it was a damned shame.

"There you are," Murien said in warm voice, smiling at him.

"Here I am."

"You're dressed for riding."

"Indeed."

She laughed softly. "I am sorry. I didn't mean to state the obvious. Where are you riding today?"

"The woods." He wondered if Kat's laugh was as seductive as Murien's; he'd seen her smile, but had never heard her laugh. He resolved to fix that situation today.

"How lovely!" Murien said. "I daresay it will be nice and cool in the forest." And with that, she took her place at the pianoforte, leaving her sister to entertain him.

Devon had to give Murien credit, she knew what she was about. She didn't press him for his attention, but merely indicated that she was there and was a pleasant and beautiful companion. Which was why he had no intentions of spending more than a minute's worth of time with her, not while the talisman ring was still in his possession.

Devon wasted no more time making his escape. If he waited until Murien began to play, he'd be stuck there for the next hour. As quickly as he could, he made his excuses and left.

As he walked out of the castle, his step grew lighter, his mouth began to widen in a real smile. Just to be certain that he did not develop an unnecessary passion for Murien, he'd spend the rest of the day trying to wheedle kisses from Scotland's most ineligible woman.

It was a perfect plan. His grin widened, and it was with a lift to his spirits that he finally rode out of Kilkairn and into the woods surrounding it.

Simon leaned in the window. "Miss Kat?"

Kat looked up from where she sat at a desk in the front room of the cottage, poring over the account books. "Aye?"

"Do ye wish to see the new shipment of glass?"

"Of course! I'll be there shortly."

Simon nodded and pulled his head out of the window.

Kat looked down at the account books. She'd been trying to stay busy so that she wouldn't think too much about St. John and his devastating smile. Though she hated working on the accounts, it was an absorbing business and should have kept her mind busy and off things better not thought about.

It hadn't worked. Instead she'd spent a good hour alternately staring out the window and drawing little horses representing her upcoming ride with St. John.

Sighing heavily, she put away the quill and closed the books. It was nice having something to look forward to other than work. Not that she didn't enjoy the glassmaking. But there was something special in being pursued.

It really wasn't that she'd been totally without masculine attention. Malcolm had enough of his Edinburgh friends to visit that she'd had numerous occasions to slap hands and kick shins. Like Mr. St. John's. But none of them had really *pursued* her, taken the time to get to know her, asked her questions, even something as simple as offering to take her for a ride . . .

She sighed and rose, making her way to the front door. St. John's offer to go riding had been so unexpected, so . . . pleasant. And while she knew she should have said no, she also knew that she would have regretted saying the word. Some of it, she suspected, had to do with Mr. St. John's blue eyes. They had a way of looking at one as if he understood everything there was to understand, a curiously empathetic look for one so obviously spoiled by life.

"Hmph," she told the air as she stepped outside, "he's probably still in his room, sitting on his bed, waiting for his valet to come and dress him."

"Whot's that?" Douglas asked, looking up from the wagon bed. He was Simon's right-hand man, and as suspicious as they came.

Her face flushed. "Nothing. I was just talking to myself."

Simon nodded. "Bad habit, that."

"Indeed it is," she agreed. "Fortunately I only do it when faced with extreme circumstances." Before he could ask anything more, she said, "Did the new glass make the journey?"

Simon brightened. "Indeed it did, Miss Kat. Donald got us a right good price for it, too." He unlashed the canvas and lifted it, standing back to say with great satisfaction, "I'll wager you've never seen a prettier blue than that."

She leaned over the edge of the cart and ran her finger down the large sheet of glass. It was a deep, rich blue. Simon was right—it was beautiful. But she had seen a blue just this color—in the eyes of the man who had held her in his arms not a week hence. "It's a lovely color."

Douglas grunted. "'Tis fair. Would like to see more green glass, but that is neither here nor there."

"We need more green if we're to complete this new order," Kat said.

"Aye, and we need to find it fast," Douglas agreed. "'Tis coming on a rain and the roads will suffer. Miss Spalding's man said the way to Sterling is washed out."

Kat tried to look uninterested. "I'd heard that Miss Spalding was in residence at Kilkairn."

"Arrived earlier this week. I don't think she was going to stay at first, for she didn't unload her trunks. Daresay all of the servants at Kilkairn were glad to see that. But then she changed her mind and had the entire place in an uproar, directing this trunk here and that one there. She even made Janie wash the sheets on her bed, she did, claiming they were dusty."

"They probably were," Kat said absently.

Simon drew the tarp back over the glass. "Miss Spalding has been trouble since she put on her first petticoats. I hope ye stay clear of her. There's no reason to stir her up; 'twould be like jamming a stick in a beehive. You're bound to get stung."

"Of course I'll stay out of her way. I have no reason to so much as talk to her to begin with." If that was the type of woman Devon St. John admired, then he was welcome to her. Murien was beautiful, there was no doubt about that, but she wasn't particularly pleasant. At least, not to Kat. There had always been a certain superior air to the woman, as if she knew her beauty and valued it more than anyone else.

"Should we put the glass away?" Simon asked, drawing on his leather gloves.

"Aye," Kat agreed.

"Very well, Miss Kat." He and the others climbed into the seats and hawed the wagon in the direction of the workshop.

Kat entered the house and caught sight of the clock that hung over the mantel.

Good heavens! Where had the morning gone? St. John would be here soon and here she was, still wearing her work clothing. She gathered the account books and ran up the stairs in her work boots. She halted on the fourth step when she realized that

Annie stood on the middlemost step, disapproval in her clear gray eyes.

"Fie on ye, Miss Kat!" the housekeeper said, sending her a stern frown. "Ye'll tear the runner wid those shoes of yers."

"Sorry," Kat mumbled, slowing down and walking more or less sedately up the final few steps. It was difficult to walk up the stairs in such a mundane manner when seconds ago she was flying up them, but she managed to take three or four more-or-less properly feminine steps until Annie was out of sight.

The second Annie could no longer see her, Kat kicked off the offending shoes, hiked her skirts, and dashed the rest of the way to her room, skidding on her stocking feet as she rounded the door.

An emerald-green habit lay on her bed, spread out in luminous glory. Kat had to pause before she touched it, just to admire it once again.

" 'Tis a lovely color fer ye, mistress," Annie said from where she'd followed Kat into the room. "Deep green and severely tailored. Ye'll look pretty as a picture, ye will."

Kat's face heated. "Thank you." It was the only article she'd kept out of the generous wardrobe Malcolm had ordered. Mainly because she so loved to ride. On a horse, flying down a path, she felt light and thin and pretty.

"Ye'd best hurry," Annie admonished. "Or His Lordship will be here afore ye're ready."

"He's not a lord."

"Och, he looked like one. Lord Handsome is what he should be called. Now come and dress."

Later, Kat stared at herself in the mirror. Annie had been right—the habit fit perfectly. And the plain, almost severe style suited her, too. The coat was simple, following the nice line of her shoulders, angling down to her waist and ending there, at her waistband. The sleeves were long and narrow while the skirts were full, but not too much, so that they could be adjusted on her side saddle.

The only levity in the entire ensemble was a starched white cravat that filled the gap at her neck, and a fluttering white scarf that draped over her shoulder. The splashes of white served a purpose for they emphasized the full curves of her breasts. Kat frowned at that. She had more than her fair share of curves, a fact that made clothing difficult to fit.

Kat turned to Annie. "Well? What do you think?"

Annie sighed again, her grin belying her exasperation. "I think the same thing I thought two minutes ago. Ye look like an angel. If ye don't believe me, ask the lads. They'll tell ye what they think, will ye or nil ye."

That was true. "Thank you, Annie." After placing a quick kiss on the housekeeper's cheek, Kat snatched up her hat and dashed down the stairs and across the clearing to the workshop.

She stopped outside the wide door, pausing to gather her nerve. Inside was the warm murmur of masculine voices as the men worked, joked, and teased one another.

Kat fingered the stiff material of her riding habit.

Perhaps she shouldn't ask them what they thought. It was just that she wasn't certain it was the type of clothing to appeal to a man. Perhaps she should wear her black habit instead. It wasn't as fitted, but was of a more modern design.

She took a deep breath and then stepped through the wide open doors. "I've a question," she announced, waiting until every eye was upon her. Then she held out her arms to either side. "What do you think?"

With the exception of the crackle of the fire in the large pit, silence reigned.

Finally, Simon set down the lathe he'd been using to smooth a rough board. He rubbed a thick finger alongside his nose, staring at her intently. "Och now, lassie. Ye look perfectly well."

Donald nodded quickly. "Aye. And, ah, your hair looks well, too." He darted a nervous glance at Will, who was firing up the bellows for the soldering. Donald jerked his head toward Kat.

Will frowned, his heavy jowls quivering. He was a massive man, more than six feet tall, his arms bulging with muscles from his work at the forge. He blinked hazily at Donald, who was still motioning toward Kat. "What?"

" 'Tis Kat," Donald said with a meaningful jerk of his head. "She wants to know what we think."

"Of what?" Will said, plainly bewildered.

"Her *hair*."

Will turned to look at Kat, squinting thoughtfully. "Hm . . . weeel, it don't look a mite different than the last time I seen it." His brow lowered. "Least I don't think it looks any diff—"

"*Will*!" Simon hissed, glowering.

Will reluctantly smoothed his dirty hands on his smock. "Och now, I dinna know what ye want me to do!" He turned a bewildered eye on Kat. "Miss Kat, ye look loverly, whatever ye done wid yer hair."

Kat sighed. "I didn't do anything with my hair."

"Ah ha!" Will turned an indignant eye on Simon and Donald. "She didn't do nothin' to her hair!"

"I heard her," Donald hissed. He stared at Kat as if perplexed. "What did ye do then?"

Simon nodded, crossing his arms and studying Kat as if she was a puzzle to be solved. "If I know one thing about women, 'tis that they do love to ask ye what ye think of their new locks or new trappin's."

Alistair rubbed his chin, rasping his blond whiskers. "Mayhap 'tis her boots."

Seven pairs of eyes fastened on Kat's boots.

She dropped her arms to her sides. "Oh for the love of—It's not my hair and it's not my boots, either." Encountering yet more looks of bewilderment, she finally sighed and said, "It's the riding habit. Do you like my riding habit?"

Neal sent a covert glance around the room, then offered, " 'Tis a new one, then? How loverly."

She stomped her foot. "No! 'Tis my old one, but I had it brushed and pressed."

To a man, they appeared relieved.

" 'Tis brushed! O' course!" Simon said.

Donald beamed. "That was me next guess."

"Whist, now," Will said, sending a stern glance at Donald. "Ye weren't a-goin' to say nary a thing aboot her habit and ye know it."

"I was, too," Donald protested, his face flushing. "Was goin' to say that if 'twasn't her hair, and 'twasn't her boots, then it had to be her riding habit. Whot else could it be?"

"Donald has a point, he does," Neal said, nodding wisely.

"Whist now, all of ye," Hamish said in his quiet way. "Miss Kat looks loverly in her habit, she does. And that's all she needs to hear from us."

The others nodded their agreement.

Simon appeared relieved the moment had passed. "There ye are, Miss Kat. We all agree ye looks wondrous."

Kat had to smile. Over the last few years, these men had become her family, and she loved them dearly. It was wonderful how they each added to Kat's life and livelihood. After years of practice, Simon was better than she was at glazing, his touch delicate and smooth. Both Donald and Hamish had a way with soldering that made her shake her head in wonder. Alistair could get the most cuts out of a pane of glass. Neal was a marvel at etching, while Douglas's ability to trace and replicate a design was almost uncanny. He had but to see a picture to reproduce it. And Will's exquisite woodworking skills made suitable frames that blended the beauty of the glass with the more functional aspects of the windows and doors Kat's patrons demanded.

But for all the talents of her apprentices, none had

her eye for design and not one understood the use of color, though she'd tried time and again to explain it to them. It was the combination of all their skills that made the glasswork so unusual, so exquisite.

A noise arose outside, and Simon crossed to the window. He frowned. "There's that Sassenach again. Does he have nothin' better to do than come here?"

"He came to see me. We are going riding."

The warm glow of approval evaporated as quickly as it had come. "Riding?" Donald said. "With a Sassenach?"

"With one of Malcolm's guests," Kat said a bit defensively. "Besides, I get to ride his gelding."

" 'Tis a bonny horse," Simon said, "but I hope ye'll have a care. I don't trust any of Lord Macdonald's guests, particularly not the Sassenach ones."

Kat placed the hat on her head, tilting it to a jaunty angle, then she went to the door. "I will take care, Simon. You have my word on it."

"Like ye'll remember oncet ye're cavorting with the Sassenach," Simon said sourly.

"I promise not to let the 'cavorting' go to my head." She grinned at the lads. "I will be back soon, and then we'll begin working on the designs for the windows for that London church. I've an idea for a panel that will leave them all breathless."

With that, she waved a good-bye and then almost danced out the door, closing it behind her.

Chapter 9

Most men are trustworthy providing you trust them only after they've proven themselves worthy.

Miss Elizabeth Standon
to a rather distraught Lady Lucinda Sutherland
upon discovering Mr. Poole's duplicity

Every eye focused on the closed door.

Simon raked a hand through his hair, wondering what he should do now. He didn't trust the Sassenach, or any man. Not around Miss Kat.

Donald pursed his lips. "Is it just me, or is Miss Kat actin' a wee bit strange?"

Neal nodded. "I was thinkin' the same, I was."

"And I," Hamish agreed.

The others murmured an agreement.

Simon cocked a brow at Donald. "I think she's actin' mighty strange. And it all has to do wid that St. John fellow."

"It canno' be another," Donald said.

"Have ye spoken to him?" Neal asked.

Donald shook his head. "Nay, but Annie has,

though what good that does, I canno' tell ye. She said he was a bonny Sassenach. Went on about his blue eyes till I was near to castin' up me lunch."

"Sassenach." Simon spat the word.

The others nodded glumly.

Silence filled the workroom. It was one thing for Miss Kat to have a beau. God knew she was a taking lass and needed a strong hand. But for it to be a Sassenach; that was another matter all together. He'd bear watching all the more closely.

Simon flexed his shoulders. "I'll say this: if anythin' untoward seems to be happenin', then we'll take a look at this man. Perhaps we'll invite him to a meetin'."

Donald brightened. "That's a right good idea. But . . . what if we do no' like him?"

Neal rubbed his nose. "Then we'll make certain Miss Kat knows aboot it. What she does then, well . . . that's up t' her."

The others nodded, muttering agreement.

Feeling better by the minute, Simon stood, smacking his fist in his hand. "Good then. When the time comes, I'll see if we can convince His Lordliness to join us fer a brief spate o' conversation."

"But—" Hamish's blond brows were drawn low. "What if he won't come to see us? He is a man of wealth and position, and we are just apprentices."

Simon considered this for a moment. Then he shook his head. "Don't ye fash that he might refuse; I can be mighty persuasive. 'Deed I can."

A slow grin traveled about the room. Neal picked

up the hammer he'd lain down when Kat had entered the room. "'Tis done then. If things seem to be gettin' out of hand, Simon will collect the Sassenach and we'll test him fer Miss Kat, whether he wants to or not."

Devon wasn't quite sure what his expectations for the ride were . . . and later he'd tell himself that perhaps it was better he didn't have any except to escape Murien's cloying presence. Yet the day turned into one of surprises, most of which involved Kat.

His first surprise had been on arriving. Kat had looked tantalizingly beautiful, even more so than she had before. Perhaps it was the green habit, for it clung to her curves as if painted. Or perhaps it was that her hair was now pinned up, away from her face so that the loveliness of her features was even more evident. Whatever it was, there was something about Kat Macdonald that appealed to him. While Murien might be lovely in the conventional sense, something about Kat whispered of tangled sheets, damp skin, and other deliciously earthy matters.

Even after mulling it through, he could not distinguish what it was about her that made his thoughts instantly turn lascivious. It was not her manner, for she was neither brazen nor suggestive. It was more the curve of her cheek, the plumpness of her lips, the fullness of her hips. They all told Devon that if he was ever fortunate enough to win his way into her highly protected bed, it would be an experience he would never forget.

Which brought about the second surprise of the

day—from the moment he saw Kat walking across the clearing toward him, his body reacted. But that was not the end of it. For the rest of the day, all he had to do was rest his gaze on her hips as she rode before him, and his manhood would stiffen instantly.

Never had Devon felt such lust for a woman. But perhaps that was a good thing, for it greatly dimmed his memory of Murien until he scarcely thought of her. He soon found that thinking of another woman around Kat Macdonald was an impossibility; she was so vibrant, so uninhibited, so different from any woman he'd ever met.

The third surprise of the day was less spectacular, but even more perplexing. For all the attraction he felt for Kat, it appeared that it was completely one-sided. He was the one sneaking glances, trying to catch her eye, and feeling bereft when she didn't notice. She was totally caught up in experiencing Thunder, a fact that Devon found somewhat insulting.

In fact, Kat was so engrossed in the blasted horse that they rode for almost twenty minutes without speaking a word. Devon's pride was pricked. He wasn't used to being slighted. And while a part of him acknowledged that it was unintentional and he was probably due his fair share—for God knew he'd danced with numerous young ladies only to promptly forget their names—it didn't make the experience any less irksome.

Finally, Devon decided he'd had enough. He urged his mount forward a bit until Kat saw him. She blinked as if surprised, and then smiled, her teeth white between her lips.

Devon's ire evaporated instantly as she pulled up.

She glowed with enthusiasm. "What a lovely horse! Where did you get him?"

"Italy. My brother deals with a trader from there who dabbles in breeding. When the trader couldn't pay, he offered to send the horse to close the debt."

She bent over to rub Thunder's neck. "Your brother is to be commended! I don't know what the trader owed him, but Thunder was worth every guinea."

Looking at Kat's face, Devon realized that he would have paid twice the amount had the smile been for him and not his horse.

Devon wondered if Murien could even ride, and if she did, how she would compare to the effortless way Kat rode Thunder. No woman he knew had such a confident seat, and certainly none of them could have handled Thunder with such ease.

She sighed happily. "It has been so long since I had an opportunity to ride like this. I'm afraid I'm being rude, leaving you behind."

"Nonsense," he said, forgetting his ill feeling from a moment before. "Trusty and I were doing well on our own." He had to admit that she'd given him a pretty animal in exchange for Thunder. They were no match in stride, of course, but the bay had a neat mouth and a steady pace. "This is a good animal."

"Trusty is one of my favorites, though I fear riding your mount has spoiled me for all my horses. I shall have to sell them now."

He grinned. "How many do you own?"

"More than I should," she confessed ruefully,

tucking a stray strand of hair behind one ear. "I felt rather decadent when I first began buying them, but I can afford them, so why shouldn't I?"

"Why shouldn't you, indeed."

"Besides, having to keep them in grain helps me to get out of bed when the lads do. It's a marvelous incentive."

Devon chuckled. He'd never met a woman who paid her own way in the world. Not once. Previous to meeting Kat Macdonald, he'd always thought a woman who dabbled in trade would be brutally harsh and unfeminine. Instead he was finding that it added a pleasant aura of confidence.

She sent him a curious glance, her skin smooth as silk beneath the flicker of sun that broke through the trees. "How many horses do you own?"

He didn't know for certain, so he shrugged and said, "Far more than I can ever ride."

"Me, too. I am forced ask the lads to exercise the horses whenever they can."

"The lads?" A smile quirked his lips. "Is that what you call them?"

"Aye," she said. "That's what they are."

"Even Simon?"

"He's the oldest lad." An answering smile curved her mouth. "And as such, he is in charge of a great deal."

"Including your virtue."

The smile left her mouth. "No one is in charge of my virtue but me."

"I think Simon would disagree with you. He glares at me every time I see him."

"That's just his way."

"Hm," he said, unconvinced. He knew a challenge when he saw one and, having a sister himself, recognized a protective stance for what it was. "Well, if you ever decide you need someone to watch over your virtue, he would be an excellent choice." Devon looked around. They were on a wide path that seemed a great deal used. "Where are we going?"

"This is the road to the village. There's a path off to the right that leads to a stream. We can water the horses there, if you wish."

"Excellent," he said. He followed her onto a narrower path, and soon the rush of moving water could be heard. Once there, he dismounted and tied Trusty to a low branch, then went to where Kat was gathering her skirts and preparing to dismount. He reached out a hand.

Kat shook her head. "Thank you, but I don't need any help." She got on and off a horse at least four or five times a day, and it would be very irksome indeed if she couldn't do it without help.

"Too bad," he said, holding out his arms. "For I insist."

She paused, uncertain what to do. But even as she hesitated, he stepped forward. His warm hands encircled her waist, and he set her on her feet as easily as if she wasn't an ungainly size.

He didn't release her, though, but stood smiling at her. His hands were warm through her habit, his mouth only a few inches above hers. If she wished to kiss him, all she'd have to do was raise ever so slightly on her toes and . . . To her chagrin, her body softened in response. With his devilish smile and black hair, he was an incredibly attractive man, far more so than most of the visitors who tried to trick her into their beds.

But this stranger with the quick smile and flashing eyes hadn't attempted to hold her against her will. In fact, she was quite certain that were she to move now, his hands would drop from her waist and he would make no more effort to touch her. It was that knowledge that kept her still, enjoying the almost forgotten feel of a man's hands on her body. A feeling she'd tried her best to leave behind.

St. John smiled, a dimple flashing in one of his cheeks. "Know what I'm thinking?"

"What?"

"That you smell as good as you look. Of warm summer days and hot scones with butter."

This man seemed made up of words; some soft, some urgent, some funny, but all of them seductive. For the first time since she'd agreed to ride with him, a genuine stirring of alarm rose in Kat's chest. Blast it. She should have never agreed to help Malcolm keep Devon away from the castle.

As if he could see her distress, he reached up to smooth the hair from her forehead, the touch gentle, his eyes darkening. "I'm thinking something else, too."

"That you are hungry and should leave and hurry home?" she asked hopefully.

He chuckled. "No. Although the word 'appetite' did flicker through my mind."

Her cheeks burned. "That's quite enough, Mr. St. John."

"Do you mean that?"

Kat wet her lips. If she was honest with herself, she'd admit she rather liked the feel of his hands on her waist.

As if he read her thoughts, he asked, "What is wrong with me holding you?"

She thought about this for a moment. Why couldn't she just enjoy a man's hands on her waist? She forced herself to relax the tiniest bit. "I suppose there is nothing wrong with it. I am just used to others telling me what is and isn't proper."

"Society is a capricious mistress."

"She is vicious," Kat said, remembering a time when she'd felt the full brunt of disapproval.

His hands tightened slightly and he pulled her closer, his face only inches from hers, his gaze intent. "Listen to me. When you and I are alone, there is no society. No Kilkairn. No Simon. Just Devon and Kat. Do you think you can remember that?"

There was sincerity in his gaze and something more. Kat bit her lip. "Mr. St. John, I have to ask you a question."

He raised his brows.

"What are your intentions?"

He looked at her for a long moment, his blue eyes searching. "For today?"

She nodded.

"For today, I plan on kissing you again, which is a

realistic goal, I think. There is nothing wrong with a kiss between newly formed friends."

"Friends?"

"Like us. Then, after today . . ." He shrugged, his eyes gleaming with humor. "That is up to you, though I must admit I hope that a kiss might eventually lead to other things."

Kat blinked. "Well. You are certainly honest."

"I didn't think you'd accept anything less."

She wouldn't, of course. She just wasn't used to having the truth tossed at her in such a bald way. In her experience, the truth was something elusive and hidden, something one had to ferret out on one's own.

Perhaps there was more to Mr. Devon St. John than the other wastrels who had visited her brother. And he was right about one thing—there wasn't anything wrong with a kiss between new friends. He'd already stated that he'd allow her to decide how far that kiss would go.

Besides—she stole a glance up at him through her lashes—perhaps another kiss would assuage her curiosity about Devon and break the tug of longing his presence sent through her. Even now, she was achingly aware of his hands on her hips, of his chest just inches from hers. "I suppose one kiss won't hurt."

"Excellent," he said gravely. "We'll get to that in a moment. Now, relax and just enjoy being held. Isn't this pleasant?"

It was more than pleasant. It was warm and increasingly sensual. She caught his gaze and managed a smile. "You are right; it does feel well."

"So I think. Kat, you are beautiful, intelligent, and quick-witted. All of which make me want to hold you even more. If there is something wrong with that, you have to tell me."

When he said it like that, it made her want to wrap her arms about his neck and kiss him in earnest. The feeling startled her, and she cleared her throat. "St. John, what if I say I want to be released?"

He dropped his arms and stepped away immediately, leaving Kat feeling strangely bereft.

"See?" he said quietly. "That is all it takes. One word and I'll stop."

She nodded. He meant the gesture to comfort her fears, but it only raised more.

"So," he said, moving back into place, his thumbs tracing small circles on her back. "May I tell you what I am thinking at the very moment?"

Good Lord, a man who *liked* to talk while holding you in his arms. It was . . . frustrating. Kat wanted the kiss he'd promised, and being so close to him was making it hard to even think. Perhaps if she pretended to listen, then she could get her kiss more quickly. "Yes? What are you thinking?"

"I'm thinking of all the reasons a dalliance with a tall woman can be beneficial. For one, neither of us has to bend so far." He lifted a hand and drew his fingers down the side of her face.

The soft, simple touch sent a shiver through her, as did the almost somber tone of his words. "I—I have never been glad I was tall," Kat said breathlessly.

"You should be. You have amazing legs." His hand returned to her waist, and he was once again holding her before him.

She looked down at her skirts. "How would you know? You can't even see them."

He wagged his brows. "Couldn't I? When you were riding Thunder, your skirts outlined them. Along with other things."

Her cheeks heated. "Oh."

"You have legs that could capture a man and never let him go."

Heavens. He was certainly bold. And handsome. And yet . . . there was something almost wistful about him. As if he was searching for something.

She managed a small smile. "Fortunately for us both, I don't intend to use my legs to capture a man."

"No?"

"No." She took a deep breath, aware of the slow build of heat that surged between them. "Mr. St. John, I—"

"Devon."

The name crept into her thoughts and wrapped about her brain as if never to leave. She closed her eyes for a moment but refused to say anything more. She didn't think she could. The moment lengthened, stirring restless feelings she'd thought she'd forgotten.

She shook herself mentally. *It is just a feeling, and sometimes feelings are not real.* Thank God she was immune to men who bandied soft words and warm hands. Men who declared their love on Monday, only to realize by Tuesday that they'd made a mistake. Yet here she was, with a man who promised nothing more, yearning for his kiss. She put her hands over St. John's and pulled them off her waist, then moved out of reach. She crossed her arms over her, as if warding off a chill.

For some reason, that tiny moment caught at her, lodged in her chest like a weight. She searched desperately for a safe topic of conversation. "How was Malcolm? Did you see him this morning?"

St. John smiled as if he knew what she was doing, but he turned and gathered the horses and led them to the water. "He was fine. A little distracted, perhaps. But that's all."

She followed him to the edge of the stream. "I suppose he and Fiona have been fighting again." Kat knelt by the bank and picked up a smooth rock.

Devon turned to look at her. "There is a lot of tension at the castle."

"Aye. Whatever their argument is about, it is very desperate because neither will budge an inch."

Devon's brows lowered. "I've arrived in the midst of a domestic dispute."

"That is Malcolm's entire marriage." Stormy, violent, and flush with passion. There were indeed times Kat yearned for peace. She hefted the rock in her palm. "I don't think I believe in marriage anymore."

"Nor I." He caught her gaze and shrugged. "Not for me, anyhow. My brothers, however, seem to be rather fond of the arrangement. My sister, as well."

"Only one sister? Poor woman."

He grinned, his eyes crinkling in the most disarming manner. "Don't pity her. Sara more than held her own. When I was eight, I hid a snail in her bed. I waited and waited for her to scream, but she didn't do anything at all. Two nights later, I found an entire army of ants in mine. She'd poured sugar in the sheets, and it took me weeks to get rid of them."

Kat chuckled. "Served you right."

"Indeed it did, though at the grand age of eight, I felt sorely misused."

"Poor man." She dropped the rock and stood. "Would you like to ride into town?"

"What's there?"

"Nothing really. But it's a beautiful ride."

He looked directly at her. "It's beautiful here."

"Yes, but—you'll want to eat soon."

"You're right." He turned to Thunder and unbuckled the bag that hung across the horse's back. "Which is why I brought a luncheon."

She laughed then, the sound low and musical. "A man of resources." Devon found himself chuckling with her as he pulled out the picnic lunch.

They sat beneath a tree and ate. Devon tried to keep the conversation light, talking of this and that adventure with his brothers and sister, but it was difficult. Every time Kat opened her lips to take bite of the flaky pasties that he'd filched from the kitchen at Kilkairn, Devon's mind would burst into flames of heated, sultry imagination. He barely ate himself, but simply watched Kat.

He welcomed the building heat. It was what he'd

counted on to save him from the ring. With every breath, every word, Kat was proving herself to be the woman to keep the ring from working its magic.

Still, she needed some gentle wooing. Though she didn't flinch from his touch, he felt both her hesitation and her yearning, and something in him wanted to change that, to soothe her fears away. So he talked, and better yet, he listened, learning from her every word.

Soon the conversation turned to glasswork. He was amazed at the process and the length of time it all took. He wondered what other skills she possessed. Looking at her pouty mouth, he decided there were one or two that, if she didn't already know, he'd take great delight in teaching to her.

The shadows grew and lengthened, and before either knew it, the sun was slowly descending. Kat started. "St. George's dragon, it's late." She jumped up, brushing leaves from her skirts.

"Must you go?"

"Aye. The lads will be wondering what has become of me and we've an order to fill before—" She colored. "You don't want to hear this."

Devon realized with surprise that he did want to hear it. "Please go on."

"No," she said, smiling ruefully. "We really should go. The lads will be out looking for me if I don't return soon. They tend to expect the worst."

He could see that she was determined, so he rose to his feet as well and began putting away the remnants of their lunch.

As he went to help her onto Thunder, her clear

green eyes met his, measuring and seeking. He knew she was thinking of the promised kiss. He wasn't sure if she was looking for reassurance of some sort or was just curious. He smiled, and took her hand in his.

The touch of her fingers sent a wave of awareness over him. She gathered her skirts, preparing to mount the horse and he wondered again exactly what horrid happenstance had turned her from society, so scared that she hid deep in the woods like a princess asleep, waiting for a prince.

Well, he was no prince. Not even close to one. And charming companion or no, he had no plans for staying at Kilkairn longer than the short time he'd intended. But if nothing else, perhaps he could at least give her something to make the next two weeks memorable. Perhaps he could even get her to lower her defenses, show her that trusting was not always painful.

With that thought in mind, before Devon lifted Kat into the saddle, he tilted her face to his and kissed her.

Devon couldn't remember all the women he'd kissed. Still, it was novel to kiss someone whose mouth was so tantalizingly close to his. He didn't have to bend down at all.

But what really sealed the kiss as one of the best he'd ever had was Kat's reaction. She held nothing back, but threw herself into the embrace with her heart and soul.

Her arms crept about his neck, her body molded to

his, and her mouth opened, her tongue running over the edge of his teeth and setting his body aflame.

How long he kissed her, he didn't know. But every stroke of her tongue, every movement of her hips, threatened to send him over the edge. He finally broke the embrace, his breathing harsh, his mind numbed at a flood of demanding lust.

She met his gaze, her own breath quick between her lips. "That was . . . memorable."

He laughed. "Yes, it was. Memorable indeed."

She gave him a smile that was touchingly sweet, then turned and let him assist her into the saddle. He wondered at that smile the entire way back to the cottage.

The truth was, Kat Macdonald fascinated him. She offered an uncomplicated friendship tinged with a taste of passion so wild that he found himself unable to stop thinking about her. Of course, he was certain that once he sampled her passion, she would fade from his mind like all the others. But in the meantime, she offered a unique and fresh challenge, one perfectly suited to his rather jaded palate. One designed to protect him from the treachery of the talisman ring.

When they reached the clearing the lads came pouring out of the workshop. Simon was foremost. He planted himself before Devon. "Where have ye been?"

"Riding," Devon said calmly, though he was irked to be questioned in such a fashion. He pointed to Thunder and then to Trusty. "On horses."

Simon's face reddened. "I knew ye were on horses, ye bas—"

"*Simon.*" Kat sent him a warning glance from beneath her lashes.

The huge Scotsman pressed his lips together and said nothing more, though if glares could melt a man, then Devon would be a puddle.

One of the other lads growled, "We've been worried about ye, Miss Kat."

"Why?" she asked coolly, dismounting from Thunder without any help at all. "Because you believe I'm not capable of taking care of myself?"

Silence ensued as well as some uneasy shuffling. More than one uncomfortable glance was exchanged.

Devon had to pretend a sneeze just to hide his amusement. Kat's cool glance and calm demeanor had cut a swath through the rowdy men and reduced them all to abashed youths.

Simon cleared his throat. "Miss Kat, ye know we weren't sayin' that ye *couldn't* take care of yerself. Just that we worried about how the Sassenach might—well, ye know."

"No, I don't know," she answered. "You were worried about how the Sassenach might *what*?"

Simon rubbed his neck, clearly miserable. "Och, lassie. Don't ye look like that. Ye know what I mean."

She crossed her arms. "Simon, I am disappointed in you. How can you think such rubbish?"

Simon scuffed his toe on the ground, his face so red, Devon thought the man likely to burst into flames. "Miss Kat, I didn't mean to suggest—it's just that the man's a Sassenach, and ye were gone fer so long—then Hamish suggested that perhaps the Sassenach had—"

"*I* suggested?" one of the largest lads said. "'Twasn't me."

Simon gave a dismissive wave of his hand. "'Twas Neal then."

"No," returned one of the other lads in a huge rumbling voice.

Simon gave an exasperated sigh. "I don't know which of ye said it, but one of ye did!"

No one volunteered a word.

Kat gave an impatient gesture. "It doesn't matter. Simon, you owe Mr. St. John an apology."

"I owe him a *what*?" Simon shook his head as if to shake something clear from his ears.

"You owe Mr. St. John an apology." Kat's green gaze narrowed. "You owe me one, as well."

"What fer?"

"For having such indecent thoughts."

"Ye can't apologize fer yer thoughts," Simon protested.

Devon had to agree with the man there. Certainly had Devon been forced to do penance for every indecent thought he'd had while being with Kat, he'd have to spend a fortnight in a confessional talking nonstop.

Simon sighed, then mumbled an apology, though he glared the entire time. Devon nodded curtly. Simon had best get used to Devon's presence, for this would not be his last appearance at the little clearing in the woods.

Devon turned to Kat. "Thank you for a lovely day."

She shrugged, though her color was a bit high. "Thank you for a pleasant ride. And for allowing me to use your mount." She reached up to stroke Thunder's neck. "He's a lovely animal."

And she was a lovely person, both inside and out—a fact Devon was just beginning to realize and appreciate. He took her hand and pressed a kiss to the back of it, her fingers trembling against his lips. Ignoring Simon's muttered curse, Devon kept Kat's hand in his as he smiled at her. "Tomorrow?"

"No. I must work."

"The next day then?"

She pulled ever so slightly on her fingers and he released her. "The next day," she agreed.

With a final smile, he mounted Thunder. A short time later, Devon was riding toward Kilkairn, dreading his upcoming dinner with the warring Malcolm and Fiona, and the wily Murien. Perhaps he could slip in unnoticed.

With that in mind, he took the back stairs. As he rounded the corner to his room, he came to a halt.

"Mr. St. John!" Murien appeared from the shadows.

That gave him pause; her room was not on this level. He glanced around uneasily, then bowed. "Miss Spalding. Forgive my clothing. I just returned from my ride."

"How delightful for you." She smiled at him, the picture of a lovely, gracious, well-bred lady of fashion. "I daresay Miss Macdonald has worn you out. She is quite a . . . robust woman."

Though Murien's expression didn't change at all,

Devon felt the contempt beneath her voice. His mouth tightened. "She is a *lovely* woman," he corrected softly. Dangerously.

Murien knew a threat when she heard one. Her heart contracted at the realization. Yet her pride would not let it go. "Did you have a good ride?"

He looked at her for a long moment, then said in a deliberate tone, "Yes. I had a delightful time."

Murien's jaw ached where she clenched it. She was not used to doing all the pursuing. He *should* have made a comment about being sorry he had not been home, that he wished he'd spent more time with her. That he'd thought of her, at least once.

This was not going well. How could she captivate him if he was gone all the time?

Frustrated and uncertain of how to proceed, she toyed with her handkerchief, a gesture she'd adopted after a lovesick swain mentioned that it drew his gaze to her graceful hands. "Mr. St. John, you aren't from here . . . I don't mean to pry, but Strathmore's sister is—" She broke off as if embarrassed to go on.

"What?" St. John prompted her.

"You should ask Malcolm what happened in Edinburgh. I'm certain he'll tell you even though it was quite embarrassing at the time."

St. John leaned a shoulder against the wall, a smile on his handsome face. "Is that what you think I should do? Collect information from Malcolm about his sister?"

Murien nodded, adding in a gentle undertone, as

if loath to say more, "I am not one to gossip, and heaven knows I don't blame poor Miss Macdonald. But if your attention is being engaged, then you have the right to know all." She watched him from beneath her lashes, hoping he'd deny that his attention was anywhere near engaged.

But all he did was cross his arms, his coat stretching over his shoulders, a lock of dark hair falling over his brow. She wet her lips. He was quite attractive, her equal in looks. They would make a brilliant couple, feted for their beauty, admired for their culture and breeding, and envied for their fortune. Well, it was his fortune now, but it could be hers if she played her cards correctly.

Resolution grew in Murien's breast. She was not going to let Devon St. John get away. He was the perfect man for her, the one she'd been waiting for. "Mr. St. John, I wondered if perhaps tomorrow you might like to ride out with me and—"

"Do you ride?" he asked, surprised as if she'd admitted to vaulting off roofs as a hobby.

"Why yes. Of course I ride."

"Ah. But do you ride *well*?"

What was this? She frowned. "Of course I do."

His gaze narrowed, and she found herself fascinated with the way his lashes tangled at the corners of his eyes. It was unusual, black lashes and those blue, blue eyes.

"When *was* the last time you rode a horse?"

She wasn't quite sure. All she remembered was that she had received several compliments and two impulsive proposals of marriage before she'd even mounted the nasty animal someone had saddled for her. "I think it was two years ago. Perhaps three."

He laughed then, the sound startling her. She lifted her chin. "I fail to see what is funny."

"Don't worry, sweetheart," he said, shoving himself from the wall and walking past her to his room. "I wasn't laughing at you, but at myself. For being afraid of a silly legend. Apparently the St. John talisman ring can be beat, after all."

With that cryptic comment, he went into his room, shutting the door and leaving her all alone in the hallway.

Chapter 10

I was lying in bed, unable to sleep, when a truth was revealed to me. Mama, men are boils on the backside of the earth. If I had my way, I'd take a knife and lance them all.

The once gentle Lady Lucinda,
to her astonished mama, the Countess of Bradford,
when that gracious lady came to see why
her daughter did not appear at breakfast

"He is never here."

Fiona pressed her fingers to her forehead where a raging headache threatened. "Murien, you have only been here a week or so. How can you—"

Murien whirled to face her. "Don't be a fool, Fiona! How can I make him fall in love with me if he won't even stay within arm's reach? He has been riding with Malcolm's sister three days in a row now. I *never* see him."

Murien had a point and Fiona knew it. But her head ached too much for her to do anything but nod dumbly. Something was going dreadfully wrong with her plan; not only was St. John unaffected by Murien, but Malcolm, even though he was winning the wager, was becoming colder by the day.

It was as if the closer he came to winning, the angrier he became.

Her lips trembled and she hastily took a sip of tea to stave off the tears. Murien hated to see people cry.

Murien sank into the chair opposite Fiona's in a cloud of pale blue muslin, a petulant expression on her face. "We have to think of some way to keep St. John here, at the castle. At least for an evening or two. I just know that if I could spend more time with him, he'd begin to see how well we would suit."

Fiona sighed. "I don't know what to say. St. John comes home every night, but goes straight to bed or closets himself with Malcolm in the billiards room. He's only been to dinner twice in the time he has been here."

Of course, part of that could be her fault. She had to admit that the cook was horrid—part of Fiona's original plan to force Malcolm to remove from Kilkairn. How Malcolm managed to get such breakfasts out of the man was beyond Fiona's ken. She imagined that the cook, like all of the other men in the household, was siding with Malcolm.

Murien's mouth thinned. "My brother-in-law does not wish me well."

"Nonsense. He merely enjoys St. John's company and likes a good game of billiards."

"Oh Fiona, stop it. Malcolm does not care for me;

he never has. That's fine with me for I don't care for him, either. How you could marry such a—"

"Don't." Fiona wasn't sure who was more surprised at the icy tone of her voice.

Murien recovered first. She leaned back in her chair, a placating smile on her lips that did not quite reach her eyes. "I was just teasing, sister. There is no need to get in an uproar."

Fiona tilted her head in acknowledgment, mainly because she didn't trust herself to speak again. Heavens, what had caused that reaction?

"This is all so very perplexing." Murien placed her elbow on the arm of her chair and rested her chin in her hand. Her brow pulled down as she considered her options. "I wish there was some way we could expose Kat Macdonald for what she really is, gauche and unformed."

"Actually, she would have a very pretty figure if it was not for today's fashions," Fiona said absently. "They do not suit a woman with such curves."

"Curves? I wouldn't call them that. But it scarcely matters for the woman has no name, is practically two stone heavier than she ought to be, and has ruined whatever reputation she possessed. There is simply no reason for St. John to be dallying with her unless she is rewarding him in some way."

Fiona's cheeks heated. "Murien! Do not even suggest such a thing. I know Kat Macdonald and she's nothing like that."

Murien curled her nose. "Kat Macdonald hasn't

the least call to think herself worthy of St. John. She has no real beauty to speak of."

Fiona didn't understand it, either. Not that she harbored ill will for Malcolm's half sister, for Kat had been very kind to Fiona when she'd first come to Kilkairn.

But Fiona had to admit that there were far more reasons that St. John would avoid a woman like Kat rather than wish to be with her, unless of course . . . Fiona sat up straighter. "Murien, do you believe St. John might have developed a true tendre for Kat?"

"Lud no," Murien said, her lip curled. "He is just amusing himself at her expense. It is painfully obvious he is running from that blasted ring. He even said something to me about it. I didn't really understand it at the time, but now that I think about it, it makes perfect sense."

"Oh? When did you speak to him—"

"It doesn't matter. I think he is afraid of being forced to marry. And with Kat . . . how could she claim that she was ruined when she has already been so? She's safe for him. Perfectly safe."

"You don't think he's going to marry her?"

"No! He's not a foolish man." Murien's impatience was clear to see. "If only he would spend more time here." Murien leaned back in her chair, her gaze hard. "What we need is a reason to keep him here while proving how horridly unsuited Malcolm's sister is, even for a flirt."

Fiona tried to will her tired brain to think, but it was nearly impossible. She pressed her finger to her forehead. "Perhaps I should have a dinner party. A large one. Then we could invite Kat and he might see—"

"Fiona! That's it! But not a dinner party." A slow smile curved Murien's mouth. "A ball. An honest-to-goodness ball. Oh, I can picture it now. All of Edinburgh will be here and we'll dazzle them with Kilkairn Castle!"

Fiona looked around the room. Though it was one of the cleaner rooms in the castle, the rugs were still dusty and the mantel hadn't been wiped in weeks. She'd thought of seeing to it that the house staff did a better job, but that would only pander to Malcolm's comfort. Besides, why should she make such an effort to make Kilkairn a lovely place when Malcolm refused to allow her to live elsewhere for even part of the year?

She shook her head. "Murien, it would take weeks to get Kilkairn ready for a large ball. I don't know how—"

"Then have a small one and hire help from the village. I don't care. I just know that you have hit upon the perfect plan to show Miss Katherine Macdonald that she does not belong in the same room as St. John. That she is outclassed by far. Meanwhile . . ." Murien tapped her fingers on the arm of her chair, a sly smile on her lips. "Meanwhile, I shall do what I can to show St. John I am indeed the one to fear—that I am the woman he is to marry."

"And how will you do that?"

"Leave that to me. You just take care of the ball. We'll show St. John the pitfalls of having a consort like Kat."

Fiona bit back a sigh, wishing Murien didn't appear quite so happy about seeing Kat in such a humiliating situation. But Fiona would do it—she'd have the ball if for no other reason than to win the wager and keep her marriage intact.

Feeling miserable, she excused herself and went to her room to indulge in a good cry.

To the chagrin of more than one person, Devon came back to the clearing twice more over the next two days. Both times, despite Murien's attempts to lure him into staying at the castle and Simon's attempts to convince Kat that there was too much work to be done, Devon succeeded in carrying Kat off on Thunder. They rode far and wide, exploring pathways and galloping over meadows. And every day they'd have lunch beneath a tree of Kat's choosing.

Devon kept the conversation light on purpose. And at the end of every ride, before they mounted up for the ride home, Devon would kiss Kat. Just once. Just enough to leave her—and him—wanting more.

It was the sort of seduction he'd never before carried out, one slowly paced and carefully planned. Every day was a tempting challenge, and Devon found that he was enjoying every minute of it.

Of course, he didn't really think he needed to protect himself from Murien anymore . . . her charms did not appeal to him, which somewhat surprised him since she truly was the exact type of woman he'd pursued over and over. Perhaps that was why Kat was so appealing; she was just . . . Kat.

It was nice, too, to get away from the castle. Fiona continually attempted to throw Murien in his way, even though he'd been plain in his desire to stay away from her. And Murien, the gold standard gleaming in her beautiful eyes, encouraged Fiona to do just that.

In the end, there was nothing for it but to avoid Kilkairn until the time came for him to leave for Edinburgh, a day he should be looking forward to, but strangely was not. In fact, he refused to allow himself to remember the exact day. Every time he began to think ahead, an uneasy feeling rose in him.

Kat, of course, could have told him exactly how many days until he was due to leave, for it was a thought that was never far from her mind. In fact, this very morning she had awakened and lay in her large bed staring up at the hangings overhead, her mind immediately humming. She went to sleep and woke up thinking about Devon St. John. Strange how some people came into your life and then left without making a mark, while others came for only a short time and made such a dent that it would take years to fill the hole. Kat knew she was beginning to care for St. John. Oh, not in a romantic way, of course, though she enjoyed his kisses. It took far more than a kiss to sway her heart. But she was beginning to value his friendship. Yes. That was what it was.

Still . . . though he made a good friend, he was only passing time, avoiding being at Kilkairn Castle, any fool could see that. Kat needed to remember that fact.

She sighed. Who was she fooling? "Thank goodness he leaves soon," she muttered. That was the only reason she'd allowed the relationship to progress as far as it had; she knew that it would all be over in a week or so and her life would settle back down to the routines she'd developed. But for the rest of her life, she'd have memories of rides through the woods, picnics beneath the trees, shared laughter, and the enjoyment of a good friend. What could be wrong with that?

A brisk knock sounded on the door and Annie entered. The petite woman was dwarfed by the huge silver tray she carried in her hands.

Annie set the tray on the night table and began arranging the dishes. A pleasant clank and clatter filled the room.

Kat pushed herself upright, tucking her hair behind her ears. "What's this? Breakfast in bed? But Annie, I am not ill!"

"Neither is the prince, but I daresay he has breakfast in bed every day."

"Yes," Kat said, "and look how fat he has gotten."

Annie waved a hand. "Ye're not fat, m'lady. Ye're rounded. 'Tis a different thing. As fer the prince, I would no' know aboot him as I try to avoid the scandal sheets whenever possible."

Kat laughed. Annie brought back every scandal sheet she could procure from her cousins in London. Kat knew because she'd read them all to Annie at one time or another. "So why did you bring me breakfast in bed?" She lifted first one cover and then another, the scent of hot bacon and ham wafting through the air.

"Whist now, Miss Kat. Can't I do something pleasant fer ye without bein' accused of false pretenses?"

Kat raised her brows. "No."

Annie sighed and took a seat on the edge of the bed, the mattress barely sagging with her weight. "Ye're talkin' nonsense. Come, lass. We can coze a bit whilst ye're eatin'."

Here it came. "Yes?" Kat said politely, cutting her ham into small bites.

"I've been thinkin', I have."

Kat took a bite.

Annie sighed and folded her hands in her lap. "See, Miss Kat, 'tis like this; whilst I know ye think ye have everything under control where the Sassenach is concerned, I have to wonder if 'tis so."

"Why is that?"

"Because there are signs ye're not so immune to him as ye think."

"Oh for the love of—Annie, I've only gone riding with him a few times. I'm not planning a hand fasting."

"Aye, 'tis a good thing, that, fer you'd not get it. From what I've heard, the Sassenach is a libertine."

"A liber—Who told you that?"

"Me cousin, Janie. She said she heard Miss Spalding say Mr. St. John's only purpose in comin' to see ye was—" Annie broke off, glancing away, her face red. "Ye know what I mean."

Kat considered this. After a moment, she said

slowly, "And if that is true? How would that change things?"

"Miss Kat!"

"Annie, he has been nothing but gentlemanly, though I'd not allow him to be else. Besides, he's leaving in a week. I've nothing to worry about."

"Are ye sure?"

"Aye. That I am."

"Oh? How will ye feel if he leaves? I worry that ye're already too attached."

Kat picked up her bread and became very busy spreading butter over it. "I am fine. Really I am. Once Devon is gone, I will have some lovely memories. Where's the harm in that?"

"Hmph. Just see to it that ye don't have a baby full of memories."

"Annie!"

"Whist now. Ye know what I mean. A man who looks like that, why, if he so much as stumbled, I'd fall flat on the floor and pray that he fell atop me."

Kat had to laugh. "You are incorrigible."

"I don't rightly know what that means, but it sounds well enough, so I'll thank ye." Annie stood. "Now eat up and I'll come in a wee bit to collect the tray."

"Thank you, Annie."

"Whist. It was nothing." The scrawny housekeeper waved a hand. "By the by, Simon is gettin' worried about you. Ye might want to set his mind at ease afore he does something silly."

"Simon is a worrier. He always has been."

"Aye, and that makes him all the more dangerous, fer he's apt to get involved if he decides things are not progressin' as he thinks they should or shouldn't."

Kat nodded. She'd have a word with Simon. Meanwhile, her mind returned to Devon. Was Annie right? Was Kat getting too attached? All she knew was that she was not going to stop seeing Devon. Not yet, anyway. She'd just let the days unfold and enjoy them all, and then worry about Devon's departure when that day arrived. She'd just have to make certain she didn't let go of her heart.

That settled, she pulled the tray closer and ate.

Devon rode into the clearing, but unlike the previous days, Kat did not come out to welcome him. But of course, he was well over an hour late thanks to Murien's machinations. She'd caught him in the stables and had quizzed him mercilessly about his horse. Devon ground his teeth.

He dismounted and tied Thunder to a rail, then tilted his head and listened. He could just make out the faint sound of voices from the workshop. Deep masculine voices and a lone, husky feminine voice.

Devon walked to the workshop, pausing outside. Was Kat angry at him for not arriving when he'd said he would?

" 'Tis a complete ruin." Kat's voice filtered outside.

"Aye," agreed one of the lads. "The fool couldn't even draw a proper bead."

Another lad added, "An' look at the bit o' a smudge that's on the bottom."

"Aye," came a voice that Devon recognized as Simon's. "A cow-handed job if I ever seen one."

"We'll have to melt the seams and take it all apart," Kat said.

Devon stepped quietly into the workshop. It took a moment for his eyes to adjust, but they eventually did. He was intrigued with what he saw.

Rows of large tables ran the center of the shop, strewn with pieces of glass of every color, as well as several large squares. To one end of the room was a fire that was banked and covered until it smoldered. Beside it was a large, flat table strewn with long sticks and covered with drips of dried metal.

He turned his head toward the side of the shop that had no windows. Against the wall stood racks of glass, each sheet stacked on end and arranged by hue. There were cobalts and sky-blues, deep greens and mints, sun yellows and rich golds, royal-purples and pale violets, and every color in between. Truly, the room bore so much color that it seemed magical.

Yet the colors were not so much what caught him as Kat herself. Gathered with her lads around her at a table, Kat stood in one of her plain gray gowns. She was looking down at a seemingly finished piece of glasswork, a large square that depicted a unicorn grazing in a grass field.

She traced a line between two colors with one finger. "I've never seen such a horrid piece of work."

Simon rubbed his chin. "Do ye think we can—" He caught sight of Devon. Simon's jaw clenched.

Kat's gaze followed Simon's. Her face reddened. "St. John."

Never had his name sounded so unwelcoming.

He had to stifle yet another surge of irritation for Murien's clinging ways. There was nothing for it but the truth. "Kat, I am sorry I am late. I was detained at the castle by a very determined committee of one."

Kat's brow cleared. "Murien."

"Aye. I tried to get away, but she made it impossible."

There was a short moment of silence, and then Kat shrugged. "We can go riding another day."

Another day? He'd be damned if he'd return to the castle without spending at least a little time with her. Besides, he wanted their kiss. For some reason, the thought of going without that simple embrace made his jaw set. Ignoring the hostile gazes of the lads, Devon clasped his hands behind him and walked to the table. "You know . . . you did promise to show me your workshop."

"Indeed I did." She gestured around them. "Here 'tis."

He looked at the glasswork before them. "Did you just make this?"

Kat looked startled. "This?"

Simon spat on the dirt floor. "We're good at our trade. Don't think we aren't."

"Easy, Simon," Kat said, unrolling her sleeves and buttoning them back around her wrists. " 'Tis time ye were all back to work. Simon and I will find a way to at least make this better, if not fix it all together."

The lads left to go about their work, except Simon, who stayed in listening range.

Devon managed a rueful smile for Kat. "I'm afraid

I don't know much about glasswork. What's wrong with this piece that it offends you so?"

"A thousand things." She tilted her head to one side, her eyes narrowed. "See the line of the solder, how 'tis thicker on one side than t'other?"

He nodded.

"That is poor workmanship. Now see here, where the corner is patched and you can tell? Again, poor workmanship."

"Your men would never turn out such work as that, would they?"

"Not if they valued their jobs, they wouldn't. Oh, we all make mistakes now and again, and I'm well aware of it. But this type of work where the metal is heavier in places than it should be leaves the window weak and prone to cracking."

"Ah. So the problem with this piece isn't the uneven metal, but the weight of what is there."

"Aye. The secret is balance. If you're heavy on one side and not the other, the window can warp. The metal's only purpose is to link the glass together and lend some form to the whole. The frame is where the real strength of the window is built."

Devon watched her glowing face, faintly envious. "You like doing this."

"I cannot imagine not doing it," she said honestly. "I love the whole process, from the design, to cutting the pieces, to applying the metals, to seeing the finished window."

He tapped the glass on the table before them. "What about fixing other people's errors?"

She laughed, the sound infectious. "Even that,

though 'tis fortunate we are not oft asked to do such a thing. Truly, had this one not kept cracking, no one but the lads and I would have ever noticed the flaws. 'Tis a lovely piece despite the errors."

Devon leaned his hip against the table, facing her so that he could see every nuance of her face. With the exception of Simon, who stood glaring not five feet away, it was as if Kat and Devon were alone, for no one else was near enough to hear. "You are very different from the women of my world."

Her face shuttered. After a moment she said, "Not so different."

"But you are. Most of the women I know think marriage their goal. But not you."

"No," she said. "Not I."

He had to smile at her flat expression. Usually he was the one with that particularly unimpressed look. "Would you give up all of this for the right man?"

She snorted, then caught herself and blushed. "I am sorry. See the hazards of working among men all day? I've no delicacy left."

Oh, but how he disagreed. Even dressed in servant's clothing and with soot streak down one cheek, she was beautiful, womanly, and ladylike. He couldn't explain how she did it, but she did. He reached out and wiped away the soot with the pad of his thumb.

He dropped his hand when the mark was gone. "I have to wonder if you snorted because you would never give up your calling for the right man?"

"The right man wouldn't ask me to give up anything." She turned her gaze on him, clean and clear, as if looking right through him. "The right man would accept me as I am, and learn to love the things I love, or at least appreciate them."

One of the lads came up to discuss the cut of a pane of glass, and Devon was left alone for a moment.

He wondered what it would be like to be loved by a woman like Kat. He suddenly realized one reason that his previous affairs seemed so unsatisfactory; those women had been pale shadows of what a woman could be; Kat was beginning to show him that.

In fact, the passion he'd shared with his past loves didn't seem nearly as exciting to him as it once had. It had been about the chase, and nothing else. No wonder none of them had lasted more than a few weeks.

He looked down at the picture of the unicorn, absently noting that though the metalwork was uneven, the animal itself was well rendered. What *would* it be like to be loved by Kat, both physically and emotionally?

Emotionally, he didn't know. But physically, he could vouch for her reactions—at least partially. He'd kissed her no fewer than six times now, each one more scorching than the last and though he'd attempted to keep the kisses sweet, chaste even, in an effort to reassure her, she'd been the one to tug them both closer to the edge. She was responsive, wildly and passionately so, a fact that warmed his blood and heated his soul.

He knew the time was approaching when he wouldn't be able to stop at just one kiss. He both looked forward to and hated the thought of that day, for it would signal the beginning of the end of their relationship. Just as it did in all his previous relationships. Because once that occurred, the chase was over.

He thought of their last kiss, the memory enough to make his body react. Devon glanced at the door, wondering how he would get Kat away from the prying eyes of her lads so that he could taste her once again.

Suddenly he realized that he had only a week and a few days before he left.

Blast and hell, what was he waiting for? It was time he moved the relationship forward, at least some. If he didn't do so soon, he'd be gone before he could discover the true extent of Kat's passion, and Devon was determined not to let that happen.

Kat's voice sounded at his shoulder. "Do you like the unicorn?"

He realized he'd been blindly staring at it. "Just trying to see all the flaws."

"Sometimes 'tis best just to focus on the beauty."

He smiled. "Miss Kat, would you do me the honor of walking me to my horse?" He held out his elbow, and after a moment's hesitation, Kat tucked her hand in his. Out of the corner of his eye, Devon caught a glimpse of Simon, who stood watching, arms crossed, a fierce scowl on his craggy face. "Kat m'love," Devon whispered. "I think we have a problem."

She looked at him, surprise in her wide green eyes. "What problem?"

"Your friend Simon does not think much of me."

"He's just a mite protective."

"Hm. I see. He also does not like me. At all."

She seemed to consider this as they strolled outside to the railing where Thunder was tied. The horse had been there so many times that he was quite comfortably reaching through one of the barn doors to nibble some hay that stuck out around a corner.

"Simon is like a member of my own family. He watches out after both Annie and me."

"Annie is your housekeeper? The little bird of a woman?"

"Aye. She's his sister, and he treats us much the same."

"Hm." They were at Thunder's side. Devon looked around. Even from here, he could make out Simon's shape in the window of the workshop.

Devon took Kat's hand and pulled her around to the other side of Thunder.

"What are you doin—"

He kissed her. But this time, he didn't do the chivalrous thing and hold back. Instead, he kissed her with every ounce of his desire. He wrapped his arms about her, held her tightly to him, pressed his length to hers as he plundered her mouth, hotly and passionately. He kissed her until he could feel the tremors in her body and her knees weakened and he had to hold her upright.

When he finally lifted his head, he looked into her eyes and said, "Kat, I want more. More of you."

Her breath rushed through her lips, her eyes were

wide and luminous. He could see she was as affected as he. He set her back on her feet. "Think about that, would you? I will return tomorrow."

Then he mounted Thunder and left, whistling all the way back to Kilkairn Castle.

Chapter 11

A disappointment in love is one of the hardest things for a woman to overcome. One would like to blame the entire male gender from youngest to oldest, for it always seems that, as a group, they have a peculiarly uniform method of failing. As if at some point, they held a meeting and simply voted to underperform en masse.

Countess of Bradford
to her favorite sister, Mrs. Compton,
while taking the waters in Bath

Tilton held out Devon's riding coat. "Your coat, sir."

Devon shrugged into it. "Thank you, Tilton. Did you call to have my horse saddled?"

"Yes, sir." The valet sniffed. "Again."

Devon grinned. "I am sorry if you find my habits so tedious."

"Indeed I do, sir. But I try not to fall asleep whilst performing my duties. I consider it a matter of professional pride."

Devon grinned and began to answer when his gaze fell on something small and shiny on the floor. He retrieved the object. "My sapphire cravat pin. I wonder how it got on the floor?"

Tilton frowned, all levity gone. "I don't know, sir. I've kept all of your pins in—" He picked up the jewelry box from the dressing table and flipped it open. He began sorting through the pins and fobs inside, his brow lowered.

"What is it?" Devon said.

Tilton paused, looked one more time, then closed the box. "The talisman ring, sir, it's gone."

"Gone?" Devon stared at the box. Surely the ring wasn't—hadn't been—"Are you certain? Perhaps it's on the floor like the cravat pin."

Tilton shook his head. "There is nothing else on the floor."

"Then perhaps it is behind the dresser." Devon began to search, his heart sick. Bloody hell, his brothers would kill him. And he'd let them, too. If he had lost the talisman ring, he deserved a beating and worse.

"Where in the hell is it?" he asked no one in particular when a thorough search turned up nothing.

"I don't know, sir. Someone had to have come in and stolen it."

Yes, but—who? Who would bother with such a theft, leaving the assortment of other, more valuable jewels? Devon raked a hand through his hair, wondering what in the hell he was supposed to do now.

As much as he disliked having the ring in his possession, it had been Mother's favorite. The entire family cherished the thing because of that, in spite of the horrid curse it supposedly carried.

He sat on the edge of the bed and yanked on his riding boots, consumed with the need to do something. He'd speak to Malcolm, have him question the household staff. It had to be one of the servants. Who else could benefit from the thing? "I'll speak to Lord Strathmore. Perhaps he has an idea of where we might look."

"Hmph. Well, the first place they should look is inside the pockets of that lazy upstairs maid. I've seen her sleeping under the steps on a number of occasions, reeking of gin."

"I'll mention that to Malcolm," Devon said. He grabbed his riding gloves and let himself from the room. He had just reached the bottom step when he caught sight of Fiona coming out of the front room. She was walking quickly, her head down, her hands clasped before her. While he watched, she then spun on her heels and turned back the other way. She was pacing, he realized, marching back and forth, her agitation clear.

"Lady Strathmore?" Devon said, pushing aside his own anxiety.

She came to an abrupt halt, swinging around to face him. "Y-yes, Mr. St. John?"

"I seem to have mislaid something. A ring. It was in my room and now it has disappeared."

"Oh dear. Do you think one of the servants stole it?"

"I am casting no blame. But do you think you might make some inquiries for me? It is the talisman ring, and my family would be loath to lose it."

"The talisman—Oh dear! Of course I'll make inquiries."

Devon could only hope she was more thorough in her inquiries than she was in overseeing the housekeeping.

She suddenly seemed to notice his clothing. "Are you going riding? Again?"

He hesitated, not quite sure why. "I am meeting Miss Macdonald, and we are going to visit the North Wood. Malcolm says it is quite magnificent."

Fiona's eyes flashed. "Malcolm? Has *he* been giving you suggestions for your rides?"

"Why, yes. I don't know the area, and he has been most kind in determining which trails would be best."

Her lips tightened. "He has been doing that, has he? And there is Kat, ready to escort you. How convenient."

Devon raised his brows. "Miss Katherine has taken great pains to assure me it is not at all convenient. She's quite busy, and I gathered that she wasn't very excited about becoming a guide."

"Oh. Well, if that is so, then perhaps you should take Murien instead. I'm certain she'd enjoy the exercise. If you'd like, I could return to the sitting room and—" She turned as she spoke, but Devon caught her arm.

"That's not necessary, I assure you." He hesitated, feeling the need to offer something more. "Besides, I will see Miss Spalding at dinner."

Fiona's face cleared as if by magic. "Excellent! That will give you a much better chance to talk than riding about on horses."

It would be much better chaperoned, too. Lately Murien's attempts to capture Devon's attention had seemed more determined than he liked. Still, he could afford to spend an hour across the dinner table from her, and if she was polite, he might even take her to the garden, providing there was a chaperone in the vicinity. If there wasn't, then Miss Murien was going to find herself alone among the roses.

He bowed now to Fiona. "I hate to leave so quickly, but Miss Katherine will be waiting."

"Oh. Yes, well—" Fiona took a deep breath as if to gird herself. "By the way, I meant to mention it to you, but I quite forgot. I . . . well, Malcolm and I thought to have a small gathering in your honor. I sent out the invitations yesterday. I would have told you sooner, but you have not been around much."

Devon almost winced at the gentle reproof in her voice. "I sincerely hope you haven't gone to any trouble. I'm not sure how long I'll be staying and—"

"It is planned for Wednesday next."

Four days after he'd planned to leave. He really needed to make the trip to Edinburgh but . . . He supposed he could stay a few more days. It would give him a little more time with Kat. "Very well. I look forward to it."

An uncertain smile swept over her face. "Excellent. I shall see to it that the servants are made aware of your missing ring, Mr. St. John."

"Thank you. Now I must be off. Pray have a good day, Lady Strathmore."

She flickered a smile, then watched him leave. He made his way outside, halting on the steps. The day was not as fine as the others, a low scattering of clouds and a hint of a breeze promising rain.

Devon took the pathway to the stables. Just as he rounded the last corner, he paused. Kat stood in the courtyard with the largest bay he'd ever seen. She was holding an apple behind her back, and the horse was attempting to reach behind her and steal it.

As beautiful as the horse was, Kat outshone it. She looked adorably mussed as she dodged this way and that, trying to avoid the horse's velvet nose. She glowed of health and laughter.

Devon waited until he was almost even with her before he spoke. "That is the tallest horse I've ever seen."

"Shhh!" Kat twinkled up at him and gave the apple to the horse. "Lady thinks she's a tiny, delicate thing. I try not to disabuse her of those notions. If she had any idea how heavy she really is, she'd refuse to take another fence."

Devon patted the horse's velvet nose, grinning a little. "She'd wait to sprout wings, hm?"

"Or for someone to carry her. She's dreadfully spoiled."

"Surely not that badly."

"Oh yes. She is everyone's darling. Even Malcolm brings her carrots and sugar when he thinks no one is watching."

Devon had no doubt about that, though he rather thought Malcolm did not bring treats to the horse, so much as he brought treats to his sister's favorite pet. "And here I thought Trusty was your most prized horse."

"Trusty? Why would you think that?"

"Because Trusty is the mount you gave me when I allowed you to ride Thunder. When two people trade, there is an unspoken implication that the two will strive to trade something of equal value."

Her green eyes sparkled with mischief. "Oh? Are you saying that Trusty was not an equal?"

"Not compared to this horse, no."

"Well . . . of all my horses, Trusty has the sweetest temper."

"And?"

Kat pursed her lips. "She also has a lovely mane."

Devon tried not to look too long at her lush lips. "What else does Trusty have?"

"Isn't that enough?"

"Not after seeing Lady." He reached out and patted Lady's neck. "I suppose I should ask if *this* is your finest mount rather than just assuming that it might be."

She grinned. "Yes, she is. I haven't ridden her for a week because she had a strained foreleg. But it seems healed now."

"She's a beauty and will make my poor mount appear lame."

"Thunder?" Laughter shining in her eyes, Kat covered Lady's ears. "Please do not get her hopes up. She can be quite despondent if she thinks to win and then doesn't."

It was nonsensical, but it helped dissipate some of the tension he'd felt earlier, though it did nothing to alleviate his concern over the lost ring. He put away those thoughts; surely the ring would turn up. "What brings you here this morning? I thought I was to meet you at the cottage."

"I'm escaping," she said. "Simon has been most obdurate about things of late. Besides, I thought we might ride out from here, to the north. You've only just a few days left, and should it rain, you might not have another opportunity."

"Actually, I may stay a few days longer than I'd originally expected." He didn't have to wait long to see her reaction.

She gave an impulsive hop. "Wonderful!"

The natural eagerness of her voice made his heart lighten. "Lady Strathmore is planning an event of some sort," he said. "It appears that I don't have a choice in the matter but to postpone my business in Edinburgh."

"Your brother will not be happy."

"Marcus will be fine; he's rarely happy, anyway."

"Poor man! Still, I am glad you'll be staying."

"Oh?"

"Of course!" Kat's smile lightened the cloudy day. "I am selfishly hoping that means that all of us can have more rides together."

"All of us?"

"You, Thunder, Lady and I. In fact . . . would you like to ride Lady today?"

"That is very kind of you," Devon said, touched despite himself. He reached over to pat Lady's neck. "She's a lovely horse."

"Aye. You know, if she didn't already have a name, I might consider calling her St. John, but she's not in the least bit averse to being held to bridle, so . . ." She shrugged, an impudent grin on her lips.

"So this magnificent beast could have been my namesake. How lovely."

The horse nudged Kat's pocket, sending her stumbling to one side. "Easy!" she ordered. "That is for later in the day."

"Another apple?" Devon questioned.

She nodded, patting her pockets where two round bulges could be seen. "I have one for her and one for Thunder."

The horse sniffed her pocket loudly, leaving a damp imprint, and then reached up and tugged on the white scarf that hung from Kat's shoulders. Kat sighed as she rescued her scarf. "Oh for the love of—"

Devon chuckled. "We had better go before she nibbles off your clothing in an attempt to win another apple." Although . . . nibbling off Kat's clothes held some appeal. A lot of appeal, if he was truthful.

They were soon riding, down the path. They rode on for some time, the slight wind rustling the leaves, the sun soaking the world with light.

After a while Kat pulled up, and they trotted along beside each other. "How are things at the castle?"

Devon hesitated. He wanted to tell her, but wasn't sure how much to confess.

She caught his look and said, "I know how it is there. I lived there once, too, you know."

"You are right, of course. I hadn't thought of that." He sighed. "Things are tense, with Malcolm and Fiona glaring at one another when Fiona isn't crying on the settee or Malcolm storming about the house. And Murien—" He stopped and shrugged.

"I know all about her, too. You should be on your guard, I heard that—" Kat's mouth clamped shut. "You should just have a care."

He managed a wry smile. "You may not credit this, but I have been on my guard against marriage traps since I was fifteen. I have no wish to ride out a bachelor and return an engaged man, and yet I have seen it happen to friends of mine."

"You need not worry about it with me. I do not find the thought of marriage attractive."

He looked at her quizzically. "May I ask why you're so set against it?"

She shrugged, looking away. "Some people are born for that sort of thing. I find that I am not."

"People . . . you mean women."

"Like Fiona."

"And Murien," he added.

Kat sent him a sharp look. "Has Murien been trying to get her claws into you?"

"I wouldn't say that, exactly."

Kat raised her brows.

Devon laughed. "Very well, perhaps I would say that."

He looked so mischievously sexy that the thrum of attraction that Kat was battling suddenly swelled and sent a bolt of heat through her. She instantly repressed it, though her body ached as if she'd deprived it of something crucial.

"I apologize for prying," Kat said. "I shouldn't be speaking of Murien or any of your other flirts."

"If we are going to talk about my flirts, we most definitely have to talk about yours."

"I don't have any."

"Well, not now. In order for someone to find you to flirt with, they'd have to have a map to the cottage and a cudgel to get through those lads of yours."

She grinned. " 'Tis true, that. Which brings me to my problem; they just don't make men capable of reading maps."

"I read maps. But only *if* there is a treasure to be found." He pulled Lady up short. "Perhaps we should find somewhere to eat before this rain lets go."

She glanced over their heads, then nodded. She led them to a small bluff, looking out over the wind-tossed fields. Devon dismounted and tied Lady to a low shrub. Then he went to Thunder and helped Kat dismount. The feel of her in his arms sparked the heat that had been growing all day. She was so perfectly made for him, her hips at his, her face only an inch or so lower. To kiss her, all he had to do was bend down ever so little—

Somehow, in thinking about kissing her, he did. Kat responded immediately, kissed him back, her arms sliding about his neck, her body melting to his. He devoured her, his mouth seeking, demanding. His hands splayed over her back as he melded her to him. Passion exploded and flared. Devon slid his hands lower until he was cupping her backside and holding her hips firmly to his.

She moaned beneath his mouth and pressed herself against him. God, but he wanted her. Every day with her had fed his desire. Every time she laughed, he wanted to kiss her. Every time she tilted back her head to look up at a bird or at the canopy of trees overhead, he wanted to open her gown and free her lush breasts, to hold them and cup them and taste them until she sighed his name. Every time she talked about the glasswork or Malcolm or her horses, or anything that ignited her passion, he wanted to sweep her from her feet and sample that passion for himself, let it sweep them both away.

And now he held her in his arms, her body moving as restlessly as his. Devon finally broke the kiss, but he did not release her as he usually did. This time he just held her. She clutched his coat, her face buried in his neck, her scarf on the ground at their feet. Her warm breathing tickled his overly active body, but all he did was hold her a little tighter. He waited for his breathing to still, resting his cheek against her silky hair, before he said, "One day soon, we are going to have to do something about this."

She lifted her face and met his gaze. "What do you mean?"

"You know exactly what I mean."

Her cheeks colored, but she didn't deny it.

"It is building between us. Can you feel it?"

She nodded.

He lifted his fingers to brush them across the line of her cheek. "I want you," he said simply. "I want to make love to you."

"Perhaps . . . perhaps we should eat." She moved out of his arms, stopping to retrieve her lost scarf.

Devon watched her open the leather bag that held their food. She hadn't agreed, but she hadn't refused him, either. For now, he would have to at least pretend to be agreeable to that.

He laid out their lunch while Kat fed apples to the horses, talking to them in a soft voice as if they were children. Thunder and Lady loved the attention and nickered in return, searching for more apples among Kat's pockets.

Devon watched from the corner of his eye. When he caught himself envying the attention she was bestowing on the horses, he shook his head ruefully. He was so randy he was beginning to act like a lovesick swain, something he never did, even when deep in the throes of a new love.

Thank goodness none of his brothers was about or they'd tease him mercilessly. Especially Marcus who, at the age of thirty-nine, was becoming something of a tyrant.

Devon gestured toward their lunch, now spread upon a blanket. "The wind is picking up, and it is beginning to look more like rain. We should eat quickly."

She smiled, finally leaving the horses. "Aye, Captain!"

He realized that her color was still high, and he wondered what she had been thinking. "I don't believe I like being called 'Captain.' "

"Oh." Some of her smile faded.

"But you may call me 'Admiral,' if you'd like." He made a magnanimous gesture. "Or 'Admiral, sir,' if it trips off your tongue any better."

Laughter gurgled in her throat, and some of the tension left her face. "I hope you're not pulling rank on me to get the largest apple tart."

"All is fair in love and . . . tartdom."

She giggled, and Devon found himself reaching out to brush a strand of hair from her face.

She jerked back at his touch. Devon frowned. "You just had a strand of hair on your cheek." His gaze narrowed. "You don't trust easily, do you?"

Kat's face heated, and she said with a slight touch of defensiveness, "I trust people. I trust Malcolm and Donald and Annie and Simon and Neal and, oh, all sorts of people."

"Just not me."

She bit her lip, wishing she knew what she did feel. Her instincts were at war with her head, and she wasn't sure which to believe. Her head told her that Devon was a rake and just wanted a few moments of pleasure. That there was nothing but pain at the end of that road.

Meanwhile, her instincts told her that she could trust him, that he wouldn't attempt to lure away her heart. That he'd been honest—painfully so—and didn't deserve her mistrust.

The idea of sleeping with Devon wasn't, in itself, a horrible thing. In fact, judging by the way her body reacted every time he was near, a few hours of mutual pleasure might be satisfying to them both. The very thought made her breasts ache as if he'd already touched them.

But even while she acknowledged the temptation that was Devon St. John, a thought clamored in the back of her mind. He would make love to her and then leave her. He had offered no more. Could she accept such a bargain?

Truly, Kat did not know. So instead of mulling it further, she bided her time. "Perhaps we should eat first and then discuss this . . . situation."

His eyes darkened and for an instant, she thought he'd refuse. But then a smile glinted in his blue eyes. "A reprieve then. But only until we've eaten."

Chapter 12

The worst part about dealing with the opposite sex, poor souls, is that they never seem to realize that even when we tell them that they are in control, they are not. Nothing would ever get done correctly, else.

Mrs. Compton to Madame Bennoit,
at a fitting at Madame's establishment
on Bond Street

Kat was agonizingly aware of Devon throughout lunch. He, meanwhile, seemed the same as ever—talking and teasing and several times making her laugh at his nonsense. Only once did she catch him looking at her with an intense expression.

Just as they finished lunch, the clouds overhead darkened. The wind rose and the plaid blanket was puffed away while they were packing the remains of their lunch back into the saddlebag. Kat had to run to catch the blanket, laughing as she did so. The wind was quick and freeing, tugging her skirts and hair, blowing fresh and cool.

Her spirits began to lift even though a part of her still dreaded the upcoming conversation.

Devon put the blanket away, then looked up at the darkening sky. "I don't know if we're going to make it back to Kilkairn."

She followed his gaze and agreed. It was looking dark, indeed. "There is a copse of woods where we can take shelter."

He glanced at her with a lopsided grin that sent her heart spinning in place. "I suppose it would be too much to ask for a cottage like yours."

"Far too much. All there is for shelter is a shed that was once used by the toll keeper. It has only three sides and probably leaks like a sieve."

"Just my luck." He untied the horses and led Lady to Kat. "Good thing I'm an admiral. We may have to swim home."

She allowed him to help her into the saddle. He set her up without effort, then stood looking up at her, his hands still on her waist.

Kat grew uneasy under the intensity of his gaze. "What? Is my hair mussed?"

He grinned. "I was just thinking that the wind had made you look as if you'd just been thoroughly rolled in the hay, even if I've yet to touch you."

But he had touched her. In many, many ways. In the weeks since Devon had arrived, Kat felt as if he'd awakened her. Brought her back to life after a long, lonely sleep.

The question was, if she allowed the relationship to go further, could she ever be satisfied to go back to the lonely sleep again, or would it be torturous to remember what she had and could no longer have?

Her smile must have faltered, for he removed his hands and said a little harshly, "Come. It's about to pour. Where is this shelter?"

She waited for him to mount and then took the lead, directing them back down the path to where the shed was almost completely obscured by a copse of trees and brush.

Just as they reached the shed, the heavens opened and rain came down in buckets. Devon slid off Thunder as soon as they reached the shelter, then helped Kat down. She was already drenched and could barely see for the sheets of rain.

He took Lady's reins, then pushed Kat gently toward the shed and yelled that he would be there soon. Kat stumbled forward, the water obscuring her vision. She could barely decipher the outline of the shed.

The old building was small and damp, but the roof wasn't as bad as she'd thought, leaking in only two or three places.

She hugged herself, shivering a little at the cold. The breeze, which had felt so good before the rain, now seemed chilly and unwelcoming. She looked around the shed to see if perhaps there was enough wood to make a fire, then decided that if she attempted to start one, the entire place might catch aflame.

Devon appeared, wet to the bone, something tucked beneath his coat. He wiped the water from his face and glanced around. "It will do."

"It has to," she answered, offering a smile. A slight shiver wracked her as she spoke.

Devon pulled the picnic blanket from beneath his coat and handed it to her. "Here. Take off your jacket and put this over you. It's fairly dry and will keep you warmer than that wet wool."

Her teeth were beginning to chatter, so she took off the jacket and the bedraggled white scarf. After looking around, she hung them both on a stray nail. "I wish there was more furniture. Some chairs, at least."

She turned to take the blanket from Devon when she saw his gaze on her chest. She looked down and winced. The rain had soaked her white linen shirt and her chemise all the way to her skin. The cloth clung to her, revealing far more than she'd intended.

Devon thought he'd never seen a more beautiful sight. Common sense told him that Kat would have beautiful breasts, but the large, full mounds revealed by her wet shirt far exceeded even his lustful imagination.

He was awash with the desire to see them, taste them, cup them in his hands. "We must have our talk," he said, wincing a little when his voice made the words seem harsh.

She colored, almost snatching the blanket from his hands and wrapping it around her. "So talk."

He wiped water from his neck, pulling off his own wet coat and loosening his cravat. "Let's sit." He searched through the ruined remains of the shed, finding a chair with a broken bottom and a bucket that, turned upside down, could be used as a stool.

He placed the chair against the driest wall and put a board across the broken seat, then overturned the bucket and made a companion chair. "After you, m'lady."

Kat took the chair, sitting primly on the edge of her seat. Whether it was because she was anxious or because the rain had wet her hair until it was slicked back from her forehead, her eyes seemed unusually wide.

"Well," he said, sitting on the bucket bench and raking a hand through his own hair. "I don't believe I've ever had a more awkward situation. But then, I've never desired to talk about having a relationship before."

She looked at him curiously. "Never?"

"No. They pretty much all just . . . happened. Mutual consent, as it were." Most of the women he'd had relationships with hadn't expected or wanted conversation. They'd wanted jewels, admiration, and his attention, all the while thriving on the hope that once he'd sampled their charms, he'd become so enamored that he'd desire something more—like marriage.

That never happened, of course. The more they wanted, the less he wished to give.

Kat was different. She didn't ask for or expect anything his former loves had craved and demanded. And it made him want to do more for her.

It was a new and perplexing feeling. Added to that was his decision to be truthful at all costs. For the first time in his life, he was enjoying a relationship based on simple truth—he didn't feel pressured to utter platitudes and inane compliments. Nor did Kat seem to want to hear false pledges of undying love. He knew that while the truth was sometimes difficult to express, Kat wouldn't accept anything less.

He glanced at her now, noting that she was thoroughly covered, the blanket clamped about her throat and hiding her wet clothing. "Kat, I'm not very good at talking about things. I'm a man of action. But for you, I'll try."

She nodded, her eyes warm in the silvered light. "I know."

Devon slid the bucket directly beside her chair, then reached over and pulled her to him.

She stiffened.

"You're cold. The least I can do is keep you warm."

She relaxed a little, glancing up at him through eyelashes that were spiked with wetness. "If that's all you're going to do."

"Until you say otherwise, it is."

They sat there, listening to the rain, their bodies gradually growing warmer. Devon rested his cheek against her hair, the faint scent of lavender drifting through the air. He always associated that scent with Kat now. Lovely and light, it seemed just like her.

Kat sighed and moved, her shoulder rubbing against his chest. Devon's body reacted immediately. God, but she was a lovely woman. A lovely person.

The tension between them that had begun at lunch

grew with each passing moment. The longer they sat together, his arm about her, her head resting against his cheek, the more insistent the urge became.

Devon lifted a strand of her hair and pressed his mouth to the tress. Wet, it curled about his fingers, clung in a way he wished Kat would. "At least your hair likes me."

She blinked at him, a quiver of humor curling her lips. "I never said I didn't like you."

"Yes, but you haven't said you did. I take that as a bad sign."

She turned and, to his surprise, trailed her lips across his cheek. It was an innocent touch, though his reaction was anything but.

He almost gasped. "If you don't wish me to touch you, you'll have to forgo little demonstrations like that."

Her brows rose. "Just a kiss on the cheek?"

"Any kiss, anywhere. They are maddening and make me want to pull you into my lap and savor you correctly."

For an instant, heat flared in her eyes, but then her lashes slid down to hide her reaction. "I have a puzzle to solve."

The soft words lingered in the air.

"Oh?"

"If I agree to take this relationship to a more physical level, what guarantee will I have that it won't hurt when you leave?" She sighed, the sound sweet in the rain-wet air. "My mind and my body are at war over the answer."

He drew her hair over his lips, savoring the silken stroke. "Sometimes the body is more truthful and uncomplicated than the mind."

"And sometimes what seems an honest and truthful response is no more than a thoughtless reaction that would happen in a variety of other circumstances. For example, the way you might jerk away if a bee were to fly close by, or how you'd react if an ember from the fire landed near your foot."

He smiled. "Has anyone ever told you that you think too much?"

She tilted her head to one side, her wet hair now more red than gold. "No."

"Then they were only being polite."

Her lips quivered with a smile, but she ruthlessly repressed it. "I don't believe it is possible to think too much."

"Hm. Would you care to put that statement to a test?"

Her wariness grew. "What kind of test?"

"We try a kiss while you are thinking . . ." He lowered his mouth to her cheek and whispered, "And a kiss while you are not."

Her skin was not the creamy white of most debutantes, but a luminous pink. He brushed his fingertips along the line of her cheek. "Sometimes, thoughts can stop us from experiencing the moment we're in. They can block feeling, emotion, energy, even pleasure."

"All by thinking?"

"All by thinking."

"I'm surprised anyone bothers to think at all,

then," she said in a slightly acid tone, though her lashes fluttered on her cheeks.

He smiled. If he merely listened to her words, he'd quit this seduction now, before it had really begun. But though she stoutly refused to give in to his verbal blandishments, she was not immune to him physically. If he could just show her that they were meant to touch, meant to be together. Not forever of course, but for this moment. "Well? Care to test your theory?"

She shrugged. "I suppose we might as well. We can't leave until this rain quits." She leaned back against his arm. "Go ahead, kiss me."

He started to lower his mouth to hers, but then stopped. "Is this the thinking kiss or the nonthinking kiss?"

"I am not going to tell you. I don't want you using any tricks to win your point."

"Very well. But you have to be honest with me about which kiss was which."

"You'll trust me?"

"With my soul."

Her face pinkened.

He didn't give her time to think that through. He tipped her face to him and kissed her. He put into the kiss all his longings, all his desires. Everything.

She was limp in his arms when he finished. The blanket had slipped and she was panting heavily, drawing his gaze once again to her nearly visible breasts.

"Ready for the next one?"

She held out a hand. "No. I've already proven my

point. That was the thinking kiss and I was reciting the names of all the kings and queens of Scotland all the while. I never made it past the twelfth century." She pressed a hand to her throat. "Thinking most definitely does not interfere with feeling."

He had to laugh. "I think you need the next kiss, too. Just to make certain."

Her gaze dropped to his mouth, and he could see she was wavering. "Just one more kiss." He bent toward her, his lips a whisper away.

"I can't," she gasped, pulling away. "No more, please." She looked at him, her green eyes sparkling with sudden tears. "I beg of you," she whispered. "No more."

Devon loosened his hold. "Kat, I don't understand—"

She shook her head, the gesture dislodging a tear. It fell from her eye and clung to her cheek. "I—I am not a fool, you know. I can see what you're doing. You are trying to seduce me."

He pursed his lips. "Yes, I am. That is what happens when there is an attraction, such as the one we have."

"I know. I am no innocent."

He chuckled. "I would beg to differ."

"Devon, I am no innocent." This time she said the words firmly.

"Ah," he said, realizing what she meant.

A grimace of anguish passed over her face. "I have made mistakes."

"We all have, sweet," Devon said. He wanted this

woman. Wanted her more than any other woman he'd ever known.

The problem was that if he succeeded in seducing her, he might damage the part of her he admired the most—her spirit.

Devon was not selfish. Not intentionally, anyway. And he knew from the conversations they'd had that Kat was not a woman given to sadness or histrionics. That fact made the tear in her eye mean all the more.

He sighed, rubbing his neck. His desire was subsiding, but only slightly. He wanted Kat in his bed, but not at the cost of her pride. "In no way do I wish to harm you."

A bitter smile touched her lips. "I've heard that before."

"But not from me. When I tell you something, I mean it. And I expect you to do the same for me."

Kat swallowed the lump of emotion that threatened to close her throat. Devon's black hair fell over his brow, his blue eyes never left her face. He'd discarded his jacket, and his black breeches hugged his narrow hips and outlined his muscular thighs. Her gaze traveled over him to where his throat was exposed. His cravat was undone and hung loosely about his neck, his shirt untied. A faint edge of chest hair showed in the opening, and she was assailed with the desire to touch it, to thread her fingers through it and feel the crispness of the tight black curls. God, but he was beautiful. Beautiful and . . . listening to her. Asking her what she thought, what she needed.

In that instant, she knew why he was different from Stephen. Stephen had swept her off her feet with smooth words and urgent hands. And she, feeling gauche and ugly after being paraded through cold receiving room after cold receiving room, had lapped it up like a starved cat.

Devon had the same passion as Stephen, but Devon had something more. Perhaps it was patience. Perhaps it was caring. Whatever it was, it had him sitting beside her, his arm offering warmth and nothing more, his head bent attentively, his eyes on hers.

In all the times she and Stephen had met, never once did she remember him looking at her with such a serious expression, or waiting to hear what she thought about anything. She wondered that she'd never before realized that.

Funny how one's expectations at seventeen were so very small. Then, years later, those same expectations transformed into a list of required virtues so long that she sometimes feared the man she wanted to meet did not exist.

She didn't want just passion, though that was part of it. She also wanted someone to talk to, someone who would listen, someone who would laugh with her and share himself the same way she wanted to share herself.

Devon reached across the space between them and drew his finger down her cheek. The touch left a trail of delicate fire that lit a heated pathway down her neck to her breast and beyond.

"What do you want, Kat? Because whatever it is, so long as it is not marriage, I will give it to you."

She tilted her head to one side. "Why do you hate the thought of marriage so much?"

His humor faded. "Because . . ." A shadow crossed his eyes. "I have a confession to make. It is not a pretty one, and you may never again wish to speak to me."

She waited, unwilling even to speculate on what he might say.

"Kat, as much as I wish it was otherwise, I cannot seem to remain . . . enamored of a woman for more than two months."

"*Two* months?"

He winced. "It sounds bad even to my own ears, so I cannot imagine how horrid it sounds to yours. I cannot help it; I grow bored after a short time, so I know I can never marry. I will not make a promise I know I cannot keep."

Kat nodded. "That is how it should be. You are very honorable."

His lips twisted. "Kat, I will not pretend I am not attracted to you—I am and you know it. And I will not pretend I do not wish for a more physical relationship than we have now. Honestly, I would give up Thunder just to spend one hour in a bed with you and nothing between us but tangled sheets and the dampness of our own bodies."

A delicious shiver tremored through her. He was so delectable, his gaze so blue, so intense. Better yet, honesty shone through him. For an instant, she thought she could see the truth shimmering over him like a light.

He raked a hand through his wet hair again, and she saw that his hand trembled the slightest bit.

"This is foolish," he said with a rueful smile. "I am ruining my chances with you, but I refuse to be less than truthful." He took her hand. "Kat, I don't know what happened in Edinburgh, but—"

"You should know."

"No. That is not necessary—"

"It is, too." She met his gaze directly, gathering courage. "If we are to continue this . . . relationship, brief though it may be, I will not have any secrets."

He hesitated, then sighed. "If you want to tell me, then do so."

She took a breath, her hands fisting at her sides. "I have thought this through a hundred times until I think I finally understand what I was doing and why. I was not raised at the castle like Malcolm. Our father really had little to do with my mother once I was born."

"He neglected her?"

"He made sure we didn't go hungry and that we had enough to survive. But sometimes whole months would go by and we'd never see him."

"That is sad."

"It was hard for us both," she agreed, "mainly because we knew he lived such a short distance away. It was especially difficult for Mama because she was the one he really rejected. I think he was always sorry he'd met her. At least, that was the impression he left us with."

Kat spoke simply, without pain. But Devon had an idea what even that gesture had cost her. "I see," he said, unable to think of anything better to add. He wondered if he should take her in his arms, but her next words forestalled him.

"It doesn't hurt so much now. Once Father died, I got Malcolm." Her face softened. "I have never regretted that trade."

"Malcolm knew of your existence?"

"He overheard his mother telling one of the stewards that my mother and I were to be ejected from the cottage. He was only twelve, but he stepped in and demanded that we be left alone. I think he'd seen us and had guessed the truth. We have never discussed it."

Devon smiled. "Malcolm's stubbornness is as legendary as my determination."

She returned his smile, her eyes warming slightly. "Determination or stubbornness? Aren't they the same?"

"I like to use the word 'determination' when applied to myself, and 'stubbornness' when applied to others."

He was rewarded with a quiet chuckle that made his heart ache.

"It is a flaw we three share, then," she said. "Anyway, after Malcolm knew of our existence, he came almost every day. His mother tried to stop him, but he ignored her and . . . he became my brother. Whatever I needed, he has been there for me. I am ever conscious of his kindness, which makes it difficult to say him nay."

"He can be persuasive."

"Indeed. When I turned sixteen, my mother died. Malcolm wished me to live at Kilkairn. Against my better judgment, I did so."

"Thus the blue room."

"Thus the blue room," she agreed. "He offered me one of the larger rooms, but I was uncomfortable. Besides, his mother resented me enough."

"I begin to dislike Malcolm's mother."

"Och now," Kat said softly, her voice gently chiding. "I reminded her of a time between herself and her husband that she wished gone. I cannot blame her for that."

"I suppose not," he said, unconvinced. "Did you like living at Kilkairn?"

"No. For so long, I had been on the outside of the castle. I thought being on the inside would be magical. But it wasn't. I felt lost, and I think Malcolm sensed that. He decided I needed more companionship, that I should be 'launched' on society as if I belonged."

"As if?"

"I was illegitimate, and everyone knew it. I had no money other than the dowry Malcolm was willing to settle on me. And—" She shrugged. "I am not a beauty. I never have been. But Malcolm was determined that I go. He coerced his mother to sponsor me, and for once she and I were in agreement; I didn't want to go any more than she wanted to take me. But Malcolm won the day and we went."

"It sounds as if the conditions were perfect for a disaster."

"It was horrid. And it got worse before it was over. I believe Lady Strathmore was sincere in her attempts to dress me well and show me about, but I did not take."

"I am sorry."

"So am I. Every event was painful and punishing. And the clothes she chose . . . now that I know more about color and texture, I can see her mistakes and mine."

Devon shook his head. "Men have it so much easier."

"Indeed they do. By the second week of arriving in Edinburgh, I was miserable. Meanwhile, Malcolm had met Fiona and he was gone a good deal, wooing her. I was left with Lady Strathmore and that . . . that was when I met Stephen."

"A rakehell of the first water, I take it."

"Worse. A rakehell of the worst water. He was unacceptable in almost every household, a fact I thought grossly unfair."

"Ah, words of the young."

"Words of the foolish. He was glib, and he spoke to me." A faint color touched her cheeks. "I'm afraid that was all it took. I eventually thought I was in love and I agreed . . . I-I absconded with him."

"You eloped?"

"So I thought. But apparently even that was too much for Stephen. It turned out later than he never intended to marry me, but merely wished to cause a scandal so that Malcolm would be forced to buy his silence." Her cheeks were deep pink.

Devon had to swallow a bitter lump of anger for

the long-absent Stephen before he could speak. "We all make mistakes."

"Most people do not embarrass their entire family with their errors," she replied sharply. "I was foolish enough to let practiced words muddle my thinking."

"Which is why you wish to think rather than feel. You believe it will keep you from making a similar error."

"Aye." She met Devon's gaze steadily. "You should know I was with Stephen for two weeks before Malcolm caught up with us. And here is where I am supposed to assure you that I am untouched. But . . ." Her lips thinned. "I cannot say that. I thought I loved him."

"Many things are done in the name of love."

"And many things undone. I believed his assurances that he wanted to marry me and that he would do so as soon as Malcolm gave his approval. But of course Stephen never asked for Malcolm's approval. Instead he asked for a thousand pounds to return me home and to keep his silence."

Devon had never been so angry in all his life. Never. "This bloody Stephen, wherever he is, deserves to be horsewhipped." B'God, if anyone had dared treat his sister the way the nefarious Stephen had treated Kat, Devon would have beaten the bastard into a bloody pulp. And then, for emphasis, all his brothers would take their turns. "If I cannot horsewhip him, then I would at least see him drawn and quartered. That might serve to punish the bastard."

"I fear you will have to dig a hole to do that; he

died two years later. I heard that he drank himself to death, though I was never certain."

"That is still too good for him."

She waved a hand. "What is gone is gone."

The gesture softened his anger, and he was once again assailed with the desire to hold her. He took her hand in his. "Kat, you are a passionate woman. There is nothing wrong with that."

She grimaced. "As Malcolm's mother was quick to point out, I am just like my mother."

"Then your mother was a joyous, warm person."

A flicker of emotion crossed over Kat's face, followed by a deep sigh. "Thank you. At the time, facing Malcolm's anger and his mother's bitter disappointment, I felt a fool."

"You were seventeen and alone." Devon pulled her closer and kissed her nose. "Listen to me, Kat. You are not a bad person. You are not an evil person. You are not a confused person. You are a strong and beautiful woman. And there is nothing wrong with being passionate with someone you care about."

"Not everyone sees it that way."

"So, who are you are going to listen to? Me? Or Malcolm's bitter mother? And let me point out that I have never lied to you, nor have I asked you to wear fashions that do not complement your gorgeous body."

Her lips quivered, her tears fading from her eyes. "You are a wretch to make me smile while I'm perfectly happy being miserable."

"It's a gift." He cupped her chin, rubbing his thumb over the softness of her cheek. "There. Do you have anything more to confess? Something of real import?"

"That was important."

"If that was your only sin, then I feel as if perhaps I should begin making confessions of my own, for my life has not been so lily-white."

"Oh?"

"I just hope you do not wish me to confess *all* my sins of a passionate nature. I fear my voice would give out before I could cover half of them."

She fingered the top button of his waistcoat. "Have there been many?"

Before now, Devon would have answered without a twinge of guilt. After all, he had never transgressed the bounds of society. He never philandered with innocents, never compromised a lady's reputation unless she initiated the event herself, and never ever mentioned names, even when deep in his cups.

But somehow, looking down into Kat's green eyes, he felt the faintest hint of a blush on his own cheeks. In all his years, Devon didn't think he'd felt a blush more than two or three times, and all before he was fourteen. "Yes," he finally said. "There have been that many sins in my life."

"Hm. And according to what you said about never staying interested more than a few months, there are going to be hundreds, perhaps thousands more."

Devon didn't answer. He couldn't. A deep loneliness gripped him. Was she right? Was he doomed to spend his life wandering from bed to bed, searching for the perfect woman, a woman he was beginning to think didn't exist?

Of course, Kat was close to his vision of perfection, and coming closer all the time. She was smart, attractive, capable, strong, and passionate . . . He frowned. Was she getting closer to his image of perfect or was he merely beginning to mold his image of perfection until it looked like Kat?

Whatever the truth, it didn't solve the problem of his own fickleness. His own lack of strength in committing. His own tendency to hurt those who came to care for him.

Whatever he did, Devon did not want to harm Kat. She'd suffered enough. So it was with the greatest effort that he stood and pulled her to her feet. "The rain is lessening. It will be over soon."

A shadow crossed her face. "Does this mean . . ." Her gaze lifted to his face. "You don't wish to be with me now that you know—"

"No! It just means that I don't want either of us doing anything we might regret. I enjoy your company too much to allow it to turn counterfeit."

"I see," she said, disappointment deep in her voice.

He almost laughed. That must be what he looked like every time she pulled away from him. She was simply adorable. So natural and free. And he was beginning to like spending time with her a bit too much. Thank God he was leaving soon.

But the thought brought as much of a twinge of pain as it brought relief. He'd be gone and Kat would be left here, to live her life in the woods while more of Malcolm's guests came to stay. Perhaps, one day, one of them would realize exactly how special Kat was, and sweep her away. It was as if, in a moment of extreme clarity, Devon could see the future.

Bloody hell. That was exactly what would happen.

"Devon?"

He realized Kat was looking up at him. "Yes?"

She wet her lips, the innocent gesture sending his senses reeling yet again. "Devon, what if I decide that *I* want for us to be closer? What then?"

"Kat, if we were to get closer than we are now, that—"

"You think my heart would be affected."

He paused. Then nodded. "I don't want to hurt you."

"You think I would fall in love with you if we slept together. That would be my problem and not yours." She placed her hands on his chest, then tilted her mouth to his and encompassed him in a kiss.

Devon's manhood stiffened immediately. He could no more resist Kat's lush body pressed so firmly against his. Her plump breasts were so close, just a waistcoat and a shirt away from his bare chest, her hips held intimately to his.

He was afire, hot and wanting, his thoughts breaking apart, dissolving before the onslaught of her soft mouth, her delicious body.

She broke the kiss, and he realized that he was once again holding her, pulling her to him. Her green eyes sparkled into his, and she said with a definite purr to her voice, "Tomorrow, we finish this."

He knew in that second that she was right; they would finish it. And for some reason, that thought made his very soul quake.

Chapter 13

Mon Dieu! *I awoke to discover that my house had sprung a leak, the cook had quit due to an unfortunate incident involving a chicken liver, and my son had written to say that if I do not provide him with financial assistance forthwith, he will be forced to become the plaything of a certain elderly lady who has no hair and very bad teeth. Remind me not to wake up again.*

Madame Bennoit to her assistant, Pierre,
while searching the storerooms
for a particular shade of violet muslin to be used
for the Countess of Bridgeton's new ball gown

Fiona opened the door to the green guest chamber and peered around the corner. Breathing a sigh of relief that it was empty, she quietly closed the door behind her and crossed to the window, her skirts whispering over the thick rug.

Once there, she pushed back the curtains and lifted on her tiptoes. She could just make out St. John talking to Kat in the courtyard below.

Fiona's gaze traveled over Kat, her eyes widening. Poor Katherine had been caught in the sudden storm and was bedraggled and wet. Kat's habit appeared black and sodden, her hair fell in long strands about her face, a sopping wet scarf trailed water into a puddle behind her. Devon was no better. His breeches were now indecently molded to him, his coat open, his shirt undone. By all accounts, the two should be miserable, but instead, they were laughing.

A pang formed in Fiona's heart at the sight. They looked so happy, just as she and Malcolm had once been. Her lips quivered at the thought. She had to win the wager with Malcolm. The only thing that could save her marriage was if she could get him away from Kilkairn, back to Edinburgh where they'd been gay and carefree. Once there, she was certain he'd forget about having children, and there'd be no more discord.

Perhaps then he would realize he still loved her, if he did.

Meanwhile, she was going to have to be more underhanded in her methods. She hated that, but it was necessary. Fiona eyed Kat for a long moment, deciding that while the habit looked wondrous on Kat's generous figure, a ball gown would not be nearly as attractive, with the high waistline and voluminous folds.

Murien was, as usual, quite right. Kat, dressed in a form-fitting habit on a horse, was one thing. Kat in a ballroom was quite another thing altogether. And as much as St. John might enjoy his flirtation, he would not tolerate a companion who could not hold her own in public.

Fiona dropped the curtain just as a voice said in her ear, "What do you think you're doing?"

Her heart jumped and she fell back, pressing a hand to her pounding heart. "Malcolm! Do not sneak up on me in such a manner! I thought you were St. John's horrid valet. I vow, but the man frightens me to death."

Malcolm looked past her to the window. "Hm. Spying on Devon and Kat, were you?"

"No," she said, her cheeks heating. "I was just here to—to make certain the room was clean."

Malcolm didn't look convinced. "What a lovely hostess you are, m'dear. Always worried about the health and welfare of your guests."

She stiffened. "I do my best, though how anyone can keep a castle clean is beyond me. It's like scrubbing the earth, all it does is make more mud."

"How would you know? You've never scrubbed a thing in your life."

" 'Tis not my fault. You are the one who brought me here to this horrid damp place."

"It's my home, Fiona. I thought we could share that, at least."

There was a tiredness to his voice that twisted deep into her heart. "Malcolm, I—" She what? She loved him but would not have his children? She adored him, but could not stand the home of his birth?

His gaze met hers, searching, seeking. "Yes, love. What is it?"

"Malcolm, you know I care for you. That I—"

Could she say it? Could she tell him that she loved him dearly, desperately? And if she did, would she lose something because of it?

She looked at Malcolm, at the way he regarded her so seriously. At the curl of his hair over his ears. At the dimple in his chin that she'd kissed so many times. Fiona took a deep breath and said, "Malcolm, I love you. But I do not wish to have children until I know for certain that you will not love me the less. I have to have your promise that it will not be that way."

He stiffened, as if she'd delivered a blow of some sort. "Fiona, I love you. I think I always will."

I think. She needed more than that. More than he seemed capable of giving. "I want us to be the way we used to be, before we came here and everything became so horrid." She bit her lip, fighting the tears. "I do not wish to live here, in this castle, watching our marriage fade away."

A flicker of pain crossed his face. "Fiona, we can't go back. No one can. We can only go forward."

He was right. Her heart pained, she collected herself as best she could, lifting her chin. "Of course. Forward. We will let our marriage rest on our wager then." She met his gaze evenly. "You may think you have won, but you have not. Not yet, anyway."

Malcolm sighed, disappointment evident. "Your sister is looking for you. She's in the sitting room."

"I'll go to her at once."

"I thought you would." Malcolm's sharp gaze rested on Fiona's face. "Murien mentioned something about a ball."

Fiona heard the note of accusation. "Yes, I have decided to give a small ball. We never use the ballroom, and I thought we might do so while we have both St. John and Murien here."

Malcolm's expression hardened. "I know what you are about, Fiona. I will not let you embarrass Kat."

"Then she needn't attend. It will be her decision."

"I see. You will invite her in such a way that she cannot refuse."

Fiona nodded, suddenly feeling miserable. She didn't wish to use Kat in such a way, but Fiona had no choice.

Malcolm looked at her a moment more, then moved past her to the window. "Murien is waiting for you."

That was it. He'd dismissed her as if she were nothing more than a bothersome chambermaid.

"I—I'll go at once."

"Do so." He lifted up the edge of the curtain, his gaze on Kat and Devon. "I will be down shortly," he said absently, as if he'd already forgotten Fiona's existence.

She stood a moment more, waiting for some sign. Some indication from her husband that he cared. But no such reassurance was forthcoming.

After a long, silent moment, she turned on her heel and left the room, and Malcolm, behind her. Disconsolate, she made her way to the sitting room.

Murien whirled on Fiona as soon as she entered. There were lines of tension on Murien's usually smooth face. "Thank God you have come. I was dying of ennui."

"Yes, it has been a rather dull day. Perhaps because of the rain."

"That didn't keep St. John from going out," Murien said in a discontented voice. "I don't understand how he can continue to see Kat. Surely the attraction, if it ever was that, has paled by now. The time has come for us to separate them."

Fiona sighed at the waspish note in Murien's voice. She hated it when her sister was out of sorts. Which lately was more oft than not.

"Where is St. John now?" Murien asked. "I am so tired of sitting around, waiting on him to return."

"He is in the courtyard saying good-bye to Miss Macdonald. It appears they were caught in a rain shower."

Murien stood and raced to the mirror over the fireplace. "Why didn't you say so?" She patted her hair. "Come! If we go out on the terrace, we can see them from there."

"Yes, but—"

"Come along. I can't go alone." Murien turned on her heel and swept from the room.

Fiona stared at the empty doorway. She was beginning to believe that her sister was a wee bit selfish. Sighing, she followed Murien down the hall to the library and then out on the terrace.

They had a prime spot to witness Devon's goodbye to Kat. Though he never touched her, there was something intimate about the way they stood. Watching them, Fiona felt a wrench of jealousy. Why should Kat have what Fiona had been denied?

Murien, meanwhile, was having similar thoughts.

It burned her soul to see a man, any man, that she deemed hers, paying attention to another woman. But there were ways to deal with such inconveniences. A word here, a word there.

More was won by innuendo than by fact. Murien found a smile. "Do not fear, Fiona. I will make certain our dear friend Katherine appears at our wondrous ball."

Murien watched as Devon said one last thing to Kat and then left the courtyard. He strode away, an amused expression on his face.

Murien decided it was quite telling the way Kat gazed after him, a rather wistful look in her eyes. "I can certainly take care of that," Murien murmured.

"Take care of what?" Fiona asked, blinking as if she had just awakened from a long sleep.

Really, what had Fiona so distracted of late? It was most annoying. "Fiona, why don't you return to the sitting room and I'll join you there. I believe I should extend the invitation to our ball to Katherine."

"But I can—"

"This one needs a personal touch. I will see you in ten minutes in the sitting room, and we can begin planning the entertainment for the ball." Without waiting for a reply, Murien made her way down to the courtyard.

She caught up with Kat just as she was getting ready to mount her horse. "There you are," Murien said brightly.

Kat turned. She was soaking wet, her hair reddish and straight to either side of her face, her riding habit molded to her frame. The sight gave Murien pause, and for the first time she found herself admitting that perhaps there was more to Kat Macdonald than Murien had first thought. "Kat, I'm so glad I caught you."

"Indeed?"

There was a decidedly guarded look to Katherine's expression. No fool was Malcolm's little sister. Murien put on her best smile. "Fiona and I have been dreadfully bored, so we've been planning a little ball. Malcolm insisted we invite you."

"That was kind of him."

"Yes, well, Fiona and I argued that you wouldn't want to come, but he was quite adamant."

Kat regarded her flatly, no expression on her face.

Murien took that as encouragement. She allowed her gaze to wander past Kat. "I don't know much about horses, but that one seems rather untamed. How do you ride him?"

Kat's hand rested easily on the horse's neck. "One mile at a time."

Murien managed to keep her smile in place, but only with the utmost effort. "How humorous."

"What do you want, Murien? You didn't come to talk about my horse."

"No, I didn't. I came to give you the benefit of my advice." Murien paused as if embarrassed. "I hope you don't take this wrong, but I realize that you've been on your own for a long while. I've also noticed that you are . . . shall we say 'fond' of Mr. St. John."

Kat's cheeks colored. "I don't know where you got that idea, but what I think and feel is none of your business."

Murien's brows rose. "There's no need to be embarrassed. I'm certain you have every reason to be infatuated. Mr. St. John is all that is amiable. He is handsome, well off, of impeccable lineage, and possesses a very pleasing manner." She gave a light laugh. "I daresay half the women in the castle are enamored of him. Poor Fiona can't get the upstairs maid to do anything."

"The upstairs maid never did anything before Mr. St. John's arrival, so I fail to see a connection."

Murien's false laugh faded from her lips. Really, it was annoying to speak to someone who did not follow the customary rules of polite conversation.

"Murien, I don't know what you want, but out with it. I don't have a lot of time."

That irked. "Very well," Murien snapped, "if you wish it, I will be plain. In addition to all of his obvious charms, St. John is an accomplished flirt. He is pleasant to *every* woman he comes in contact with, including me."

Kat's hands tightened about the reins. "For your information, I am not infatuated with Mr. St. John. And second, even if I were, it would not be your place to inform me of that fact. If you wish to protect a heart, then watch for your own."

"Oh dear. I've offended you. I'm so sorry. It's just that—well, someone should drop a hint as to the way things stand."

"And how do they stand?"

It was obvious the woman was embarrassed to the teeth, which was exactly what Murien wanted. To add vinegar to the wine, she sighed softly, as if regretting what she had to say. "This is so unpleasant. But you *are* Fiona's sister by marriage, which makes us almost sisters. This is the least I can do. I just didn't want you to embarrass yourself at the ball next Wednesday."

"Embarrass? How would I do that?"

Murien smiled gently. "The ball Malcom and Fiona are holding in honor of Mr. St. John will be well attended. It is quite obvious how you feel about the man. Though you might think you were being circumspect, your face will always betray you, and everyone will know. *Everyone*."

There was a stiff silence during which time Kat stared fixedly at Murien. Her face was inscrutable, but the way her knuckles were white on the reins told all. Kat Macdonald was boiling inside. Boiling and just the littlest bit shamed, just as Murien had planned.

Murien waved her hand. "You've been warned. Rest assured that whatever you decide, I will do what I can to smooth things over for you." Murien smiled as kindly as she could.

"I don't need anyone to smooth things over. No one would dare ridicule me in my brother's house."

"Not to your face," Murien said gently. She paused to let that sink in, then said in a staunch voice, "But you are right. You should attend the ball; after all, it is in your brother's house. I'd just forget all those who will be whispering. I'm certain Mr. St. John won't notice anything, either."

"You don't want me to go."

"Me? Oh, I don't care, one way or t'other. In fact . . ." Murien's gaze slowly traveled over Kat. "I sincerely hope you *do* come. It will make it all the more enjoyable for the rest of us."

Kat's lips thinned, and Murien knew she'd drawn blood with that one. "Murien, I don't know how to thank you."

"I'm certain you'll think of something. Perhaps, one day I'll have you do some glasswork in my house. There are a number of windows that could use some decorating glazes." Smiling over her shoulder, Murien turned and left.

She hid her triumph as best she could as she made her way back to the terrace. Kat would attend the ball now, Murien was certain of it. Better yet, Kat would be awkward around Devon, as well, wondering if he could see the same things on her face that Murien mentioned.

Overhead, the late afternoon sun shone warmly, the blue sky decorated with a faint scattering of puffy clouds. Murien decided that it was a beautiful day. A beautiful day to win.

Kat tromped into her bedchamber, Annie hard on her heels.

The housekeeper shut the door and then turned to regard Kat with a flat stare. "What's happened to put ye in such a mood?"

Kat slumped onto the bed. "Nothing." Blast

Murien Spalding and her little blond airs. Kat wasn't the type of person to develop a hatred for anyone, but Murien had certainly managed to ignite a strong dislike inside Kat's usually forgiving heart.

"Don't tell me ye aren't fashed about something," Annie said. "Ye near took off puir Donald's head fer nothing more than a cheery good afternoon."

"I did not snap at Donald."

Annie lifted her brows, her skinny arms folded beneath her breasts, one foot tapping in disbelief.

"Don't look at me like that." Kat kicked at her skirts, frustration boiling. Should she go to that silly ball? Murien would simply make a mockery of her, and Devon would . . . Kat frowned. What would Devon do?

She caught Annie's minatory gaze and suddenly remembered that the housekeeper was waiting on an answer. "I'm sorry, Annie. I just didn't wish to hear Donald complain again about the flue in the new chimney. I know it needs to be fixed but I'm not in the mood to hear him harping on it day and night whilst he—"

"He said 'good afternoon' to ye and not a word more."

Kat's shoulders slumped. She supposed she had been a little harsh. "You are right. I was just angry at—Never mind. I'll apologize to Donald as soon as I finish."

"Finish what?" Annie asked suspiciously.

Kat scooted off the bed with an energy she was far from feeling and went to the wardrobe. She threw open the door and waved at the assortment of clothing that hung there. "I'll apologize as soon as I finish deciding what I'm going to wear to Fiona's and Malcolm's ball next week."

Annie brightened. "A ball? Och now, that sounds promising."

"I don't know about that." Kat straightened her shoulders and stared at the gowns, most of them too plain to be of use. "I wish I had time to have a gown made."

Annie hopped up on the edge of the bed so that she could watch Kat pulling first this old gown and then the next out of the wardrobe. "We should order one now fer the next time ye are invited. *If* they do. I'm a wee bit surprised they remembered ye this time." She sniffed her disdain loudly. "They've been somewhat remiss aboot that in the past."

"No, they haven't. They always invite me. And I always refuse. They know I don't like their puffed up affairs and I know they would find my company at such a formal event quite onerous. But this time . . ." Kat pulled out her best gown. Of sky blue silk, it was quite fashionable. Or had been, several years ago.

She held the gown before her and looked in the mirror, mentally comparing it to the gowns Fiona wore. Good heavens, how fashion changed.

Kat sighed and dropped the gown on the bed beside Annie. "What is different about this ball is that Fiona's sister, Murien, is going to be there, and she seems to think I'll be an embarrassment."

Annie made a face. "Och, that one. She's catty, she is."

"Yes, she is." And rude and possessive, too. And if one was so inclined, one might notice that Murien's eyes were just a wee bit too closely aligned. "She's a haughty vixen, and I don't mean that in a good way."

"They say she runs with the devil," Annie said in a mysterious undertone.

Kat had to grin at that. "I can't argue with you there. She's also very determined that every man in a fifty-mile distance should pay her homage."

"Oh ho! I suppose ye're talkin' about St. John. So ye have Miss Spalding worrying that you're getting too close to him, eh?"

"I am not getting too close to him." Not yet, anyway. Tomorrow, now . . . that might be another story. Although, now that Kat had tasted Murien's poison, things seemed far less clear. If Kat did allow Devon closer, wouldn't her feelings become even stronger? Even more obvious to anyone who looked at her?

Not that she was in love; she wasn't. But she was close to it, she knew. If she looked down at her toes, she was certain they'd be flush against the line that marked friendship and love.

Perhaps it wouldn't be a good idea to allow her relationship with Devon to progress into a more physical area. Perhaps—

"Hmph. I can see why ye're hesitant about takin' up wid the Sassenach. He's well enough if ye like the tall, handsome, wealthy, titled sort o' man."

Kat sighed. "Don't start, Annie."

"Lord love ye, Miss Kat, but what's not to like in a man like that?"

Kat wisely didn't answer. She dug deeper in the wardrobe, but found nothing else even approaching an acceptable evening gown. "I should have never let Murien goad me so."

"Aye, ye haven't a decent gown."

"I know, I know. But I cannot refuse to attend now."

Annie snorted. "She taunted ye, did she? Now ye'll go, come heaven or hell, come good weather or bad. Ye'll go if ye have to walk the whole way barefoot and naked as the day ye were born."

"I was rather hoping I could find something less dramatic to wear than my bare skin," Kat said dryly. "Unfortunately, my wardrobe does not extend into our present decade." She touched the sky-blue gown on the bed and sighed. "It looks as if I'm going to have to play the part of rustic dowd for the night or not go at all."

From her position perched on the edge of the bed, Annie picked up the gown and shook it out. "Won't this do? 'Tis of quality silk, and the color would look good on ye."

"It's sorely out of fashion. I'll be a laughingstock, I suppose, but that's nothing new. At least I won't be sitting at home, moping about because some puffed-up piece of fluff ordered me to stay away. To Hades with Murien Spalding and her airs."

"That's the spirit, Miss Kat!" Annie jumped up off the bed, her thin face resolute. "And I'll help ye, I will. I might have time to turn this gown into something acceptable, if we keep things simple."

"Annie!" Kat said, touched by her housekeeper's show of spirit. "Thank you."

"Och, 'tis only right that ye go and that ye look well doin' it. Besides, I should help ye after all ye've done fer me." Annie pursed her lips thoughtfully. "The last time I saw Lady Strathmore, she had on a right lovely gown that was . . ." Annie's eyes narrowed, and she nodded, folding the gown over her arm. "What we need is one of them fashion books as are stacked in Lady Strathmore's dressing room. That fool, Jane—a lazy wench if there ever was one—tends to the upstairs. We'll borrow one of those books fer a bit and then we'll fashion ye up a gown that will show that Murien hussy just who is the real lady."

"Yes, but we've no time to—"

"Hesh, Miss Kat! We've plenty o' time. I've still yards and yards of that lovely straw-colored silk left over from making the linings for the curtains in the front room. I'll start with that and perhaps . . ." She held out Kat's old gown, shaking it a bit so that the sky-blue silk rippled in the light. "Perhaps we can put this one to use, as well. I can use the bodice and the skirts and jus' add new sleeves and perhaps—" She smiled. "I can do it, never ye fash."

Straw colored silk combined with the sky-blue—it would be stunning, Kat decided. She couldn't help but think it would add some drama to her rather drab appearance.

"Annie, do you really think you'll have it made by next week?"

"Aye, Miss Kat! Just leave it to me." Annie tossed the gown over her shoulder and went to the door.

"I'll send Donald to the castle to fetch the book. He's still lingering downstairs, moping because he thinks ye are upset with him. Then we'll have a look to see what's needed. I may have to borrow a bit of ribbon, though I've plenty of thread left."

"It seems such a huge undertaking. Can you—"

"Och now, don't ye worry! All we need is one gown, simple and elegant. 'Twill allow yer beauty to show through."

A new gown that was simple and elegant—Kat couldn't help a burble of happiness from flickering through her. "Annie, you're priceless."

A half hour later, a lone rider arrived at Kilkairn Castle. Donald, armed with specific instructions from Mistress Annie, rode up to the servants' entrance and requested to speak with her cousin Jane.

Jane was a while in coming as Lady Strathmore had decided that the castle had to be cleaned from top to bottom for the upcoming ball, a fact that had horrified Jane. Normally, she made it a point not be easily found when there was work to be done. This time, she'd hidden behind the curtain in the library and had promptly fallen asleep, propped against the windowpane. She'd been fortunate only John the footman had found her as she'd drooled a bit and marred the glass. Lady Strathmore was not the fussiest of employers, yet Janie couldn't help but think perhaps window drool was a bit much. So, sighing as if greatly put upon, Jane had wiped the window with the dust rag she'd let drop to the floor on the onset of her nap, then trudged back to the kitchen.

She halted on seeing such a huge man waiting on her. "Och now, who be ye?"

"Donald. Mistress Annie sent me to ye."

Jane looked the man up. Then down. She lingered on the appropriate places and raised her brows in admiration. "Annie has always been a good cousin to me."

The man's brows lowered.

Janie quickly said, "So ye're one of the lads from the cottage, eh? Fairly large, aren't ye?"

"I'm no' the largest."

Well! That was difficult to imagine. The giant who stood before her was every bit of six and a half feet tall, his head barely clearing the ceiling. He was a fine-looking man, too, Jane decided. With large hands as could hold a lass just right whilst tupping.

Suddenly feeling more awake, Jane smoothed her hair and hoped she didn't have a red spot on her forehead from napping against the window. "Whot's Annie wantin' from me?"

Donald glanced around the busy kitchen. Preparations were already under way for the ball and there was a fervid air to the many maids and cooks who ran hither and yon. 'Twasn't a good place for private speech. "Mistress Annie wrote ye a note. Can we speak somewhere where there's less noise?"

Jane pursed her lips. "There's a shed by the barn."

"A shed?" Donald blinked. "There's no need fer that. Everyone is in here so no one would hear us talkin' if we just went outside."

"But the shed is very private." She leaned forward

and placed her hand on his thick, bulging arm. "No one will even know we're there."

Donald shook his head. "Mistress Annie said I was to hurry, so the courtyard 'twill do." He turned and went back the way he'd come.

Jane sighed her disappointment as she followed him. She wondered what Annie could possibly want. Annie was always in a tizzy about her position with Miss Kat. Which was a silly thing to be, because everyone knew it was more of an honor to work for the viscount and viscountess in the castle than to work for Miss Kat in her cottage in the woods. Although . . . Jane looked once more at the massive man who walked before her, noting his tight rump and muscular thighs. Perhaps there were some benefits to working in the cottage for Miss Kat, after all.

Donald led the way to an area near the outer wall. Except for a few maids gathered on the other side of the garden, they were quite alone. He reached into his pocket and withdrew a crumpled note. "Mistress Annie said to give this to ye."

Jane opened the hastily scribbled note, smoothed it out, and then squinched her eyes at it.

Donald looked at her with suspicion. "Can ye read?"

"O' course I can read," Jane said indignantly. "Not well, of course. But well enough." She squinted back at the paper, slowly working her way through the rather scrambled writing. "She wants a book?"

Donald nodded.

Jane studied the note a bit more, then nodded

once. "What Miss Kat needs is one o' Lady Strathmore's fashion plate books."

"Can ye get one for us?"

Jane folded the note and carefully stowed it in her pocket, taking the time to admire Donald's wide shoulders and how he dwarfed even the huge shrubbery around the herb garden. "Possibly."

"What do ye mean 'possibly'? Are ye goin' t' help Miss Kat or no'?"

"I'll have to steal from me own mistress."

"Borrow," Donald said firmly.

"If she don't know 'bout it, then 'tis stealin'."

He eyed her for a long moment, his eyes traveling over from her head to foot. Eyes of dark blue that left a shiver everywhere they went.

Janie wished she'd worn her good gown today of all days. She had to settle for thrusting her bosom forward and sucking in her gut. She wished she had the time to comb her hair, too.

"I have to hurry back," he finally said. "Mistress Annie said 'twas important we no' waste any time in gettin' that book to her."

"Then ye'll have to make sure she gets it. But first we're goin' to have to visit the shed."

He blinked slowly. "The shed?"

"I want a kiss," she said firmly, giving him a direct look that gave him pause. "And more."

Lord love the woman, but she was daft, she was. But she was also young, clean, and rather attractive with her brown hair and blue eyes. Besides, he was not a man who took well to returning from an errand empty-handed. Not Donald.

She wet her lips. "The woodshed behind the stables is empty."

Donald rubbed his neck. The things he had to do for Miss Kat. Still, he was not about to give this hot young miss a ride for nothing. He wasn't one who liked his women ordering things about as if they thought they was better than he.

He eyed her up and down as boldly as she had him. "We don't need a shed."

"We don't?" She glanced around, finding the small knot of giggling women on the other side of the garden, watching them with knowing glances.

"We don't need a shed or any other place. Here will do just fine." He reached down and undid his belt. Several of the maids began to giggle, whispering furiously to one another.

Jane caught his wrist, casting a furiously red-faced glance at her friends. "Whist now! Not here!"

"No? But—"

"The woodshed," she hissed. She caught his gaze and must have realized he was teasing, for a smile broke over her features. "The woodshed?"

He didn't move.

She added softly, "Please."

There it was. He reached down and patted her bottom in a way that pleased her very much. "Very well, ye little strumpet. To the woodshed wid ye. But don't go getting' any ideas. This is fer Miss Kat and no one else."

Face pink with pleasure, Jane sniffed, then sashayed off, nose in the air, wiggling her hips as she went.

Following behind, Donald noted that not only was she pleasantly brass, but she had a lovely sway to her cart, too. And he was a man who appreciated swaying carts.

Feeling rather pleased with himself, Donald closed the shed door behind him. It was amazin' the things he had to do fer the mistress.

Chapter 14

Ah, ma chère. *You are wrong when you say this is not the time for love. Love makes its own time. It always has.*

Madame Bennoit's assistant, Pierre,
to Sabrina, Lady Birlington's kitchen maid

Life, Devon decided, was a complex proposition. Just when you thought you had everything figured out, something would occur to prove you wrong—again.

Wet and bedraggled, he found the library, where he knew a fire would be waiting. He was right; a merry blaze met him as soon as he opened the door. To his relief, the room was also empty.

He made his way inside, found a chair, and pulled it close to the flames, then dropped into it and stretched his booted feet before him.

His mind was so full of the day that it raced. He was aflame with Katherine Macdonald. Tomorrow was much, much too far away, and the knowledge was torturous.

Devon reached over and retrieved the three-week-old edition of the *Morning Post.* He would read and get his mind off such things as Kat's luminous green eyes or the curve of her hips as she rode Lady through the fields.

He idly leafed through the paper, seeing nothing to stop his rapid thoughts. Finally, irritated, he threw it down. In a way, it was strange seeing a remnant of his previous life. Since he'd come to Kilkairn, he felt as if he'd been living in a distant, mystical land. Even Kat in her sturdy little cottage in the woods, surrounded by her seven scowling giants, seemed unreal.

But real she was, as evidenced by his growing feelings. And they were growing, he admitted. Though not in his usual manner. Normally, by this point in a relationship, he was well on his way to proclaiming his love. Somehow he knew Kat would not appreciate such an impulsive, and eventually worthless, display. If he told her he loved her, he'd better mean it with every ounce of his heart, soul, and body, for she'd accept nothing less.

Up till now, his life wasn't a very pretty picture. If he ever wanted a relationship that was more, then *he* would have to be more, do more, give more. That fact was slowly becoming obvious to him.

He moved restlessly. It was strange, but he didn't miss London nearly as much as he had expected. He remembered his astonishment at discovering that his brother Chase planned to close his London residence except for a paltry two months of the year, so that he could reside in the manor house he'd purchased near his new bride's childhood home.

Devon couldn't imagine how his sophisticated, onetime dissolute brother would find anything to do in the country. Yet when he'd mentioned his concerns to his brother, Chase had laughed and then categorized about two hundred chores and efforts he and Harriet already had planned, including a new system to shear sheep and store wool that he'd been certain would revolutionize the entire industry.

It was then that it had dawned on Devon how much Chase had changed. Now, though, he wondered if perhaps Chase hadn't changed at all, but had only found a place to expend his energies. Energies he'd been wasting before he met Harriet.

Devon grimaced. It was all nonsense. Chase might have needed to change, but God knew that Devon didn't. Except for his irresolution with women, he liked who he was and what he was, and if he sometimes worried about his inability to feel anything substantial, it was merely because he wasn't yet ready to settle down. Yes, that was all it was.

A soft knock sounded at the door.

"Come in," Devon said over his shoulder, glad for the interruption.

The door opened and Tilton entered, dressed and pressed into the perfect rendition of the perfect gentleman's gentleman. "I beg your pardon, sir. May I have a word with you?"

"Of course."

"Thank you." Tilton came to stand beside Devon's

chair, standing a precise two feet from the arm. "Sir, I still have not located the talisman ring."

"Blast!" Yet another thing to add to his list of things to think about that he'd rather not.

"Indeed, sir. I took the chamber apart but other than discovering a ruby cravat pin that most definitely was not yours, I found nothing."

Devon scowled. He'd been certain Tipton would find that damned ring, so certain that he hadn't really bothered to think about it. Now, though . . . Devon rubbed a hand over his face, wondering what he should do next.

He remembered seeing the ring on Mother's hand, the light catching the carvings whenever she moved. It was the one thing that was uniquely hers. He suddenly realized how much the ring meant, not just to him, but to his brothers and sister. "Damn, damn, damn. We have to find it."

"Yes, sir. I shall continue to make discreet inquiries among the servants, though so far, no one seems to know a thing."

"The hell with discreet. Offer a reward. I have to find that bloody thing before next week." When he would leave.

The thought depressed him, a feeling he resolutely repressed. "I will ask Lord Strathmore about it."

"Yes, sir." Tipton eyed Devon's wet riding habit. "You will be changing prior to visiting His Lordship, I presume?"

"No. I want to see him now."

"But you're wet."

"I won't sit on any of his good chairs. Only the old ones that appear ready to fall apart."

"How fortunate for the good chairs," Tipton said, eyeing him severely.

Devon hefted himself from his seat, glad to have something to do other than mope about. "And how unfortunate for my arse; most of the bad chairs have fallen springs. I daresay I will be sorry I did not heed your advice and change my clothing."

"You always are sorry for ignoring my suggestions, and yet you are never slow in disregarding them."

Grinning, Devon left the room in search of Malcolm. He found him standing outside the sitting room, loitering in the hallway as if listening to the murmured conversation inside.

Malcolm gestured for him to be quiet.

"What are you doing?" Devon asked.

"They are discussing the ball. I want to know who they are inviting."

"Oh. May I ask why?"

"Because it's all a plot. I know it is. I just cannot discover what their intentions are."

It was interesting how a perfectly sane man could become insane once he married. Keeping his voice low, Devon said, "Malcolm, I have lost something."

"Oh? What?"

"The talisman ring."

"The talisman ri—" Malcolm snapped his mouth closed. Silence issued from the room inside for a moment, and then the murmured conversation continued.

Malcolm grabbed Devon's elbow and dragged him around the corner. "Good God, when did that happen?"

"A day or so now. I told Lady Strathmore about it, and she said she'd ask the servants. Do you think she has?"

"I don't know, though she's said nothing to me. I'll ask about and see what I can discover." Malcolm's frown deepened. "Devon, what if someone finds it?"

"I hope they will return it to me. Though I don't want to be burdened with it, it did belong to my mother, and it is rather precious because of that."

"No, no. I mean . . . if the ring is in someone else's possession, would *they* end up married?"

Now there was a thought. Devon considered it. Finally, he shook his head. "I don't think so. I mean, it is called the *St. John* talisman ring."

Malcolm didn't appear convinced. "I hope you are right. I also hope that neither Fiona nor Murien have found the thing."

"What would they do with it?"

Malcolm frowned. "I don't know, but the way they're scheming, 'tis a possibility one or the both o' them had their hands on it."

"You're being a bit hasty."

Malcolm sighed, his shoulders slumping. An apologetic smile flickered over his face. "Perhaps 'tis just mislaid, as you said. I'll go and see if I can't find that lazy butler. Perhaps Davies has some knowledge of your ring."

Devon didn't think he'd ever actually seen the

butler at Kilkairn. "I hope Davies knows where the ring is. I must find it before I leave."

Malcolm nodded. "We shall. Never fear. It is too dangerous to leave lying around. Meanwhile, you had best dress for dinner. You look a bit wet."

Devon nodded. "I shall. Thank you for your assistance, Malcolm. I appreciate it."

"I'm looking for that dismal artifact more for my own good than yours. 'Tis the last thing I want lying about where an innocent male might chance upon it." With that, Malcolm headed downstairs, yelling for Davies as he went.

Devon watched him go. Why couldn't his mother have had a ring that caused increased health or stamina? Anything other than an illness that might lead to marriage. It really wasn't fair.

Sighing, he turned and made his way to his own room, wishing he didn't have to attend dinner that evening.

Dinner was every bit as horrid as Devon feared. Fiona was flushed and talkative, a desperate sparkle in her eyes. Once or twice Devon caught her staring at Malcolm with such a look of longing that it startled him.

Malcolm, for his part, spent most of the meal prying for hidden meanings behind his wife's every statement, while Murien did her best to play the part of The Perfect Companion.

By the time he and Malcolm retreated for brandy, Devon was ready to plead tiredness and retreat to the relative quiet of his room. But once there, he found himself resenting the stillness, for it left him far too free to think about Kat.

He stood restlessly and wandered to the window, pushing aside the heavy curtain and looking out at the starlit night. What was Kat doing now? Was she working with the lads? Was she thinking about the promises she'd made him? Was she even awake? As late as it was, she was most likely in bed, sound asleep.

That brought to mind more important questions. What did she wear to bed? A long flannel nightgown devoid of lace or trim? Somehow, he couldn't imagine her in anything so mundane. Perhaps a thin cotton rail, tied with ribbons and bows? But no. That was too ordinary. Perhaps she just wore a silk chemise. One with little tiny flowers embroidered around a low neckline. A neckline that outlined the curve of her generous breasts—

He turned from the window and grabbed up his coat, his imagination—and other parts of him—afire. It was almost midnight, and by the time he arrived at her house, it would be tomorrow already. Perhaps, in addition to showing her that he was earnest in his desire to forward their relationship, he could also model the virtue of promptness.

Grinning at his own whimsy, he made his way through the moonlit night to the stable, where he woke, then handsomely bribed, a sleepy groom to saddle Thunder.

Kat tossed her scarf on the dressing table and then found her comb. Sighing heavily, she sat in front of the oval mirror and made a face. "Comb your hair and stop thinking about That Man."

As usual, she didn't listen to herself, for the third time she drew the large toothed comb through her hair, she caught herself wondering what Devon was doing now. Was he playing billiards with Malcolm? Listening to Fiona talk about the upcoming ball? Or walking a moonlit path with Murien?

"Ow!" The comb hit a tangle. That was the problem with having thick hair, it got mussed far too easily.

She worked the comb through the tangle and smiled when it finally slid through. "There," she told her reflection in the mirror. "See what a little work will do?"

Her reflection grimaced back at her. Work was one thing, but wanting the impossible was another, which was what spending an entire day with Devon St. John tended to do to her. The man had a gift for inspiring confidences and appearing earnest, both talents that made him a dangerous man indeed.

It was funny; when she was with Devon, everything seemed so *right*. But then, when she wasn't with him, the doubts began creeping in. The damning little thoughts that asked her what she thought she was doing, spending time with a man who, by his own admission and Murien's insinuations, changed his affections as easily as most people changed their clothing.

Kat pulled the comb through her hair one last time, then braided it. The situation with St. John was too perplexing to consider this late at night. Perhaps, when she saw him tomorrow, she'd know the answer. One made all the easier by warm sunlight and a new day.

A scratch sounded at her window. Kat paused in braiding her hair, but the sound did not come again. She finished braiding, then rose and carried the candle to the bed.

Another scratch sounded, and this time she could tell it was the tree limb that, when the wind blew from the south, bent until the branches scraped the casement. She frowned. It hadn't seemed that windy before . . . was there a storm blowing in? She went to the window and flipped the latch, then pushed it open.

"Kat!" came a strident whisper.

Kat jumped, pressing a hand to her heart.

"Kat!" came the voice again, this time closer.

She blinked, then leaned forward. The tree branch was bent toward the house, but there was no wind. What there was, however, was a large man, steadily climbing the tree to her bedchamber. "St. John!"

He paused, grinning up at her. His teeth flashed in the pale moonlight. "It's after midnight." He was a scant six feet away now, and she could make out the shape of his face, a shadow of nose and eyes and smiling lips.

"I know it's after midnight. What are you doing here?" she asked, astounded and perplexed and frightened just the teeniest bit. He was getting closer with each moment, climbing with the surety of a man who had clambered countless trees as a lad.

She suddenly realized that he'd said "tomorrow."

Good heavens, he was coming because she'd promised . . . What *had* she promised?

But she knew what she'd promised . . . and she'd meant it, too. Or she had until Murien had let her know how far gone Kat already was. The truth was that she already cared too much for St. John to have a simple dalliance with him. If she wasn't careful, she'd reveal her feelings and damn what friendship she and Devon did share; a friendship far more precious than any Kat had ever had.

She pressed a hand to her cheek. Her heart was pounding, her palms damp, her throat tight. Part of her felt as if she should flee. But another part of her was flattered and excited and . . . happy. Devon St. John was climbing a tree outside her window. Her window and not Murien Spalding's, the most beautiful woman in Scotland.

He was now almost at eye level, the light from the room spilling over his face. Excitement gleamed in his eyes. "You said we would settle this thing between us 'tomorrow.' " He placed a hand on her window casement. "It is now 'tomorrow.' "

At his words, her body whispered needfully that she should move, just a step or two, and then he would be in her bedchamber and all the heated thoughts and late night longing she'd suffered would be sated. But her mind ordered her to stay put, not to be swayed by soft words.

Which was right, her mind or her body? It was torture, this double yearning to do and not to do. Kat clenched her teeth against it all.

His gaze met hers, softly quizzing. "I can't climb in unless you step back."

The old fears and questions tumbled back into her mind. "I-I do not know if I should let you in or not."

"Are you asking my opinion?" His teeth flashed whitely in the uncertain light. "For if you are, I think you should let me in so we can—"

"I'm quite certain I know what *you* think. I just don't know what *I* think."

"Whatever you decide, you'd best make up your mind quickly. I might fall at any minute. These branches are not very stable."

He was laughing at her, she could tell. And she didn't like it one little bit. "Of course, as hard as your head seems to be, one little tumble won't kill you."

"Won't it? Kat, what are you afraid of? You don't trust anyone of the opposite sex other than your lads and your brother. Meanwhile, you stay here, hiding from the world and anyone who might hurt you."

He thought she was afraid. How ludicrous! "You are sorely mistaken; I am not afraid. Not of you or anyone else."

"I see." He was silent a moment before he said, "What if I just come in long enough for a drink of water?"

"There's water in the barrel by the barn."

"Oh." He leaned on the casement with his free arm, the candlelight smoothing a golden path across his handsome face. "I'll get some water on my way out. But . . . I'm also a little chilled."

"Then you'd best return to your room at Kilkairn."

He glanced past her to the crackling fire in her

room. "But your fireplace doesn't smoke. What if I just came in long enough to warm myself a bit?"

She crossed her arms and looked at him.

He heaved a sigh. "You are the most stubborn woman. Very well, I'll leave. But I must rest first. May I come in and just—"

"No!" Heavens, but he was a determined individual. "Good night, Mr. St. John." She placed her hand on the casement to close it, expecting him to move out of the way.

Instead, he drew back instantly—and then disappeared from sight. The place where he'd been was filled with a horrid black stillness.

She gasped and rushed forward. "Devon—!"

He was still there, crouching on the thick tree limb that held him, hanging onto the branch above. His teeth gleamed faintly in the dark. "You would miss me if I was gone; admit it."

"I am not admitting anything," she said, though her heart still trembled in place. "That was a horrid trick."

"I'm a desperate man. Climbing up was one thing, climbing down in the black of night is another." He moved back into place, leaning in the casement as he smiled at her, that wistful lopsided smile that always made her melt just the tiniest bit on the inside.

"Kat, my love, what if you chose a chair for me and I promised to stay in it?"

Her gaze narrowed. "You wouldn't get up?"

"The seat of the chair and I would never part. Not unless you invited us to."

That seemed like a fair offer. Besides, if he stayed in the window, one of the lads was bound to see him. Simon in particular was a restless one and was frequently up and about in the wee hours of the morn.

Kat closed her eyes. "This is madness, but . . . blast it! I suppose I might as well."

And with that, Kat Macdonald made a monumental decision, one she'd mull the rest of her days. She stepped out of the way and let Devon St. John climb into her window.

Chapter 15

Every oncet in a while, I gets a pain in me head and I'm never sure if it is because of somethin' I've done, or somethin' I need to do.

Lady Birlington's maid Sabrina
to Cold Bob, the fishmonger,
at the market early one morning

Devon climbed the rest of the way in, stepping over the sill with ease. He paused to close the window, the sound unnaturally loud in the quiet.

"You cannot stay long." There was a defensive note to her voice.

He turned to answer her, but though he wanted to reply, her night rail prevented him. All he could do was nod. Nod and stare, for she was wearing a gown of pale green silk that flowed to her feet, clinging lasciviously to every curve she possessed. Worse—or better, depending on whether he enjoyed the lush torture she presented—the neckline was low, exposing rounded curves that made his mouth water.

"Yes, well," she said, her heightened color letting

him know she was aware of his regard, "the next time you decide to clamber up a tree and into a woman's room, you might want to make more noise."

"Noise?"

"Yes. Whistle or something. I could have mistaken you for a reiver, come to steal my jewels. 'Tis a wonder I didn't call for one of the lads."

"I don't whistle. Not well anyway."

"Then sing. That would work, I suppose."

"No," he said firmly. "I am not going to sing, not even for you. I respect my fellow man too much to put them through such a parody of talent."

"That is very kind of you."

"I made that decision after being forced to listen to I know not how many musicale performances by anxious mamas who think men admire women who can warble a song."

Her lips twitched. "Poor you, having to endure such."

He tried not to stare too long at her soft, full mouth. "I never heed the matchmaking mamas. But they have made me more aware of the fact that just because we think we're talented, does not make it so."

"A wise lesson."

An awkward silence then fell, as if they'd used all their stored-up banter and were now completely wordless. Kat glanced nervously around, then cleared her throat no fewer than three times.

Devon finally took pity on her. "I believe I was

supposed to occupy a chair. Shall we sit?" Now that he was there, he had all the time in the world.

"Sit?" She glanced at the bed, then at the chairs, as if dragging her mind from one to the other. "Oh yes! Of course we may sit." She led the way to the chairs, her gown revealing the tantalizing outline of her thighs as she moved.

Devon had to force himself to breathe. God, but she was beautiful. He eyed the long red-gold braid that hung down her back and wondered what her hair would look like splayed over a mound of white pillows. His blood heated.

She took her seat, sitting on the very edge of the chair, her hands clasped on the arms of the chair. The second he took his place across from her, she said, "Why are you here?"

"I was just riding by and thought to see what you were doing."

"At midnight?"

"It's twenty after," he pointed out politely.

Her gaze narrowed.

He shook his head sadly. "Oh ye of little faith."

"I have faith. Just not in men who knock on my window in the middle of the night."

"I should have used the front door, but I was bored and this seemed an adventure." He could tell from the quiver in her voice that she was nervous and fearful and just the tiniest bit excited. He smiled a little, knowing exactly how she felt. In his own way, he felt the same.

She folded her hands in her lap, her feet perfectly

flat on the floor before her. The prim gesture was very much at odds with her decadent gown. "Devon, I am not an adventuresome woman. I don't believe you should—"

"Nonsense. You are very adventuresome. You live here, alone except for the company of your servants and seven scowling giants. You are building a business that by all accounts is getting to be extremely profitable. And you can ride like an angel. How much more adventuresome do you need to be?"

Kat bit her lip. She'd never really thought of herself that way before but . . . he was right; she did take risks. Only not with her heart.

She was trying to figure out how to say this when he stood.

From her chair, Kat immediately leaned away, too aware of his proximity and her own lack of clothing.

"I am just going to get a drink of water," he said in a calming voice. "May I?"

Her cheeks heated. She didn't mean to overreact, but she was too nervous to think. "Of course. Pray help yourself."

She watched from beneath her lashes as he went to where Annie kept a pitcher and glasses. Devon poured himself a glass of water. Then he turned and leaned against the low edge of the dresser.

He finished the water and set the glass on the dresser, his eyes wandering over Kat. "That's a lovely gown," he said, his voice low and deep.

She had to fight the urge to shiver. The silk night rail had been a gift from Malcolm. Kat sometimes wondered if he'd perhaps ordered it for Fiona, but when it had arrived, it had been too large for her petite frame and thus it had been passed on to Kat. However it was, she loved the feel of the silk against her skin and she wore it often. Of course, she'd never worn it in front of anyone else, and she now found herself achingly aware of every inch of fabric that hugged her bare skin.

Devon absently picked up her white scarf from where she'd placed it earlier. He ran it through his hands. "I am intrigued by you."

"By me? Why?"

"Because you are such an interesting mixture of vulnerability and bravery. I wonder what I can do to prove to you that I am worth trusting."

"If we had several years to debate it, it is quite possible I might eventually come to do so. But you will be leaving soon."

Devon nodded but didn't reply. He was looking at the scarf, a strange expression on his face.

"Kat," he said, his gaze still on the scarf, "I think I know how to prove myself to you." He draped the scarf over his arm and walked toward her.

Her heart thudded faster. "What . . . what are you doing?"

"You've been wounded by words—told things that were not true. So I will prove myself in deeds."

"Deeds?"

"I am going to prove to you by action that I am worthy of your trust."

She gripped the arms of her chair. "Why . . . why is that important to you?" She waited with bated breath for his answer.

"Because if you never trust someone again, then you will be lonely the rest of your life. I don't want that to happen to you."

"I am not alone. I have Malcolm. He is all I need."

"You need more than that. You need friends, acquaintances . . . lovers."

Lovers. Not "lover," but "lovers." That certainly said a lot about Devon St. John. Kat eyed him with a dark frown. "It is none of your concern what relationships I choose or don't choose to have." Or whom she chose to have them with, for that matter. Although, if she were honest, in the years since Stephen, she hadn't really been attracted to any man. Except Devon.

His mouth quirked into a half smile so delectable that her heart thudded an extra beat. "Kat, do you think you can trust me for five minutes."

"Five minutes?"

He nodded. "During that five minutes, I can do anything to you that I want providing it doesn't hurt you in any way."

"Do?" her voice quavered just a bit, but Kat couldn't help it. Her entire body was afire with his suggestion. "What—" She licked her dry lips. "What would you do?"

"Nothing to cause you harm. Only pleasure."

It was a ludicrous idea, although . . . it intrigued her. "What if I wanted you to stop?"

"Then you say 'stop' and I stop." His gaze dripped over her, lingering on her breasts before returning to her face. "And I promise only to touch you in ways that will keep you gasping in delight."

Kat's face heated until she thought it would catch fire. "I—I don't know—"

He was before her now, standing in front of the chair. He looked so handsome. But it was more than that. Between them pulsed a physical longing that swept over them both like waves of the sea. It was a feeling Kat had almost forgotten.

The truth was, she wanted this man. But she also knew that she had begun to care for him and that any other step in their relationship would only jeopardize her heart all the more.

The question was, could she continue without further risking her heart?

He knelt before her. "Five minutes, Kat. No more."

She swallowed, aware that she only had to reach out and an entire world of pleasure was hers. "Why?" she finally managed to whisper. "Why me?"

He lifted his hand and lightly traced the line of her cheek. "Because you are the most exciting, beautiful, intelligent woman I have ever met."

When he put it that way, she *felt* exciting, beautiful, and intelligent. Strange how something as simple as a few words could have so much of an impact on her heart. But it was more than words; his gaze was painfully sincere.

"Very well," she heard herself whisper. "You have five minutes."

His eyes flared. "You will not regret it."

"What—" She had to lick her lips to continue. "What do we do now?"

"We are going to build your trust."

"How?"

"Very, very slowly." He held out his arm, the scarf fluttering at the movement. "Lean forward and place your feet flat on the floor."

She did as he asked, though it brought her knees against his chest.

"Afraid?" His voice was dark, deep, seductive.

Kat sent him a glance, one she hoped was quelling and disdainful. "Should I be?"

"With me? *Never.*"

One word. But spoken with such meaning that it gave her pause.

He took the scarf and ripped it down the middle, into two long pieces.

"Wh—" She blinked in astonishment as he took one of the pieces of the scarf, placed the end in the palm of her hand, and then began wrapping it about her wrist. While she watched, amazed, he took the other end of the scarf and wrapped it around the arm of the chair until her wrist was bound to the chair. "Devon, I cannot—"

He placed the loose end of the scarf in her hand. "All you have to do is let go and unwind it and you will be free. You are in control, Kat. Not me."

He was right. As long as she held the end of the scarf in her hand, she had the ability to release herself. She watched bemused as he did the same to her other wrist.

Kat couldn't quite believe what was happening to her. She was dressed in the decadent silk night rail in her own bedchamber, bound to a chair in front of a handsome man.

"Now," Devon said, standing. "Here is where we begin. Do you mind if I take off my coat?"

It was very warm in the room, she thought. Actually, it was a lot warm, though little of that had to do with the fire. "Of course you may take off your coat."

He did so, revealing a narrow waistcoat of deep blue. He tossed the jacket over the back of the chair he'd abandoned earlier. "Now. May I remove my waistcoat and shirt?"

Dear God, he was undressing right in front of her. A delicate shiver traced down her back, shimmering across her skin and making her breasts swell in response. Somehow, she found herself answering in a hushed, husky voice, "Yes."

Within moments, his waistcoat and shirt had joined his coat on the back of the chair. He stood before her, broad-shouldered and narrow-hipped, his arms powerful, his chest covered with crisp, curly hair. Her fingers itched at the sight, for she wanted nothing more than to touch him.

She twisted against the bonds that held her hands.

"All you have to do is release them and they are gone." He knelt before her, his face level with hers. "You are in control, Kat. You decide what you want. And if you ever want me to stop, no matter when, no matter what I am doing, I will do so." He bent forward then, his lips to her ear. "You can trust me."

She turned her face until her cheek was pressed to his. Her entire body thrummed with awareness, with need. She wanted him to touch her, to kiss her.

He pulled back slowly, his skin brushing hers as

he found her mouth. He kissed her deeply, passionately, his lips hot and firm. She moaned against his mouth, leaning forward, letting all her passion flood through the embrace.

He left her mouth to kiss her cheek, her neck, the neckline of her gown, his lips teasing, caressing. She pressed forward, offering herself to him, wanting more.

Devon's head dipped lower until his mouth was on the crest of her breast. Her nipples hardened, abrading the silk gown and tightening. She threw back her head, reveling in the sensation.

The scarf bonds tightened as she unthinkingly attempted to bring up her hands to cup his head, hold him to her. But she did not release the ends. There was something freeing about letting him have his way, about having the ability to stop it, yet not.

He slid down and pressed his mouth to her breast through her gown. She gasped, then stopped as he tongued her nipple, her gown growing damp from his efforts. The sensation of that mouth through the thin material of her gown, of the hot, damp clothing over her nipple, made her shudder already.

It felt so good, so wondrous that she could scarcely stand it. And the fact that his bared shoulders were so tantalizingly close made her torture all the more exquisite.

He slid farther down, his hands tracing the shape of her waist, her hips, her legs. On to her feet. There he stopped, meeting her gaze for a long moment. "If you want me to quit, all you have to do is say one word."

She nodded, but made no effort to say anything.

He smiled, his hands now resting one on each ankle. "This is for you, my love." He lifted up the bottom of the night rail, sliding the silk along her bare skin, pushing the material until it rested on her knees. Then he bent and kissed the inside of each ankle, sending tremors of feeling pulsing through her.

Kat had to fight a moan. The stifled noise seemed to inflame him, for he slid his kisses from her ankles to her knees. Cupping an ankle, he gently pushed up her night rail even more, parting her legs as he did so. Cool air wafted over her calves and the insides of her thighs.

She felt like a complete wanton, sitting exposed before him. But somehow, she couldn't help it. Couldn't stay away, couldn't pretend that this attraction wasn't burning through her.

He pressed a kiss to her inner thigh, the movement sudden and unexpected. So strong was her reaction that Kat thought she'd shoot right out of the chair. "Devon," she gasped.

He stopped immediately, his gaze meeting hers. "Yes?"

She knew she had but to say one word and he'd stop. She could also release the scarf ends and be free to put her gown back in place, and resume her life of unending dignity. She looked down at herself, at the wet circle he'd made around her nipple, at the way the silk gown was bunched almost to her hips.

At the sight of her own legs bared and splayed, Devon kneeling between them.

God help her, she didn't want to stop. Not now, not ever. She lifted her eyes to his and said not one word, but two. "More, please."

Chapter 16

I've had me share of the fair sex. 'Tis a pity the fair sex thinks they've already had their fair share of me.

Cold Bob, the fishmonger,
to young Peter Franshawe,
tutor to the Duke of Draventon's son
after a chance meeting in a pub

Devon leaned back, the candlelight caressing his face, tracing the line of his jaw. He looked so incredibly handsome that Kat's breath stuttered. This must have been what the angel Gabriel looked like, a vision of masculine beauty that locked the eye and sent a piercing ache straight to the heart.

Kat cleared her throat, wondering if her thighs looked fat from the angle Devon could see them. She suddenly wished for a cover. "I am a little cold."

His brows lifted. "Afraid?"

The soft words hung in the air between them. Kat's jaw tightened. "Of you? No. Of course not."

"Good. There are a lot of things I'd like you to feel when you look at me. Fear isn't one of them."

That was certainly unfortunate because a sort of fear was shivering through her that very instant. Fear that her feelings were already so deeply engaged that she could not back away. Not that her body was retreating from him. Oh no. God forbid that Devon touch her any more intimately than he already had or she'd explode into a conflagration of white-hot flames.

The fact was that Devon St. John inspired fear and more; he was also directly responsible for every last twinge of lust, desire, and unmitigated longing that had wracked her nights ever since she'd met him. And it was time she stopped fighting it and accepted the simple fact that she wanted him.

Slowly, she released the ends of the scarf and tugged her arm free, first one, and then the other. He rocked back on his heels, disappointment flickering across his face.

She unwound the scarf scraps from her wrists and collected them in a ball. Devon stood, looking down at her with an inscrutable expression. "Kat, I—"

She pointed to one side.

His gaze followed her finger, his eyes widening when he realized she was pointing directly at the bed.

She handed him the scarf scraps. "You can tie me up there, if you'd like. I think it might be more comfortable for us both."

Devon blinked bemusedly at the scarf ties, a gradual dawning crossing his face. "Kat, are you certain—"

"More, please," she said again, only this time she

stood and walked to the bed, not waiting to see if he would follow.

She stopped by the bed and reached up to undo the single tie that held on the pale green night rail, hesitating just a second when it dawned on her that for the first time in she didn't know how many years, a man was going to see her naked. And not just any man, but Devon St. John, one of London's most sought after, most feted bachelors.

He was used to having the most delicate and dainty women of the *ton* undress before him every day, if what Murien hinted was true.

Kat's lips quivered suddenly. She wished she hadn't grown so fond of pastries these last few years. But who could have foreseen that a beautiful, incredibly handsome man would even now be waiting for her to undress, his eyes dark with passion.

Life was a mystery. And so, too, was Devon St. John. She only hoped that he would not cease to be attracted to her once he saw her for what she was—too tall, too large, too awkward, too loud, and too . . . undainty.

The horrid thoughts froze her fingers over the ties.

Just as she was preparing to force her fingers into behaving, a pair of warm hands closed over hers. Devon's voice sounded in her ear. "You're going to maul this lovely gown. That, my sweet, is my job."

The humor lacing his voice made her relax somewhat. "I'm sorry. I'm not used to undressing on demand."

He quickly undid the tie, but made no move to

step away, his body warm against her back, his hands slowly sliding up and over her shoulders. "There. Now you are untied."

So she was. She took a deep breath and pulled her gown loose about her neck, but didn't remove it any further. In fact, she clutched it to her, feeling as bare and vulnerable as if she were suddenly seventeen once more, and thrust into the unwelcome arms of Edinburgh society. She couldn't bring herself to turn to face Devon, so she said with a nervous laugh, "I'm certain you made many of the women of the *ton* very happy."

There was a short silence, and then he leaned forward to wrap his arms about her. "Kat, don't be afraid. Not of me. You are one of the most natural, passionate women I know. I don't want you to feel less because of me."

"Less?"

"I won't pretend I don't wish to see you without that blasted gown. I do. So much. But not at the price of your pride."

Her pride. Was that what was holding her back? She considered this and then decided he was right. It astonished her that he seemed to understand her so well.

Her first impulse was to turn toward him, wrap her arms about his neck, press her body to his, and kiss him as deeply and passionately as he had kissed her only a day ago.

And after she thought about it, she realized it was also her second, third, and fourth impulse, as well. She wanted to kiss him. Kiss him and more. *Much* more. She wanted to kiss him, taste him, feel his mouth on her lips, her skin. She wanted to touch him, and feel him against her, inside her—

Stop it, she warned herself abruptly. Already her body was responding to Devon's intoxicating closeness. She didn't need her vivid imagination adding more stress to her already fractured brain.

Devon watched the play of emotions on her face, fascinated despite the raging ache in his loins. He had never known a woman whose face showed her feelings so clearly, and he didn't think he would ever tire of seeing her myriad expressions.

Her gown dropped to the floor.

Devon's breath stopped as he slowly took her in, from feet to glorious crown of hair. She was magnificent, even more lush and beautiful than he'd imagined. Long-limbed and rounded, every lush inch of her made his mouth water, his heart pound, his manhood rise in eagerness.

She crossed her arms over her breasts, drawing his attention back to her face. "I am not going to be the only one without clothing."

Her chin was jutting stubbornly, challenge in every line of her rich body. Devon undid his breeches and stepped out of them with an alacrity that had everything to do with the sight of the beautiful woman before him.

Kat eyed him up and down, her tongue coming out to wet her lips before she turned and climbed into the high bed. Devon watched her bemusedly, his body a raging river of want and need. Bloody hell, what was he supposed to do now? He had promised himself to be noble, to take his time and be gentle.

But he was caught by the sight of her plump white shoulders, by the smoothness of her pearly skin, by the silken threads of her hair curling at the juncture of her thighs. God, but she was magnificent. He wondered how he could have ever thought thin, tiny women would please him. They were pale wraiths in comparison to the sensuous woman before him.

He couldn't wait a moment more. He joined Kat on the bed, climbing in beside her. Immediately the smell of lavender and jasmine sent a wave of anticipation through him.

Devon lifted up on one arm and admired the prize he'd captured. Never, in all his experiences, had he seen such lovely breasts. Full and ripe, they would fill a man's hand and more. Each soft, abundant mound was topped with a guinea-sized areola, dusky pink and nipped with excitement. Beneath that, her stomach rounded down to—

He closed his eyes. She was going to kill him. Already his heart was racing, his stomach quivering, his manhood painfully erect.

He'd always loved women, loved sex. He reveled in a woman's unique scent, in the feel of her beneath him, around him. But this . . . this experience was different. More vibrant with taste, feel, color. There was something about Kat that inflamed him, aroused him, drove him mad with desire.

"I don't think we're going to use the scarf this time," he said hoarsely. "Kat, I want you completely with me. Without anything between us."

"As you wish," she said, her voice soft and breathy. "Just touch me, Devon, and hold me. I want you so badly." She ran her hands over his bare arms, across his shoulders, and then down his chest, her touch like lightning.

His tenuous control shattered and broke into a million tiny pieces. All that was left was the raging desire to make love to Kat. To hear her soft cries and make her moan with pleasure.

He took her in his arms and kissed her, his mouth covering hers, his tongue seeking. She clutched at him, opening her mouth beneath his, pressing closer. Devon cupped her to him, his hands spanning her luxurious curves.

The kiss deepened, fanning the flames ever higher. Her arms snaked around his waist, and to his pleased surprise, she pulled him even more tightly to her, pressing her hips to his.

Devon had pleasured many women and had left them all smiling happily. He knew the value of a woman who unapologetically enjoyed the physical act with all of her soul. And Kat was definitely one of those few. He gave himself over to pleasing her completely.

Kat was drowning in a sea of passion, of tangled blankets and a complete commitment to her own madness. A madness that had been threatening her own peace ever since she first laid eyes on Devon St. John.

God, but he was magnificent! All lean, rippled muscle and a firm arse that filled her with the bemused desire to nip it.

He was sublimely unapologetic in his nakedness, his attention focused on her breasts. Kat was used to men looking at her breasts; they had been doing so since she was fourteen. But somehow this was different; Devon held his hand flat over her nipples, rubbing his palm over them. They immediately hardened and peaked, but Devon continued his ministrations, as if seeking something more.

Soon she was panting, her body aching, her thighs moist with longing. "Devon," she said. "Please."

"Not yet," he whispered. "Not yet."

He grasped her rounded rump firmly, kneading and pressing. She moaned, squirming slightly, growing hotter by the second. He could see the moisture glistening on her inner thighs, and his own body tightened at the sight. She was so ripe, like a plucked peach, ready to be devoured. "Tell me what you like."

"Like?" She gasped when his fingers brushed her center.

"Do you like this?"

"Oh yes!" she gasped.

He knelt between her legs, savoring the warmth of her skin, the scent of her secretmost place. He bent forward and kissed her there, gently but urgently. She planted her heels and arched upward at the shock of the touch.

He waited only a moment before he did it again. And again. Soon she was panting, her knees splayed as he pleasured her. After a moment, he lifted his head. "Tell me, Kat. I want to hear you say it." He bent and traced a line across her most sensitive spot.

"Oh God, I love it. Don't stop." She squirmed

madly, rubbing against his mouth. He sucked her gently, then with increasing fervor. She trembled against him, her hands in his hair, clutching, pulling, trying to get closer, and at the same time trying to escape. "Devon! Don't stop. Never stop."

Her gasped request set him to even more frenzied ministrations. He slowly slid his thumb into her, marveling at her tightness.

God but she was hot and wet. He wanted to plunge into her, to run his hands over her flesh and taste her until she cried out in wonder and happiness.

That was what he wanted, more than anything. Just as he had the thought, she lifted and stiffened, then said his name as the pleasure overtook her. Devon bent to capture her once more, tasting her and increasing the pressure of his tongue.

The musky-sweet scent of her and the ripe, womanly taste were more than he could take. As her shivers subsided, Devon lifted himself above her and positioned himself between her thighs. He was so ready for her that he ached, his mind a fevered flash of desire.

He was just ready to press forward when she clutched at his arms. "Devon."

There was something about her voice, some hint of desperation or fear that made him pause, rigid and fierce as he was. He had to clench his jaw, but for her sake, he kept his control.

"Are you certain you want this?"

He almost laughed. Instead he pressed an unsteady kiss to her forehead. "I want this more than anything I've ever wanted in my life."

Relief, wonder, laughter, and unmitigated lust warred for expression on her face. To Devon's relief, lust won the day, and she clamped her legs around his waist and lifted her hips to his.

He closed his eyes as he slid inside her, the overwhelming heat sending a shudder all the way to his toes. She gasped at the fullness of him, but only for a moment. Soon she was murmuring in his ear, clutching at his shoulders, moving more and more frantically as the pressure inside built.

Devon had to grit his teeth to keep from spilling into her. She was so tight, so hot, so incredibly sexy as she moved against him and writhed seductively. She had a body built for love, his hands roaming freely, touching and tormenting.

Just as Devon's tenuous control began to slip, she came yet again, arching her back and bucking wildly.

Devon had to grasp her hips to hold on; the exquisite heat and her unbridled passion pushed him over the edge. He thrust forward, burrowing deeply as he came in a rush of heat, and then collapsed on the bed.

How long it took him to regain his breath, he'd never know. But minutes passed before he could even speak.

Never had he known such passion, such earthy sweetness, such complete surrender. Never.

Devon raised on his elbow and looked down at Kat. Her eyes were closed, her face turned to one side, her braid was still intact, if somewhat frayed.

He toyed with the silken strands that had fallen loose, a smile on his face. What an experience. It had been even more than he'd expected.

He bent and kissed her neck. "Kat, my love, are you well?"

A smile curved her lips, but she made no move to face him.

"Shy?" he asked.

That got a glance. "After that? I think not. I am just too winded to move."

He chuckled, scooping her to him, soaking in the feel of her silken skin against his. "That was incredible, my love. Simply incredible."

"Mmmmm," she answered, burrowing against him, her arms about him. "It was lovely. And next time, we'll use the scarf."

He chuckled, a deep satisfaction warming him. He pressed a kiss to her forehead. "As you wish, my lady."

A lovely peace filtered through him as he held her, their hearts returning to a normal rhythm, their legs entwined in a most intimate manner.

The bed was lovely, full of pillows and far more comfortable than the rock-hard mattress he had to sleep on at Kilkairn. And certainly his bed didn't smell of lavender and Katherine Macdonald, which was a lovely scent he could quite easily become enamored of.

The thought held him, and he turned to press his cheek against hers, holding still so he wouldn't wake her. He'd never felt this way before, such a sense of completeness. It was a good thing he was leaving soon, before this magical feeling left.

It was much later that he sighed, kissed her forehead, and slowly climbed from the bed.

Ten minutes later, Simon entered the workshop and lit a lantern by the door. Then he walked to the back of the room to a large red door.

He kicked it open and then held the lantern aloft, lighting a room lined with neat cots. The inhabitants of the room began to stir, cursing at the brightness.

"Bloody hell, Simon," Donald said. "Put down the lantern!"

"What do ye want now?" muttered Hamish, leaning on his elbows and squinting toward Simon. "Was I snorin' again?"

Simon plunked the lantern onto the table that stood to one end of the room and then sat in one of the chairs. "We need to talk."

"Now?" Neal asked, knuckling his eyes.

"Aye, now. I couldna sleep, so I went to the kitchen to see if Annie had left out a little somethin' to eat."

"Ye'd better have a reason fer wakin' us other than Annie forgettin' to leave ye a hunk of cheese," Will said, sitting up and yawning.

"I have a better reason," Simon said grimly. "I saw the Sassenach. He was climbin' down out of Miss Kat's window usin' that old oak."

To a man, they came awake.

"That bastard," Donald swore, jumping to his feet.

"I get to kill him first," Neal said, standing, fists ready.

"No, 'tis fer me to do the killin'," Hamish growled. "Ye can do the dismemberin'."

Simon sighed. "Whist now, I know how ye're all feeling. I was the same. I even thought of takin' him off his horse and doin' the deed right there by meself. But 'twould not answer. Miss Kat would skin us alive. Lads, I think the time has come to invite the Sassenach to a meetin'."

Silence met this suggestion. Finally, Hamish sighed and said, "I suppose ye're right. Miss Kat needs a beau. The Sassenach is a beau."

"But will he be good to her?" Will asked.

"He will be if we have anything to say about it," Simon said grimly.

One by one, the men nodded. Finally, Donald looked at Simon. "We're agreed then. The time has come to invite the Sassenach to a meetin'. And you, Simon, are the one who will do it."

Chapter 17

My lord, I am happy to report that your son has all the makings of a fine young gentleman once he gets over an unfortunate tendency to pinch the maids.

the dashing Peter Franshawe,
tutor to the Duke of Draventon's son,
to the duke during their daily progress meeting

Devon awoke the next morning to the sounds of tradesmen and hammering, carts rumbling over the drive, and the low murmur of a crowd. For a moment, he thought he was still in London, that perhaps Kilkairn Castle and all its occupants were naught but a dream.

The idea made him sit bolt upright, and it was with relieved eyes that he realized he was indeed at Kilkairn, the familiarity of the green chamber setting his mind at ease. Memories came flooding back and he turned onto his back and linked his hands behind his head, dwelling on each moment of the night before.

It had been amazing, an experience he would

never forget. He'd known Kat would be a passionate lover. But he hadn't realized how that would increase his own pleasure.

But most astounding of all was that though he'd slept with her last night, he'd awoken this morning, anxious to see her again. That was yet another first, in a series of firsts.

His gaze wandered over the room. Perhaps he should rise and see her. Had she awoken yet? Had she thought about him?

Good God, I'm acting like a lovesick puppy. He blinked, then sat upright. Love? Surely not. What he felt was merely explosive lust and . . . something else. Respect, perhaps. He knew of few women with Kat's capabilities or heart. So it was not love that he felt. Not unless . . .

His gaze fell on the empty candle dish beside the nightstand.

What if the talisman ring had *caused* him to fall in love with Kat? *Real* love. Bloody hell, what if the ring had meant for him to fall in love with her all along and he, thinking to trick it, had merely played into its nefarious plans and—

"Bloody hell, what is wrong with me?" he muttered. The ring had no power; that was nothing but an old wives' tale that his mother had made up to amuse six very active children. Not that it mattered, the ring was not in his possession, but someone else's.

He frowned. Unless, of course, Tilton had found it.

Downstairs, someone shouted and then dropped something with a large thump that seemed to echo down the hallways. "Bloody hell, what is all the din?" He got up from bed and began rummaging about for his clothing.

The door opened and Tilton entered carrying a tray. He raised his brows on finding Devon half dressed. "Pray tell me the buff breeches and green coat are an effort to amuse your host and not an honest attempt at fashion."

"What? This coat and breeches? I wore them to the Whythe-Stanhopes' and everyone complimented me."

"Hm. Did they appear to be smirking when they made their comments? Or perhaps the wine was flowing freely? I believe I have heard that the Whythe-Stanhopes are notorious about spiking the punch at their own parties."

Devon eyed his valet with a narrow gaze. "Are you accusing me of being out of style?"

"I would never presume to do such a thing," Tilton said primly, setting the tray on the night table, "no matter how true such a statement might appear to others."

Devon looked down at his breeches for a moment. Then he sighed. "Damn it, now you have me wondering if perhaps you're right. Find me another coat to wear."

"Excellent, sir." Tilton uncovered the dishes on the tray. "Perhaps you should eat while I do that very thing."

Devon was more than willing to eat; his stomach was rumbling so loudly he was beginning to think that was what had awakened him rather than the mill downstairs. "What is going on to cause that racket?"

"Preparations for the ball, sir. Apparently Lady Strathmore has been most lavish in her preparations and His Lordship has been complaining about it since."

"I see." Devon had forgotten the ball. Lately, it seemed that he'd forgotten a lot of things. He yawned and stretched.

Tilton shot him a sharp glance. "Tired, sir?"

"Somewhat."

"Yes, sir. Sleep riding will do that to you."

"Sleep riding? What are you talking about?"

"Merely that after you went to bed last night, you apparently got up, dressed, and went for a ride."

"I was awake. And yes, I know I did. How did *you* know? It was late and I thought you were already abed."

"I was, sir. However, the lower footman's youngest brother was apparently roused from his warm cot and offered a large sum to saddle your horse." Tilton met Devon's gaze evenly. "I assured the entire staff that you frequently rode out while still sleeping. They were intrigued of course, and I had to answer a thousand questions, most of them having to do with what would happen if you were sleep riding and had the sudden need to relieve yourself—would you be awake enough to realize it. After we surmounted that hurdle, they began to ask why you would ride in your sleep to His Lordship's sister's cottage. I fear I had no answer for that."

Devon didn't like the sound of this at all. "The staff all know, then, where I went?"

"Oh yes, sir. The wagering has been fierce. Some seem to think Miss Spalding may yet have a chance."

"What about my sleep riding? Didn't anyone believe that?"

"A few of the more dewy-eyed ones, but not enough. It would not surprise me if the story filtered back to His Lordship."

Wondrous. Devon wondered what Malcolm's reaction would be to such information, and a faintly sick feeling tightened his stomach. "Any word yet on the lost ring?"

Tilton shook his head, a frown creasing his brow. "No, sir, and I've interrogated the entire staff. No one has even seen it. I asked your footman, Paul, to make inquiries among the stablehands."

Devon took a sip of his juice to cover his relief. It was reassuring to know that the ring hadn't unknowingly been in his possession last night, when he'd been with Kat. He didn't want to think of their time together as ordained by some family myth. He wanted it to have been of her own free choice and nothing more.

Strange how that mattered. He wondered why, then shrugged it off. Devon finished his breakfast, changed his coat for another, and then made his way downstairs. Malcolm was on the main staircase, looking about the great hall with wonder. Devon waited for some sign that his friend had heard about his late night visit, but it quickly became obvious that Malcolm was as yet unaware of anything other than the fact that his house was being turned upside down.

Boxes were stacked everywhere, as were large folds of silver and blue cloth. Tables had been removed, chairs lined up, and every servant Devon had ever seen at the castle was in evidence, scrubbing and polishing and cleaning.

Devon wondered if any of them had ever worked so hard. He watched the small army, then said to Malcolm, "I thought this was to be a small, private ball."

"So did I," Malcolm said grimly. "Apparently that was a misconception. Every person within fifty miles has been invited to attend."

"How horrid," Devon said. And it was. The last thing he wanted to do was spend his last few precious days doing anything but being with Kat.

The thought of leaving was beginning to bother him. He absently rubbed his chest where a faint pressure seemed to lurk. What was it about her that tugged at him so? At first, she'd been his haven from the lure of the ring to keep him from becoming enamored of the she-witches of the world, women like Murien, for example. But then he'd begun to enjoy being with Kat for Kat's sake.

But that was to be expected, he supposed. After all, other than Kat, what amusement had there been at Kilkairn Castle? None. Malcolm, usually the brightest of companions, was consumed with his argument with his wife. And while riding was certainly a pleasant thing to do, Devon certainly couldn't be expected to do that alone. So that just left Kat.

A faint sense of relief filtered through Devon. Once he left the isolation of Kilkairn and found himself home once again among the glittering ballrooms of London, he'd forget all about Kat Macdonald.

Of course, he couldn't leave at all until he found the talisman ring. Brightening a little, he asked Malcolm if he'd discovered anything about the ring. To his surprise, Malcolm hesitated, then nodded. "I heard one thing from one of the lower housemaids, but . . . I need some time to make certain of the facts."

"Take your time," Devon said, waving a hand. "I'm in no hurry."

Malcolm eyed him curiously. "What about your business in Edinburgh?"

"For now, I'll send a letter and postpone the meeting. I'm certain they will not mind." Of course, Devon's brother Marcus *would* mind. But Marcus was in London, and by the time he discovered that Devon had changed the meeting date, there would be precious little he could do about it. "I cannot leave without that ring."

Malcolm seemed to agree, but before he could say anything, another group of workmen came clomping into the hall to add to the growing stack of boxes.

"Bloody hell, what is Fiona doing?" Malcolm asked.

Devon didn't know or care. He just wondered if Kat would be attending. He hadn't realized he'd spoken the words aloud until he saw Malcolm's lowered brow.

"I don't know if she'll come or not; she's funny about these things. But why are you asking? Are you wishful to see her?"

Devon was wishful to see her, taste her, touch her, and do everything in between. But all he said to Malcolm was "I was just wondering, that's all."

"Hm," Malcolm said, uncertain how to read the casual statement. Certainly there was a spark of interest there, only . . . was it good interest, or self-absorbed masculine interest?

For Kat's sake, he hoped it was not the latter. "It would surprise me if she attended. She's not usually one for such things."

Another stack of heavy boxes were being unloaded and he had to move so that the servants could clean the floor. When it came to getting things organized for an event, Fiona became a little general, ordering people about and making lightning-fast decisions.

His heart swelled a little at the thought. Lately, he'd caught her looking at him in a sad way, as if debating a horrible, difficult decision. Was she on the verge of deciding she'd had enough, that their marriage wasn't worth fighting for?

Malcolm wiped a hand over his tired eyes. The wager had been a horrid, foolish idea and had alienated them even further. He wasn't even sure if he really wanted to win.

Throat thick, he waved a hand at Devon. "I won't be able to play billiards this evening. Fiona has assigned us all a list of duties, and I must see to it that the library is readied."

"Is there anything I can do?"

"Just stay out of Fiona's way. She's a tyrant when it comes to these things."

Devon bowed. "That, I can do. In fact, I'll begin now."

Malcolm managed a smile, answering St. John's further comments as best as his aching soul would allow. Eventually Devon excused himself and Malcolm watched him go, wondering what had the lad in such a merry mood.

Well, Malcolm hoped Devon enjoyed it while he could. God knew that the second he fell in love, his happiness would be limited.

Sighing heavily, Malcolm quit the great hall and retreated to the peacefulness of his library.

Kat awoke with a pleasant, satiated feeling. It had been so long since she'd felt that way that she had to stop and think of the cause. As she stretched, her muddled morning mind stretching along with her, her ankle became entangled in something. She bent down to free herself and saw it was a strip of a white silk scarf.

Her cheeks heated as her memory came flooding back. She and Devon had made love in this very bed. And not just love, but exquisite, breathtaking love. Her breasts tingled with the memory of his hands, his mouth, of the way he'd tasted her and the power of his body over hers.

She shivered and gathered a pillow close, snuggling her cheek against it. If she breathed deeply enough, she could still smell him, the faint scent of sandalwood clinging to her sheets.

There was a knock before the door opened and Annie came in carrying something over her arm, Simon and Hamish following her. They were carrying the large brass tub and arguing about something, though they did break off their bickering long enough to wish her a good morning.

"Up, ye sleepyhead!" Annie called out merrily. "Ye've a bath to take and measurements to take afore I cut the cloth for yer gown."

Kat started to sit upright, but then remembered that she was as naked as the day she was born. Belatedly she snatched up the cover and held it before her.

Simon and Hamish were still arguing in heated whispers about a meeting of some sort, and had missed her error. But Annie's eyes widened, her gaze seeking and then finding the discarded night rail pooled on the floor. That sent Annie scurrying, admonishing the men to begin fetching the pails of water as soon as it was hot. She whisked them from the room and closed the door.

"Och, Miss Kat, ye went and fergot yer night rail. 'Tis on the floor." Annie placed Kat's old ball gown over the back of a chair and went to collect the forgotten night rail.

Kat held the covers a bit tighter. "I, ah, got very hot last night. So I took it off and threw it on the floor. I meant to pick it up, but I slept in."

"Hmph." Annie's gaze scrutinized her features. "I canno' fer the life o' me believe ye were so hot that ye took off yer rail. 'Twas cool last night after the rain."

Kat didn't know what to answer, so instead she

glanced at the old gown and said, "I'd forgotten about the ball."

Annie stopped, astonishment on her face. "How can ye say that? 'Tis to be a grand affair."

"I know, I know! I'm just a little—" What was the word? In lust? She certainly wasn't in love, that would require . . . well, it would require a man who was capable of caring about one for more than a two-month period.

A little of her happiness dimmed. He would leave soon, and she needed to remember that, first and foremost. Her heart sank as she realized how soon he would be gone. "I am looking forward to the ball." If nothing else, it might well be one of her last chances to see him, talk to him, laugh with him.

Ever.

Somehow, before this moment, the enormity of that fact had escaped her. In a way, she'd used it as a shield to protect her from caring too much. But somehow she had allowed her heart to become entangled. She loved him. With all her heart, she loved him.

The realization stole her breath. Tears threatened to clog her throat. Good God, when had that happened?

She loved a man who had plainly told her that he would not, could not love her.

Now what would she do? She had thought being with him was a safe venture. Safe because he wasn't the staying kind, safe because he hadn't once tried to pretend that he was something he was not. Now she realized that those facts had merely made him more dangerous.

"Ye should be excited," Annie chatted on, "for 'twill be a fine ball. Now come, listen to what I have planned fer yer gown."

Annie began to talk and Kat forced herself to smile, though she felt far from it.

It wasn't quite so difficult to really smile once she heard Annie's idea for the gown. The housekeeper had outdone herself. She would use the straw silk borrowed from the saved curtain linings to make a slashed overdress with puffed sleeves and decorate it with no fewer than eight tiny, hand-sewn rosettes of blue silk from Kat's old ball gown. Annie would then use the remaining blue silk as insets in the sleeves and for the petticoat, which would be revealed in the slashes on the overdress. The overall effect would be simply beautiful and, when combined with Kat's reddish hair, breathtaking.

At least when Devon saw Kat for the last time, she wouldn't be wearing a gown smudged with soot. She lifted her chin a little. Whatever else she did, she would not let him see how much she cared. This time, she would keep her pride intact, no matter the cost.

She caught sight of Annie's speculative gaze and hurried to paste a smile back on her lips. "Annie, it will be a lovely gown."

Annie beamed. " 'Tis glad I am to hear that ye think so, Miss Kat. Ye know, ye look a mite flushed." Annie laid her hand across Kat's brow. "Are ye taking an ague?"

Kat shook her head. " 'Tis excitement, that's all." And not just over the ball.

"Hm. Well, 'tis to the bath wid ye and then we'll see how ye're feeling." Annie went to the wardrobe and fished about for one of Kat's robes. "Here, put this on. Ye don't need to be getting cold afore ye soak in the tub."

A clattering in the hallway preceded Simon and Hamish's reentry. They carried two large steaming buckets, which they tipped into the brass tub. "One more trip will do it," Hamish said, his gaze fixed on Kat.

"Mornin' Miss Kat," Simon said, eyeing her even more closely than Hamish.

There was something odd in the way they looked at her, but Annie didn't give them time to say anything. She sent them to fetch more water while she straightened the room. Finally the tub was filled to the brim, and Annie sent the lads on their way.

Annie went to the tub and added some scent, then dipped her elbow into the water. "Perfect! Come along, now. Into the tub wid ye."

Kat didn't wait. She gratefully slid into the lavender-scented water. Perhaps her troubles would melt away if she just stayed here. Surely Annie would bring her food and the lads would keep the glasswork going . . . Why, she could stay here for the rest of her life and no one would ever know. Kat's lip trembled. Who really needed her anyway?

Stop that, she told herself. *You are being silly.* And she was, but somehow she couldn't help it. Her heart was trying valiantly not to show its cracks, and all the while it was trembling, falling to pieces. To stop from thinking too much, she scrubbed herself thoroughly, trying to rub away the hurts. It helped . . . a little.

Annie leaned out the window. "By the saints, 'tis that Sassenach of yours."

Devon? Here? Now what was she to do? If she saw him and he guessed how she felt, it would ruin everything together. But if she didn't see him, he would know something was amiss.

Which was better? Kat took a deep breath. She could do a lot of things, but pretend she wasn't affected by him wasn't one of them. Not here, or now, anyway. If she waited until the ball to see him, at least then she'd be girded in the wondrous ball gown. She would smile and laugh and dance, and no one would know her secret.

Taking a deep breath, she pushed her wet hair behind her ears and then sank into the water up to her neck. "Annie, please inform Mr. St. John I will see him at the ball and not a second before."

To say that Devon took the news of Kat's defection well would be a misstatement. He didn't. He'd been at first incredulous, and then irritated, and at last angry that she could so calmly put him off when he'd come to see her time and again.

While he was *not* in love, their night together had proven something to him. It had shown him that passion did not burn itself out, that it could satisfy even as it left one hungry for more. Never in all his days had he ever had such a delightful encounter with a woman. And if he'd had his normal reaction, once having sampled her bounty, he would be itching to be off, looking for another challenge. But this time, all he wanted was to be with Kat. More and more.

And not just physically. While riding there, he'd thought of no fewer than three things he wanted to tell her. One thought involved a nice trail ride that had a pretty little abbey at the end of it. It was a tip from one of the grooms at Kilkairn and sounded as if it might be just the thing for a lazy afternoon. The second thing he wanted to tell her was how Murien had been in the stable when he'd left. She'd been loudly demanding a horse, saying she wished to ride, too. The grooms had all been skeptical and had not hurried to meet her demands. One old groom, however, had agreed to saddle a mount for her. And he had—a pathetic old slug with a lumpy gait and a bad tendency to bite.

Devon had been hard-pressed not to laugh. But he'd made certain he wasn't around when she got ready to mount the horrid thing. He didn't want Murien tagging along when he came to visit Kat.

The third thing he thought to tell Kat was about the talisman ring and how it had gone missing. And that he could not, in all honesty, leave until it was found.

He had wondered if she would be glad, but if he agreed to her wishes he'd have to wait until the ball to discuss anything with her. It was most irritating.

It was ludicrous to wait for such a time—there were still four more days until that blasted ball. Four days of no Kat. Surely she hadn't meant it . . .

But a visit to the clearing proved him wrong. So

did a second visit. And a third. All he got from his visits was the sight of Kat's back as she whisked out of sight, and the baleful stares of her lads.

Frustrated, but refusing to make a spectacle of himself, Devon returned to Kilkairn. Preparations for the ball continued and to fill the suddenly empty hours, Devon began to assist Malcolm in the list of duties Fiona had assigned him. Devon had his servants leave the relative comfort of the inn where they'd been staying and spend the better portion of each day at Kilkairn, helping in whatever way was needed. Though he stayed busy, Devon's mood darkened with each passing hour. Without Kat, everything seemed . . . dull and lifeless. The moods of his companions were not much better. Fiona was in a tizzy, Malcolm was strangely quiet, and Murien looked as if she'd like to drag Devon off to the nearest broom closet and divest him of his clothing.

The evening before the ball, he took a long lonely ride on Thunder, conveniently missing dinner. He returned to his room well after the sun had set, muddy and tired and feeling almost despondent.

Sighing, Devon removed his coat and crossed to the window. He pulled back the curtain and stared into the distance. Cool air leaked in around the casement, making him glad for the fire, smoky as it was. The night was especially bright, lit by the full moon, the stars twinkling all around. It would have been a magical night for a midnight ride.

But only if he had Kat to share it with. God, what a coil. His last few days had been ruined. Blast it, he was locked here in a ramshackle castle with a warring couple and a marriage-minded shrew while the woman he—

He caught himself. The woman he what? Liked? Enjoyed? Lusted after? What was she? His mind seemed unable to define it, to define her.

He sighed and rested his forehead against the damp windowpane. Deep in the woods, a faint light twinkled, a glimpse of golden warmth.

He couldn't seem to stop thinking of her. Of the feel of her lips beneath his, of the fullness of her in his arms. He loved women, loved their foibles, their airs, their frivolity. They amused him, but none had ever engaged him on a serious level.

But with Kat, he found himself wondering who she was behind that enigmatic exterior. She simply did not play by the known Rules of Womanhood. She didn't flirt. She didn't laugh at his sallies unless they caught her by surprise. She didn't try to impress him or engage his interest in any way whatsoever.

She was completely devoid of the artifices most women used. Artifices that had, until very recently, amused him in a mild sort of way.

What was strange was that the more he saw of Kat, the less amused he was by what he had once considered natural feminine wiles. In fact, he was finding Murien's company onerous. What bothered him most was the realization that, had he met Murien two weeks ago, he would have been completely taken by her. At least for a month or so.

He sighed, pushing the curtain back further, to rest his shoulder against the window frame, feeling the chill of his own chamber.

He'd wager Kat's cottage was warm. There was something almost magical about that place, something uniquely comforting and homelike. Somehow, Kat had turned her cottage into everything that Kilkairn Castle was not. He sighed. Once he left Kilkairn, every day would feel like today. Every day he'd smile and talk and nod and feel utterly alone. Being with Kat had spoiled him.

He dropped the curtain and turned away. The truth was that Kat Macdonald intrigued him in a way that no other woman had. Not because he was attracted to her, but because she was a challenge, a unique, undiscovered source of amusement to his dull spirit. It had been a long while since he'd had to put forth an effort to win a woman to his bed. And such a woman, too.

He removed his boots, tossing them to one side. He had just reached for his cravat when something clinked against the window.

Devon whirled toward the sound. It came again, only with more force. Bloody hell, someone was trying to get his attention by throwing pebbles against his window. Could it be Kat? Had she missed him, too? No one else would go to such lengths to gain his attention. Malcolm would knock at the door, Fiona would never have cause, and Murien . . . well, he rather thought Murien would just walk right in and climb into his bed. And if he was not cautious, that is exactly what she would do. There was a line of brass beneath her silver polish. He could almost taste it.

Another rock hit the window, this one larger. It

clunked against the glass and fell away. It had to be Kat.

Grinning, he threw open the window and leaned out—*thunk*. A rock hit him in the forehead, and sent him staggering backward, into the long curtains that surrounded his bed.

He fell against the mattress and then lay there, blinking rapidly. Bloody hell, did she want to kill him? He straightened, carefully touching his forehead, where a bump was already swelling.

"Sassenach? Are ye there?" a heavily masculine voice called out.

It wasn't Kat after all. Irritation warred with disappointment. With one hand covering his aching forehead, Devon climbed back to his feet and looked out his window. In the courtyard below stood a huge, hulking Scotsman, one of Kat's lads, no doubt, though it was too dark to see which. "Who the hell are you?" Devon demanded. "You almost killed me!"

"Not a'purpose," the giant said in a mild tone. "'Twas a small rock."

Devon finally recognized the voice. It was the redoubtable Simon. Devon gingerly rubbed his forehead. "What do you want?"

"I came to see if ye'd like to wash a whisker wid us."

"Wash a whisker." What the hell did that mean? "I'm afraid I cannot wash my whiskers right this moment since I have none—"

"Come, Sassenach! The Lion and Boar has some fine ale, they do. I'll even foist the rowdies fer it."

Devon placed his hands on the windowsill and

leaned out so he could see his visitor a bit more clearly. The man didn't appear drunk, for he wasn't swaying on his feet, nor did his words sound anything other than crisp and to the point. "Ale, eh? Is that what 'washing your whiskers' means?"

"What else could it mean?" Simon asked, apparently astounded.

"What else indeed. May I ask why you're offering this wonderful invitation?"

"Because we thought ye'd like a pint."

"We?"

"The others are already at the inn. I daresay we'll be hard pressed to catch up wid 'em, especially Hamish. He seems solemn, but he can outdrink any man ye care t' name."

Devon's head ached from the rock, and his heart ached from the last few wretched days. But somewhere in the back of his mind, he could hear Malcolm's voice, suggesting that the best way to win over Kat was to win over her lads.

It was an unspoken right of passage for a man who wanted to judge another man's mettle, to invite him to partake, and then see who could withstand the torture with the least effect. And Devon recognized the aged ploy now.

But this contest of manly wills had a purpose—to win the trust of Kat's lads. If all he had to do was drink with a roomful of rowdies to win some time with Kat, he'd do it every night for a year.

"Very well," he called down. "I'll come. Wait for me there."

Simon's grin was evident even from upstairs. "Do

that, Sassenach, but dinna keep me waitin' long. I've a powerful thirst as 'tis."

"I won't." Devon started to close the window, but his gaze fell on the rock that had rolled to the edge of the bed. With a faint smile, he picked it up and then, after taking a second to judge the distance, he tossed it back out the window.

A faint grunt of pain and then a loud curse filled the air.

Grinning a little, Devon pulled on his boots and coat and headed out the door.

Chapter 18

I don't know how my son came to do such a thing, pinching a kitchen maid. I know he has never seen me do such a thing. I've never taken up with anything under a chambermaid in my life.

Duke of Draventon
to his best friend, Lord Rutherford,
while walking with that gentleman
into the gallery at the House of Lords

"Bloody hell," Devon said woozily. "I've died."

"Not yet," came a sharp feminine voice.

"Kat?" He started to lift his head, then groaned and dropped it back on the mound of pillows holding it. The movement made his stomach clench.

"Lie still," she ordered.

As if he could do else. "My head . . . did someone hit me?"

"The only thing that hit you was the brandy in the bottom of a bottle."

She sounded angry. He opened his eyes again, but had to close them right away. "The room is spinning."

"Put your foot on the floor."

"What?"

Two capable hands picked up his foot and plopped it on the floor. After a moment things settled a bit and he was able to say, "That worked."

"So will this," she said. "Sit up and drink it."

It took every ounce of effort that he possessed, but he lifted himself on his elbow and realized he was on a settee in a small room, most likely at Kat's cottage. His head felt swollen to twice its normal size, and his body ached everywhere that didn't feel ill.

Kat's face swam before his eyes, and for a second he forgot his woes and said the first words that came to mind. "I love you."

She had just picked up a glass holding some murky-colored stuff, but she paused, her clear eyes meeting his not-so-clear ones. "What did you say?"

What had he said? He blinked, trying to remember. Then his brow cleared. "I said I love you." Damn, but his memory was good, even when drunk.

"I see. Here." She placed the glass in his hand.

He was suddenly thirsty, so he took what she offered and brought it to his mouth. But before the rim could touch his parched lips, the scent assailed his nostrils, and he smiled. "This smells like a lemon tart."

"It's a tonic and it tastes horrid, so don't get your hopes up."

"Horrid?"

"Horrid."

He put the glass down, though it took him some

time to make it land on the floating table. "Don't want horrid tonics. Not today, anyway. Maybe tomorrow when I'm more the thing and horrid tonics won't make me want to vo—"

The glass was rudely thrust back into his hand. "Now." Irritation colored Kat's voice. "I haven't all day, Sassenach. Drink your tonic or get on your horse and go back to Kilkairn now."

The thought of riding a horse made his stomach queasy again. He waved a hand. "No horses."

"Then drink the tonic."

Devon held out his hand, and the glass was once again placed in his grip. He peered up at her through his lashes. "You sound angry."

"Imagine that," she said, waiting for him to finish the horrid beverage. Finally, after much hacking and wheezing, he managed to choke down most of it.

He wiped his mouth on his sleeve. "Bloody hell, what's in that? Horse urine?"

She took the nearly empty glass. "No, but only because I didn't have the time to collect any."

He blinked, and she could see that her wit was wasted. Sighing, she pulled the covers back to his chin. "Go to sleep."

"Oh I will," he assured her in a thick voice, the tonic beginning to do its magic. "I will go to sleep for you, though I'd rather sleep *with* you." His eyes cracked open, and he offered a devilish smile. "Can I convince you to join me on the settee?"

"There's not enough room," she said, her heart suddenly pounding.

"There's plenty of room if you lay atop me." He moved so that he was flat on his back. "See? You'd fit just fine."

"I have work to do today. Now no more talking."

"Very well," he mumbled. "I will sleep and sleep and sleep . . . and . . . sleep . . . an—" His head lolled to one side, his long lashes cresting his cheeks.

Kat sat back on her heels, her knees unable to support her. She could scarcely believe it; Devon had said he loved her. Of course he was drunk, but still . . . had he meant it? And even if he did, would it last more than his usual month or two, if that?

Whatever he felt, her love for him would continue forever. A wave of loneliness struck her, and she had to wipe away a tear.

Simon stuck his head in the window. "How's our Sassenach?" Behind him she could just make out Donald's and Neal's concerned faces.

"He's drunk."

An awed expression came over Simon's face. "Do ye know that it took over seven pints to get him like that? Even Hamish cannot drink so much."

"What's more," Donald added, "he's not even a Scotsman."

Neal pulled Donald away from the window, so he could have a better view. " 'Tis a record at the pub. We carved his name over the door."

Kat wondered if any man truly grew up. "Thank you for that wonderful information. If he casts up his accounts, I'll let you think about that while you're cleaning it up." Kat gathered the glass and stood.

"Come back in about three hours and you can return him to Kilkairn."

"Aye, Miss Kat," Simon said. "I'll take him meself."

"I'll help," Neal offered eagerly. In the background, Donald nodded.

That was the worst part, Kat decided. Whatever had happened last night, her lads were completely won over. Devon St. John had done more than drink his fill at the inn, he had also cajoled her men into believing him a man of epic proportions, or, as Simon had put it when he'd tenderly carried the Sassenach into the cottage that morning, " 'Tis a good one, is St. John. The lads an' I have promised to teach him the glasswork oncet he's feelin' better."

With that, Kat realized she'd lost her only allies in her attempt to keep her heart in check. Thank God Annie was still on her side, else she would have been quite alone.

The thought cast her down, and it was with a heavy heart that she finally left Devon sleeping on the settee and made her way to the workshop.

Devon waved goodbye to Simon and Neal and . . . well, whoever the other one was, then wandered into the castle, his head still swollen, though thanks to Kat's tonic, the world had ceased to tilt.

Malcolm had been wrong that winning the lads was the way to Kat's heart. Devon had won the lads, but somehow that effort had only seemed to infuriate their mistress until she would barely speak to him.

Or was she upset about something else? He tried

to think what it might be, but could not hit upon anything. Perhaps he'd said something, but his memory was somewhat fuzzy.

Sighing, Devon picked his way through the sumptuous preparations for the ball and then found his bedchamber, glad he didn't run into anyone who might require him to speak in a complete sentence. Once Devon reached his room, he fell into his bed, hoping to fall back asleep. He was too tired to think. Somehow, he'd find a way to solve all his problems, but not now.

As soon as he closed his eyes, it seemed that Tilton was there, shaking him.

"I'm awake, I'm awake," Devon mumbled.

"Excellent, sir. Perhaps you could prove that by opening your eyes."

Devon rolled onto his back. "What time is it?"

"After seven, sir. I ordered a bath so you could prepare for the ball."

Devon lifted his head to see a tub sitting in one corner of the room, already filled. "It can't be that late."

"Oh, but it is. Shall I open the curtains and prove it? The sunset is quite brilliant this evening."

"No! Do not open the curtains. My brain would shatter if I had to see a drop of sunlight." Devon collected himself and swung his feet over the edge of the bed. He waited for nausea or dizziness, but none came. Kat's tonic had indeed helped; he felt much better. He managed to bathe and dress without too much fuss and allowed Tilton to assist him into his formal attire.

"Any word on the talisman ring?"

Tilton shook his head. "I don't understand it, sir. You offered a substantial reward. I fully expected someone to come forth with some sort of information, but no one seems to know a thing."

"Well, keep looking."

"Yes, sir."

"Thank you, Tilton." Sighing, Devon prepared to join his hosts, though all he really wanted to do was find Kat and make things right.

Soon, he told himself. Very soon.

The Strathmore ball was an unusual event. Not only was it being held out of town in the midst of the season, but it was also being held at His Lordship's ancestral home. It was the first truly formal entertainment at Kilkairn in over one hundred and fifty years.

Added to that, the ball was given in honor of Mr. Devon St. John, and all of Edinburgh society was anxious to meet such a wealthy, eligible bachelor.

Fiona had planned everything carefully. She'd rented large pots of flowers in varying hues of violet and blue, so many that the room looked like a garden. Long silver swaths of material floated down the ancient walls, reminding one of waterfalls and reflecting the light of a thousand candles. She'd had the servants make bowers over each doorway and had threaded even more flowers there.

She'd also ordered ices, a large quantity of punch, and no fewer than three hundred iced cakes which were to be distributed at the first ring of midnight, each baked with a favor hidden inside. Most of the favors were worthless—small pairs of dice, a trumpery bit of jewelry, or some such nonsense—but three cakes had real jewels in them. The guests were already excitedly buzzing about the coming treat, many hovering over the table, wondering which cakes held the prizes.

The ball was bound to be a smashing success.

Devon caused quite a stir when he finally appeared. Fiona had been thorough in inviting all of society, and the great hall sparkled with beautiful people. Appearing somewhat harried, she introduced him to the guests. Devon instantly felt like a prize poodle on display, especially when he saw the avaricious gazes of the many unmarried women who had attended.

What was worse was that if Fiona had latched on to his left arm, Murien had positively stuck herself on to his right. He was most uncomfortable, especially when he read the possessive note in Murien's voice.

Devon decided to let them have their way—for now, at least. He was far too busy looking for Kat to worry about Murien, anyway.

Kat, meanwhile, was still at the cottage. The dress Annie had made was beautiful; straw colored silk over sky blue . . . the colors made Kat's hair gleam. She'd been astonished when she'd first caught a glimpse of herself in the mirror for Annie had altered the current style just enough to compliment her full figure.

She stood before the mirror in the sitting room

now, trying hard not to glance at the clock over and over. She'd thought to go at ten, but Simon had not yet brought the cart. "Where is Simon? I'm going to be late."

" 'Tis fashionable to be late," Annie said calmly as she pinned a blue silk flower in Kat's hair. "He'll be here soon. Just ye wait."

"If he's much longer, I shall saddle Trusty and ride over there myself."

Annie snorted. "Ye wouldn't dare! Not after I spent so much time a-stitchin' that gown."

Kat sighed. She really shouldn't go. People would talk; they always did and Kat hated it. But this was her last chance to see Devon. Perhaps ever.

Her heart pained her at the thought and she realized that she'd been right not to spend any more time with him other than these few moments in public. She was no longer in command of her own heart; she hadn't been since she'd realized she loved him.

A knock sounded on the cottage door and Annie bustled to open it. Simon stood on the stoop.

Kat blinked. He was dressed in his Sunday best suit of broadcloth, his hair meticulously slicked back from his forehead, his skin scrubbed fresh and clean.

"St. George's dragon," she said softly, blinking.

He reddened. "Aye, I look a fool. But Annie said 'twould be nice if'n ye had a way to the ball other than the old cart, so the lads and I got ye a surprise." He stepped back and jerked a thumb over his shoulder.

Kat peered past him into the dark. Neal and Hamish stood awkwardly beside an old carriage. The two lads were dressed in their Sunday best to match Simon's. Kat raised her brows, first at her lads, then at the carriage. "Isn't that Dr. Lambert's?"

"Aye," Simon answered. "The doctor loaned it on the condition that the lads and I help raise his new barn next week."

Annie nodded her satisfaction. "Off with ye now, Miss Kat. Now ye've a carriage like a proper lady should."

Kat shook her head, her heart filled to overflowing. "Simon . . . Annie . . . I don't know what to say."

"Don't say a word," Simon pleaded. "This collar is about to choke me. Just climb in and let's be on our way fer we're already late."

Thus it was when Kat made her appearance at the Strathmore ball, it was to find Fiona already looking wan and pale, Malcolm nowhere in sight, and Devon surrounded by society beauties, with Murien purring along beside him, looking like the cat who ate the cream.

Though Kat had been expecting such a thing, it didn't make it any easier to witness. Especially since nothing had prepared her for the sight of Devon in his ballroom finery.

Dressed in black breeches that hugged his muscular legs, and a coat tailored to fit his broad shoulders without a wrinkle, he stood out among the more provincial dressers. He'd done little to his hair except comb it back, but one unruly lock hung over his forehead, giving him a slightly dissolute look.

Added to that were the faint shadows beneath his blue eyes and the look of impenetrable boredom that he was sporting, and he was easily the handsomest and most intriguing man in sight.

Kat paused at the door, suddenly wanting desperately to turn and run. It was ludicrous to make an appearance in such a lovely ball gown; she wasn't sure now why it had mattered. From the cold glances she was already receiving, she was a pariah no matter how she dressed.

As soon as she was identified, the rumors would begin yet again, and there would be more stares, more whispers, more innuendoes—the vicious circle never stopped. Her spirit quavered at the thought.

This was not the way she'd envisioned the night. She'd thought to make an impressive entrance of some sort. To be accepted where she never had been.

She wasn't sure now why she'd thought that . . . perhaps because by falling in love with Devon, she felt new. Fresh. And even lovely.

But now, facing the harsh stare of society, she had to wonder . . . was that an illusion too?

Heart heavy, she decided to make a hasty retreat, but before she could move, Malcolm suddenly materialized.

He didn't give her time to argue, but led her back inside, tucking her hand in the crook of his arm so she couldn't escape. "Where do you think you're going?"

"Home," she said flatly.

"But you look beautiful." He eyed her up and down, growing appreciation in his gaze. "Where did you get this gown? It's perfect for you."

"Annie made it."

"She's a wonder. One day I shall steal her from you and I will never eat poorly prepared food again."

"She's a miracle," Kat agreed. She knew what he was doing—making casual talk so she could regain her composure. She loved him for it, even though she wished he would just let her go.

"I didn't even know Annie could wield a needle. Yet another reason to prize her over all other women."

"Except one," Kat said softly.

Malcolm's gaze grew shadowed. He led her across the room, nodding at this acquaintance and then that. "Except one. At least have a bit of punch."

"But I—"

"It has ice in it that cost me a bloody fortune. The least you can do is drink some of it and pretend it tastes as good as it looks."

Kat had to smile. "Is Fiona driving you to ruin?"

"Oh no. I can stand the nonsense. I just wish—" He broke off, something crossing his face and then disappearing behind a bland smile. "At least let me complain. All good hosts do, you know. It's their way of casually dropping their costs into the conversation."

"Is that why they do it?"

"Lud, yes. See those large pots of violets by the door? Fiona ordered three hundred of them and they cost me five pounds each. What's horrid is that the flowers will be dead by morning and we don't even get to keep the bloody pots."

He found the refreshment table and procured a glass of punch, then handed it to her. "Well?" he said with a challenging look in his eye.

"It's wretched, but cold. Very cold."

"There. You've made my evening better already. As much as this blasted affair has cost me, I demand to get the maximum enjoyment out of it that I can, so thank you, most lovely of sisters, for drinking my punch and admiring my ice."

Kat returned the glass to him.

"More?"

"Oh no, thank you. Let's save some ice for your other guests."

"Very well, but at midnight, you must be in line to snatch up an iced cake. You could end up with a prize, you know."

She followed his gaze to the tables where the cakes were set. "Why is everyone standing around the table now? There is still almost forty minutes before the clocks will chime."

"Because some of the prizes settled to the sides and you can almost make out what prize is in which cake." He lowered his voice. "I'm going for the third cake in the fourth row. You can see a jewel of some sort sticking out of the bottom."

"You had the opportunity to see the cakes before anyone else, so I believe that is cheating. Are you certain you wish to compromise your values in such a way as to—"

"Malcolm—" came a deep voice. "And Miss Kat."

Kat knew who it was without even looking. Blast

it, it had been a trick. Malcolm had lured her into the room and then kept her busy until Devon could find them.

She closed her eyes and tried to move her heart back into place before turning and smiling. "Mr. St. John. How are you this evening?"

"My, that was frosty," Malcolm said, sending her a frown. "Perhaps you had too much of the icy punch." He glanced at Devon. "Have you come to claim Kat's hand for a dance?"

To her horror, she realized the band was playing a waltz. "I don't dance."

"Excellent," Devon said. "I'll teach you." He took her hand in his, Malcolm slipping away without so much as another word.

"You cannot learn to dance while at a ball!" Kat said desperately.

"Why not?"

"Because I'll look a fool. And you will, too."

"Nonsense. I'm an excellent teacher. Just put your arm here, and your hand here." He placed one of her hands on the tip of his shoulder and held the other one loosely. Immediately all the unease in Kat's stomach grew warmer.

"Good!" he said, placing his other hand on her waist. A shiver immediately traveled through her, though she resolutely ignored it.

His eyes glinted into hers. "Now comes the easy part; all you have to do is follow me."

"What?"

"Just follow me," he repeated.

"But I—"

The music swelled, and he began to move. Aware that now, in reality, every eye was indeed upon her, Kat struggled to keep up, desperately counting. Several times she stumbled, and once she went left when he went right.

He sighed, his breath brushing her hair. "I can see we're going to have to work on this."

"There is no need," she said stiffly, wishing miserably she'd never come. What had she been thinking? She should have refused. It would take more drastic measures to escape now. Perhaps she could fall to the floor and have a fit; she'd once witnessed just such an occurrence at a ball years ago and the unfortunate woman had been immediately spirited away. But apparently Kat's boldness was back at the cottage along with her comfortable clothes.

How she hated that every eye was upon them. By now everyone knew who she was, and their entire dance would be scrutinized, analyzed, conjectured about, and exaggerated until it didn't resemble the truth at all.

"Kat." Devon's voice was close to her ear. "Relax, my sweet. Trust me to get us through this maze of horrid dancers."

She looked into his eyes. "What does trust have to do with dancing?"

"When you follow someone in a dance, they have to direct you because you are dancing backward and you cannot see where you are going. I've often thought men do not realize how difficult it must be to relax and let a partner you sometimes barely know lead you through a maze of dancers. But you and I, we do know one another. And if there is one thing we do have, it is trust."

She thought about this. Perhaps . . . perhaps he was right. Things had changed when she realized that being closer to him did have a cost—her own heart. But that was not his fault. He'd been honest with her from the beginning.

She met his gaze and found him regarding her, a quizzical gleam in his eyes. A smile was wrung from her at his hopeful expression. "I do trust you."

"I know," he said simply. "Relax, my lovely Kat. Let me navigate for a while." He pulled her a little closer. "Meanwhile, you rest."

She did as he suggested, though after a moment, it dawned on her that those dancing around them had a good foot between them while she and Devon had mere inches. "I don't think you're supposed to hold me this close."

He rested his cheek against her hair. "But I like it."

She was quiet a moment more, then she lifted her head to ask, "Why do men always get to lead?"

His lips quivered. "I've often wondered that myself. Perhaps we can trade off. Would you like to lead for a bit?"

Would she? She thought a moment, then nodded. "Certainly."

He smiled and let her begin leading. She wished she could say she was good at it, but she wasn't. Twice she ran them into another couple, and once they barely missed a low table by the door.

But eventually she began to understand how to do it, and she led them without incident. As she relaxed, she became aware of the feel of his chest against hers. Of his hand on her waist. Of being surrounded by him.

The music swelled and pulsed, yet somehow they were in the center of a bubble of pure bliss, a slow heat simmering about them.

Kat let herself drift against him. It was heavenly, being held like this.

Their bodies brushed, then touched, then stayed there.

A deep languor arose, and Kat closed her eyes, letting the music take them where it would.

They went slower and slower, lost in the tug of heat that rose and ebbed between their bodies. Everything else ceased to be. It was just the two of them and no one else. Finally, his arms encircled her and his mouth moved from her hair, to her cheek, to her mouth . . .

Kat was lost. She kissed him back as passionately as he kissed her, reveling in the feel of Devon, her Devon, around her, with her. His hands moved across her back, then lower to cup her bottom intimately. It was then that she realized that the music had come to a halt. As had all the talking.

In fact, the entire room was deafeningly silent.

Kat opened her eyes, breaking the kiss, stepping away so that Devon was no longer touching her. All around them stood the other guests.

Some were smiling.

Some were plainly scandalized.

Some looked too shocked to do more than stare with mouths agape. Dear Lord, but they'd all seen

Devon kissing her. Worse, he'd had his hands on her arse.

Kat caught sight of Murien's furious face, Fiona standing beside her, white-faced and grim.

Good God, what had she done? Kat didn't dare look at Devon; it had to be his worst nightmare. She turned toward him, her gaze locked on the top button of his waistcoat. "Do not say a word," she said in a low voice. "Let me—"

"Katherine."

Malcolm's voice broke over her. She turned to find him next to her.

He looked hard at Devon. "It appears as if this ball has a purpose after all."

"Malcolm, no—" Kat began.

He threw up his hand. "This is a conversation better had in private. Shall we retreat to the library?"

She nodded miserably, wishing she could find something to say to Devon. Meanwhile all around them came the whispers. They were low now, but Kat knew how this part went . . . first were the tiny whispers, followed by the slightly audible murmurs of disapproval. Next came the accusations. Those hit with gale force, ripping reputation and fate alike.

How had she let this happen? Kat had to find a way to fix things, a way to keep Devon St. John from being harmed by their mistakes.

It was with a sinking heart she walked into the library, Devon behind her, as Malcolm closed the door and turned to face them.

Chapter 19

I love happy endings. I had one myself, you know.

Lord Rutherford to his lady love,
Mrs. Montesque-Drumme,
while watching the fireworks at Vauxhall Gardens

"Pssh." Malcolm rubbed his neck and looked at his sister and best friend. "I dinna know where to begin. You know better than to do such a thing."

They didn't say a word, each avoiding the other's gaze. Malcolm wondered what he should do. "What happened out there? You two were supposed to be dancing."

"We were dancing," Kat said, her cheeks pink. "At first."

Devon nodded. "I was letting Kat lead for a while—"

"You let Kat lead?" Bloody hell, what was wrong with the man?

"Aye. And somehow, it just felt . . . good. So I kissed her and, well, that felt even better. So I suppose I forgot where I was and—" Devon raked a hand through his hair.

There was no mistaking the husky timbre of St. John's voice or the slanted glance Kat threw his way.

They were lovers. Malcolm had suspected as much, but the heated looks along with the passionate kiss and intimate hold he'd witnessed between them on the dance floor proved it beyond any doubts.

Perhaps he should—The door flew open and Murien stood in the doorway, Fiona peering anxiously over her shoulder.

Murien walked in, her hand fisted about an object. "Do not continue this farce."

"Farce?" Malcolm scowled. He'd never liked Fiona's sister, and every day he was coming to like her less if that was possible.

Murien's lip curled as she looked at Kat. "You are trying to trap Devon into marriage. Well, I won't stand for it."

Devon's frown was quicker than Kat's. "You don't know what you're talking about. Kat has never tried to entrap me or anyone else."

"She is not an innocent. Nor is she without fault. I think you should put her to the test."

"What test?" Devon asked, his irration mounting.

Murien held out her hand. There, on her palm, lay the St. John talisman ring.

Fiona gasped. "Murien! Where did you get that?"

"Thank God it has been found." Devon started forward, but Murien's fingers closed over it.

Malcolm had to unclench his jaw to speak. "You stole that out of St. John's room."

Murien regarded him with a triumphant sneer. "Only after I saw you, dear brother, borrowing it."

Malcolm's face heated. He glanced at Devon, then shrugged. "I just wanted Kat to see it."

Fiona looked from him to her sister. "Murien, you know St. John was searching for that ring. There is no excuse for what you did."

"I didn't steal it. I was going to return it to St. John as soon as—" She closed her lips over the words.

Malcolm unclenched his jaw. "You were waiting for the ring to prove its magic, weren't you? But nothing happened, so you kept it, waiting."

Murien's face flooded with color. "Don't laugh! You took it to Kat, but nothing happened when it was on her finger, either."

"Nay," Malcolm said, eyeing Murien's closed fist with interest. "Something *did* happen."

Devon's gaze went to Kat. She flushed and shrugged. "It grew warm, that's all."

Murien's expression tightened. "Warm? How warm?"

"Very. So much so that I—well, I could feel it inside."

"I don't understand." Murien peered at the ring. "I've held it and held it and it still feels cold. So cold that it makes my hand ache and—"

Fiona took the ring from Murien. "You owe St. John an apology." She crossed the room and handed the talisman ring to Devon. "Here you are, sir. I ask for forgiveness for the actions of my family."

Devon looked down at the ring. It lay against his palm, sparkling as if newly minted. That was one of the ring's odder characteristics—that it never appeared old, but always new.

Always new. The words echoed softly through Devon's mind. Would that he could keep his feelings for Kat always new. Then he'd have no compunction about marrying her.

Marrying her. Good God, where had that come from?

Did he *want* to marry Kat? His fingers curled over the ring and he searched his heart for the answer. It was not long in coming . . . the truth was that he loved Kat Macdonald. And in a way he'd never thought himself capable.

Of the many women he'd once thought he'd loved only to become un-enamored of them in a remarkably short time, he'd never once awakened with the urgent need to tell them some news or thought. He'd never before wondered about their opinions on matters near to his heart or found himself storing up questions that might loosen some bit of information about them or their thoughts and feelings.

The reason his love for Kat was so different was that *he* had been different. In getting her to open to him, he'd opened his own heart and soul to her. And in doing so, he'd found a woman of gentleness and compassion that answered something deep inside him.

He loved Kat Macdonald. And suddenly he knew

it was forever. The ring began to warm, sending a tingle up his arm. He opened his fingers and looked at it in amazement. How could he have ever run from it? From his fate? "Thank you," he said quietly, and then slipped the ring into his waistcoat pocket.

"Murien," Fiona said, turning back to her sister. "Perhaps you should join the other guests. We will be along shortly."

"But I—"

"That is all, Murien." Fiona's voice rose in frosty dismissal.

Murien stiffened. "Fiona, do not speak to me that way."

"Why not? You *stole* St. John's ring."

"Yes but—Malcolm did the same thing."

Malcolm snorted. "All I did was borrow it for a wee hour, no more. You've kept it for days. Had Kat not so obviously won over St. John, you would have the ring with you still."

"Won over?" Murien laughed. "What do you mean by that?"

"You saw them kiss and . . . other things. Everyone did."

"Yes," Murien said, a faint aura of superiority on her face. "But it doesn't matter. You cannot make St. John marry Kat for that; she's already ruined. She has no reputation to protect."

Kat's face flooded with color. Devon wanted nothing more than to pull her into his arms, but something about the stiff set of her shoulders halted him. She had her pride, and she would not welcome a gesture from him that might be interpreted as pity. So instead he sent a cool glance toward Murien. "I don't know what you're speaking about."

"Oh? Let me tell you, then. When she was seventeen, Kat—"

"I know about that," Devon said dismissively. "I just meant that I don't know what you mean when you say she has no reputation to protect. She has a reputation for many things, including her excellent glasswork, as well as her kindness, capability, caring, and intelligence."

Kat looked at him, bemusement on her face. But Murien was not so quiet. She made an impatient noise. "I don't know what you're talking about, but it's—"

"None of your concern," Fiona said firmly. "Murien, it is time you left. Now."

"But I—"

"Either you go, or I will tell Mother how you embarrassed us all by sneaking into St. John's bedchamber and stealing a family heirloom."

"You wouldn't dare!"

"Try me. And you know what she'd do. You'd never see Edinburgh again, much less London."

There was a long moment of silence. Murien looked resentfully from Fiona to Devon. "I suppose there isn't any need for me to stay, is there?"

"No," Malcolm said flatly.

"None at all," Devon added. "Even if the St. John talisman ring began to glow red-hot with your name printed on the side, I would never marry you."

Her face flushed a dull red, but she kept her head

high. "Very well. I will leave." She turned, but then paused. "Of course, that means that you have lost your wager, Fiona. And your marriage. I hope you're happy."

With those bitter words, she swept from the room, slamming the door behind her.

Malcolm looked at Fiona. "I've never heard you speak so firmly to her before."

Fiona gave a faint shrug, her shoulders seemingly weighted. "It was overdue. I-I suppose I shall return to our guests as well." She made as if to turn, but Malcolm's hand closed over her arm.

"Stay," he said softly. "Please? Perhaps you can help me sort this out."

Her eyes widened, but after a moment, she nodded.

Devon knew the time had come. He and Kat both knew the rules of society, but when they were together, the rules seemed to vanish. They became unimportant in the face of other things, like passion, and companionship, and love.

He turned to Kat and took her hand in his. "Kat, this is not the way I'd thought to do this, but I want to make things right. For now and for always. Will you marry me?"

"No."

The word echoed in the silence that followed. Devon could not believe his ears.

She bent her head. "Devon, thank you but . . . I do not want to marry you."

A thick ache arose in his throat, and he suddenly realized that though he knew his feelings, he didn't know hers. Or he hadn't until now. He raked a hand through his hair, wondering what he was supposed to do now, feel now, think now.

She didn't love him. She had refused his offer of marriage without even pausing. It had cut to his soul, and he found that he could not breathe, could not think. Love was not supposed to be painful, was it? Or so despairing. Had he known it would hurt so, he would never have allowed it to happen.

Damn the talisman ring. This was the retribution he received for having lost it. Unless . . . what if the legacy of the ring was not, as he'd thought, marriage? What if it was merely the act of finding one's true love? And in that act, many things could happen, marriage being one of them.

Or heartbreak.

Malcolm blinked as if as bewildered at Kat's answer as Devon was. "Kat, lassie, do you know what you're saying?"

"I know," she said, her gaze locked on her hands, clasped in her lap.

A mirthless smile touched Devon's lips. He had feared that blasted ring all these years because he'd thought it represented the inevitable loss of his freedom. Now that he would have welcomed that loss, he found that it was all moonshine . . . An untruth. A fabled myth.

Good God, it did not bear thinking of. Just as he was ready to accept marriage—even to welcome it—it was denied to him. She had said no.

Devon looked at Kat. It was then that he saw what his pain had not allowed him to see before: Kat was crying. Not just a few droplets, either, but streaks of tears, trailing silently down her face. Her lip quivered, but no sound came out. Just a soft gasp of air as if she were drowning in her own sorrows.

Her pride, he realized. That was what was keeping them apart. It wasn't that she didn't love him at all.

Relief sang through his veins and he reached for one of his handkerchiefs, but Malcolm was quicker.

The Scotsman muttered a curse and dug a handkerchief from one of his pockets and then pressed the scrap of linen in his sister's hands. "Och, don't cry. If you feel that strongly about it, you don't have to marry St. John." He sent a hard glance at Devon. "Does she?"

Devon jaw tightened and his mind sprang into action. After a long moment, he shook his hand. "Actually, I believe she does have to marry me." His chest felt weighted, but he ignored it. If he did not say and do exactly the right thing in the next few moments, he stood to lose the love of his life. And that was what Katherine Macdonald was—the end and beginning of his life. He was just starting to realize that fact.

The real beauty of it was, he'd found his true love, his soul mate, and he hadn't needed the blasted ring at all. All he'd needed was to slow down enough to listen to his own heart. And his heart told him without question, without doubt, that Katherine Macdonald was the woman he'd been searching for for so long.

Life without her would be nothing but a long string of sad disappointments, missed laughter, and aching loneliness, and he'd already had enough of that to last a lifetime.

The problem was, though he was unwilling to face life without her, for some stubborn reason, she was all too willing to live life without him. Perhaps it was because she'd spent the years since her public humiliation telling herself she didn't want someone else, didn't need anyone else . . . but what she hadn't yet realized was that love wasn't about *needing* someone in your life. It was about *wanting* someone.

There was only one way he could fix it all—mend Kat's tattered reputation, quiet the gossips at Kilkairn Castle, and never again wonder if he could love someone forever.

Devon crossed his arms and rocked back on his heels. "Malcolm, I have been compromised and I demand satisfaction."

An explosive silence met this pronouncement. Devon didn't blame them; it was never something he'd ever thought to hear himself say.

Malcolm's brow lowered. "What are you saying, St. John?"

Devon turned to Kat. She sat still as a stone, hands tightly gripped in her lap, her cheeks pale. She'd managed to partially dry her eyes, Malcolm's handkerchief twisted between her fingers. "Kat, I hate to tell your brother our secrets, but 'tis necessary."

"Secrets?" She blinked up at him, her lashes spiked with wetness. "We have none."

"We've one or two. I just want you to know that 'tis necessary."

Her brow lowered and he could see she was trying to discern his meaning.

Meanwhile, he turned to Malcolm. "Prior to this, my reputation was spotless. Reparation must be made. I demand that Katherine Macdonald marry me."

Kat gasped. "You—but I—how could you—" She clamped her mouth closed and glared. "No," she said. "I will not do it."

"You must; you seduced me."

Malcolm's brows lowered. "Seduced? St. John, have a care what you're about."

"Your sister tempted me to run away and visit her," Devon said promptly.

Kat jumped to her feet. "I did no such thing!"

"Did you or did you not allow me into your bedchamber through the window?"

Her cheeks red as could be, she snapped, "Yes, but only because I feared you'd fall from the tree."

"But . . . if she was inside her room, how could she tempt you?" Malcolm asked, apparently bewildered.

"She was walking around in a green silk night rail beside an open window that had a very strategically placed tree beside it. How could I help myself?"

"How indeed," Malcolm murmured, comprehension finally dawning on his face. Fiona started to say something, but he caught her hand and held it to him. "Devon, I suppose you blame Kat for the tree's existence, as well."

"I believe she planted it by her window for that very purpose."

"That tree is three hundred years old," Kat sputtered.

"Ah ha! So you admit that the seduction was planned in advance."

Malcolm stifled a laugh, and even Fiona smiled.

But Kat just glared. "I admit to nothing except allowing you into my room. That was my only fault."

"Well, now," Malcolm said. "This is far more serious than I thought. Kat Macdonald, you admit to allowing Mr. St. John into your bedroom at night."

"Only once."

Devon nodded, then added, "She also locked all her windows and doors so that the only way into the house was by climbing the tree. That is how devious she was. She had to know that a challenge like that would only inflame a man more."

Malcolm tsked. "He's right. Lass, what were you thinking?"

"You've always told me I should lock my doors!"

"And leave your window open with a tree right beside it?"

"Well no, but—"

"Malcolm, as you can see, your sister has led me down a dark path. And I, in my innocence, followed like a lamb to the slaughter."

A tremor of a smile touched Malcolm's mouth. "Well, Kat. What have you to say for yourself?"

Kat planted her hands on her hips. "I have nothing to say! Not a blooming thing! St. John, I will not let you get away with this. You were the one who wanted to come into my room. And you were the one who wanted to tie me up with scarves and kiss me and—"

"Scarves?" Malcolm looked stunned.

Devon just smiled.

"Who tied who up with scarves?" Malcolm demanded.

"Devon tied me up. He's the one who—" She stopped, her brow lowering as she stared at Devon. "Wait a moment. You tricked me. You tricked me into confessing about— Oh! I see what you were— You scoundrel!"

He blinked innocently. "Me?"

"You made those outrageous allegations because you wanted me to admit to—oh!"

Devon came to stand before her, a question in his gaze. "I'm sorry I tricked you, but I thought it would be best if Malcolm knew how things stood between us."

"Aye," Malcolm said. "There's no question in my mind, either. You'll marry this man, Katherine Macdonald or I'll see to it that ye nev—"

"No," Devon said, taking her hand in his own. "She has a choice. I don't want a forced bride any more than she wants a forced groom. But if she wants a *willing* groom, then here I am."

Fiona gave a murmur of approval.

Kat's throat grew tight. He knew her so well, knew her fears and her pride. "I don't know, Devon. I don't wish to be hurt again."

"Love, the only way you can never hurt again is to stop living. And not even you with your stubborn pride and seven scowling giants can do that."

Still holding her hand, he knelt before her. "Listen to me, Kat Macdonald. I want to marry you. It will stop the petty gossip that has so hurt you as well as give our sons a name. But if you cannot find it in your heart to come to me freely, then I will be content with whatever you allow. Even if I have to live in that tree beside your window until the winds blow me down, there I will go. I love you, Kat. I love you now and I will love you tomorrow and the day after that and the day after that. I will love you as long as you allow it."

Her heart filled and swelled and threatened to overflow. "Devon . . . how can you be so certain?"

"I always thought I fell in and out of love far too easily. Now I realize that until now, until I met you, I've never loved at all."

Kat couldn't speak. Every emotion she possessed had knotted in her throat. He loved her; she could see it in his eyes, in the way he held her hand so gently, as if afraid to hurt her. She could see it in the fact that he knelt before her so patient, so tender.

Malcolm sniffed and wiped his own eyes. "Och lassie, I think you're going to have to marry the man. 'Tis obvious he's daft about you. And if you don't, you'll regret it for the rest of your days."

He looked past Kat, his eyes meeting Fiona's. "So long as there is love, one can overcome anything."

Fiona took a hesitant step forward. "Malcolm? I—I want out of our wager."

"Out of it? But . . . my love, I believe I just won it."

"Yes, well, it was a stupid idea." Her lips quivered. "I don't know what I was thinking. I just feared that if we had a child, you would cease thinking of me as—" She bit her lip.

There was a moment of silence and then Malcolm held out his hand. "Come, love. We have let our pride do the talking for too long. It is time our hearts had some time together."

Fiona slowly put her hand in his, her eyes filled with tears. "But . . . what if we cannot agree on the things that have kept us apart?"

"Then we will learn to compromise." His gaze searched hers. "I thought winning was important. But now, like you, I am beginning to think there are times when losing can be more rewarding. Come, my love. We have a lot of talking to do, the two of us. And here is neither the place nor the time."

"Indeed," she said, laying her head on his shoulder and smiling mistily. "We really must return to the ballroom. 'Tis nearing midnight and soon it will be midnight. People will wish to claim their favors."

Malcolm turned to Devon. "May I announce that you are engaged?"

Devon looked at Kat. She took a deep breath. "I suppose we might as well." The flash of happiness in Devon's eyes warmed her heart.

Malcolm nodded his approval. "Excellent! We'll make the announcement once the cakes are gone." With that, he and Fiona walked out the door, hand in hand.

Devon pulled Kat into his arms. "See what persistence can do for a man? That's my one fault, you know. Persistence."

"One?" She quirked a brow at him.

"Aye," he said challengingly.

A faint quiver touched the corner of her mouth. "I

suppose everyone is allowed one." Kat's gaze dropped to where Devon's hand enveloped hers. "I have to know one thing."

"Yes, my love?"

"Will you promise on your life to always tell me the truth, even if you think it is something I might not want to hear?"

"Yes."

He hadn't even hesitated. That was good, wasn't it?

"I want a long engagement," she added.

"One month," he said promptly.

"One month? That's not long enough," she protested, though she had to laugh a little, too. It was flattering that he was so very, very eager.

"Kat, my love, trust me on this. A month will seem very long to both of us since I daresay your brother is even now looking for an ax to chop down that damnable tree." Devon captured her hand and placed a kiss on the back of her fingers. "A month may seem like a year under such circumstances."

Her fingers tingled where his mouth moved over her bared skin and she shivered. "You are right, as usual."

He grinned. "Mmmmm! I like the sound of that. Say it again."

"When you've earned it, and not before," she said, trying to be severe, though her grin would not stay contained. Smiling up at him, she traced a finger over the pocket of his waistcoat where the talisman ring was tucked. "You once said this was cursed."

"I was wrong. It was, and is, blessed." He took the ring from his pocket and slid it over her finger.

It rested there, warm and gleaming. This time, its effect was gentler, softer, but more lingering.

She ran a finger over the silvered runes. Perhaps that was a sign. A sign to open the cold, frozen doors of her heart and let in the sunshine, one gentle ray at time. A sign to let in Devon.

The warmth of the ring seemed to sense the change in her, for it began to tingle, running up her arm and into her heart.

She looked down at the ring. "I suppose I have no choice. The ring has decided."

Devon nuzzled her ear, a flare of delicate fire flickering over her. "I have decided. To hell with the blasted ring."

She peeped up at him through her lashes. "If I refused you, would you haunt me?"

"For the rest of my days."

"And make my life a living hell?"

Devon's lips quirked. "I wouldn't say that, precisely. I believe that parts of it would be very enjoyable indeed."

Kat laughed then, and it seemed that the ring warmed even more with the sound. "Yes, my dear. Parts of it would be very enjoyable indeed."

Epilogue

I love surprises. I love large ones. Small ones. Ones that come in boxes with bows. You simply cannot have too many surprises.

Mrs. Montesque-Drumme
to her daughter, Lady Mountjoy,
while playing cards at the Westons' rout

A short time later, Devon pulled Kat into his arms and danced with her around the ballroom at Kilkairn.

People were still whispering, but Kat no longer cared. "I cannot believe you wished to return here. Everyone is talking about us."

"They will be talking even more when your brother announces our betrothal." He held her a little tighter, his hips now brushing hers. "Meanwhile, let's give them something more . . . exciting to talk about."

"You are a very naughty man. I can see that I'll have my hands full trying to keep you from embarrassing me more than I've embarrassed myself."

"Which is yet another reason you love me." He sighed. "Gad, when I think of it, there are hundreds of reasons for you to love me! See why we should wed with all due haste?"

"You certainly think well of yourself."

He grinned. "I can't help it. The most beautiful woman in the room is dancing with me. I feel very superior when you're on my arm."

"Oh, if that's what causes it, then by all means, continue on." She began to say something more, when a sudden excitement began to rise in the crowd.

Voices raised in exclamation and everyone began pointing to the clock.

"Ah," Devon said. "The iced cakes. Come, my sweet. Let's see what jeweled favors we may find." He took her arm and led her forward, trying to find a way through the throng.

As they went, Kat looked up and saw Malcolm standing by the table. She lifted her arm to wave—and the clock began to chime.

There was an ebullient cry and a mad surge toward the table. Kat was knocked forward, her arm outstretched. Suddenly she and Devon were watching in twin dismay as the St. John talisman ring went flying, a silver circlet that flipped end over end, above the heads of the guests, only to drop squarely onto the table of cakes.

All around them pandemonium reigned. But for Devon and Kat, there was nothing but silence.

Kat looked up at Devon. "I-I don't know how that

happened. It fit so well; I really didn't think it was loose."

"I didn't, either. In fact, I thought it fit perfectly." He lifted up and tried to see the table and the general vicinity where the ring had landed.

He was just about to say something when he caught a glimpse of the ring sitting squarely on a small iced cake, one of the few left. As Devon looked, a slender feminine hand reached from the milling crowd and took the cake, ring and all.

And then it was gone.

Devon watched as the hundreds of guests thronged, laughing and talking, some holding their prizes above their heads, others discreetly tucking them away in reticules and pockets.

The talisman ring, so recently recovered, was gone.

Kat wrung her hands. "I cannot believe I lost it like that! What will your brother say? Isn't he supposed to receive it next?"

"Oh, I'm sure Marcus will be heartbroken." A faint smile touched Devon's mouth.

"Shouldn't we at least try to look for it?"

He shook his head. "I don't believe it would do any good. There are too many people and too many grabbing hands. Chances are, someone already has it tucked into their reticule."

"Reticule?"

"Oh yes," Devon said, smiling ear to ear. "Somewhere at this ball is the woman my brother Marcus is going to marry."

Kat looked impressed. "But . . . how will he find her? Or the ring?"

"I don't know if you've noticed or not, but when the ring wishes to be found, it is." Devon took his future bride's arm. "Meanwhile, let us talk of more important things. What do you think of an elopement? Something with a lengthy honeymoon on the continent. You may bring your lads with you, and we can gaze at stained glass to your heart's content."

"A trip abroad? Really? But . . . what about your brother? Won't he need help finding the ring? And his future bride?"

"Never fear, my dear. I'm certain *your* brother will give us a copy of the guest list for the ball. Marcus can begin there."

"But . . . there are over four hundred people here!"

"Then he had better get started quickly. He's almost forty, you know, and it is high time he found a wife. Perhaps it will liven him up some; he has gotten to be quite a tyrant of late. Meanwhile, you and I, my love, have some dancing to attend to." And with that, Devon swept his lovely bride-to-be onto the dance floor, though in the back of his mind, he was already composing the letter to his brother:

Dearest Marcus:

Life is oft full of ironies. This is one I'm sure you will enjoy . . .